The Lady's Pirate

CONRAD LEGACY
BOOK TWO

C.K. MACKENZIE

The Lady's Pirate

Conrad Legacy Book 2

Contact Information: ckmackenzieauthor@gmail.com

Cover Art by Graziana Masneri

Interior Formatting by C.E. Higgins

Publishing History

First Edition, 2023

Paperback ISBN 979-8-9850526-8-8

Published in the United States of America

For all of us who dream of a better world

Southern Portuguese Coast

JULY 23, 1808

Adelaida Machado stepped from the cover of her family's villa into the pounding vitality of the wicked summer storm. Though she reveled in the rain's energy, she wasn't foolish enough to race down the slick stone steps. Rather, she cautiously picked her way, barefoot, from the villa to the beach she so loved.

The wind whipped around her, as angry as the country, as if the weather understood the simmering hatred lurking barely beneath the surface. Despite the late hour and the driving rain, the air remained warm. Adi stepped off the last step and raised her face to the sky, letting the rain wash over her.

Another gust of wind plastered wet strands of loose hair against her cheek. Adi ignored them as she had ignored the constant frown of her mother-in-law, the worried look from her own mother, her sister-in-law's concern, and the suspicious side-eyes of the French troops currently occupying her home.

She looked up the steps, but no one followed her in this storm. No one was crazy enough.

Good. She needed peace and quiet, though finding either

outside in an angry night seemed impossible. If it'd been a beautifully clear night without a cloud in the sky, she'd have had company. She'd had company for months now. She needed time for herself.

The sand sank between her toes as she walked along the water. The waves crashed along the beach, dark and furious. She didn't blame them. Hiking her skirts, the ocean lapping at her ankles, Adi kept one eye ahead of her and one on the bouncing lanterns lining the villa.

No one followed her, at least no one carrying a light. The servants, who probably didn't need light, wouldn't bother following, and the French, who knew nothing of the terrain, didn't seem inclined to venture out into the storm.

For the first time in months, Adi breathed freely. Then she screamed.

She waded deeper into the ocean. Her fingers clenched her skirts so tightly, she wondered if she could ever release the material. She vented her anger and sorrow and helplessness into the storm until she gasped for breath.

Head thrown back, eyes closed, rain running down her face and beating on her eyelids, she took in another breath. She released it in the same venting screams, letting the wind catch her anguish and take it far out to sea.

Finally, spent, gasping for breath, knees weak, she opened her eyes. Nothing had changed. The rain continued pounding the coast like a vindictive maelstrom bent on annihilation. The sky remained black, heavy with clouds, as if it, too, wept for Adi and Portugal. Her toes had gone numb in the cool, wet sand, and she slowly uncurled them as the waves continued their inexorable rush against the shoreline.

Several minutes passed before her breath came easily again. Stepping from the ocean, Adi turned for the villa. The lanterns bobbed in the wind, a chaotic dance of light against the unrelenting darkness. She could retrace her steps, walk up the slick stone steps and back into the oppressive suspicion of the French colonel, who thought her childhood home was now his.

Or she could not. Not yet.

Adi stepped toward the distant, rocky outcropping that bordered the land. Her delay only postponed the inevitable, but for now, that was good enough.

Her fingers ached where they held her dress, and she dropped the heavy, sopping material. It didn't matter anyway; she was soaked clear through.

The wind eased, as if it truly carried her suffering out to sea. Thankful for the break in the unexpected summer storm, Adi scraped her hair from her cheek. She wiped the rain from her face and eyes, spreading her arms wide for no reason other than she could. Her lungs had eased with her screams—now all she wanted was to sleep for a week. But the tension of the occupation and the slaughter across the country made that impossible.

Suddenly, as if trying to impart a message, the wind completely stopped. Suspicion rose on her skin in a cold shiver, and she looked around the beach. It lay deserted. Wet, battered by the storm, and empty.

Had she heard a sound? She'd thought it was the rain against the rocks, but no. Now that the wind had eased, it sounded like something else.

A person.

Unease skittered down her spine. For one frozen moment, Adi didn't know whether to race for the villa or investigate. The French occupation had taught her a caution she'd never before possessed, not here in her idyllic childhood sanctuary. However, no matter how brutally they treated the coastline, she refused to cower.

Making her way cautiously over the rocks, she searched for the source of the noise. A villager, hiding from the French? There were many of them now. Perhaps the noise was merely an animal, a dog who'd wandered too far in the storm and gotten trapped.

She blinked as a gust of wind smacked her in the face. A man. As battered from the storm as the coastline, he half sat, half leaned against the rocks, clutching a satchel of some sort.

"I hope it's well-oiled," she muttered. Shaking her head at herself, Adi grimaced as she searched for a way over the rocks that wouldn't tear up her bare feet.

"Are you breathing?" she called. She carefully placed her hands on the rocks and peered over the barrier. Studying him for a moment, she took in his clothes—soaked through, obviously, and plain, but in the darkness they looked well-tailored. No hat, no uniform insignia, just a shirt, trousers, and shiny boots that would no doubt be as ruined as her gown.

He looked alive.

Sitting on one of the flatter rocks, Adi swung her legs over and scooted to the other side. She ignored the sound of rending fabric.

"Who are you, and where did you come from? Fisherman? Probably not. Smuggler? Perhaps. Pirate?" Her lips twitched. Now she was being fanciful. She pushed off the rocks and landed on the wet sand with a painful thud.

Ouch. She'd turned her ankle, but other than a faint twinge, it seemed unharmed. Adi sighed. There was no help for it now. She was fully immersed in the rocks, and she'd have to climb out one way or the other.

Crouching before the man, she brushed his wet hair from his forehead. He startled awake, clutching the satchel as if it were a lifeline.

"*Olá?*" she asked, leaning back.

"Ah." He coughed, one hand still clutching the satchel, the other holding his chest as if his lungs ached. Otherwise, he seemed unharmed. "*Olá.*"

"Can you stand?" she asked in Portuguese, suspicious. But he seemed to understand well enough.

"*Sim.*"

Adi straightened and quickly looked up and down the beach —deserted. Still, with the break in the storm, best to get moving. Just in case one of the French soldiers ventured out in search of her. "We need to move off the beach."

"*Sim,*" he agreed but didn't move. "That would be for the best."

He definitely spoke Portuguese and not that half-French, floundering Portuguese the French tried. Frowning, Adi crouched before him again. "*Can* you stand?"

"Oh, I know I can." He blinked slowly, his eyes unreadable in the darkness. His hand hadn't moved from his chest, and he looked as if he had trouble breathing. He blinked up at her again, and his lips pressed tightly together before he said, "Just perhaps not right now."

Her lips quirked, her first true smile in nearly a year. This was far from a laughing matter, but he looked so sincere, she almost laughed. "All right."

She had no time to waste—they needed off this beach before someone came looking for her. The French patrol wouldn't venture down in this weather, but with her wandering, Adi took no chances. She looked around again, but the beach remained deserted.

"Let's see if your legs remember how."

Adi shifted so she crouched beside him, then awkwardly slipped one arm around his back. It took more than a few tries before his legs held his weight. With the seconds ticking by, she feared discovery. That fear beat through her with every heartbeat.

"I don't know what you're doing here," she muttered as they started up the beach, hidden by the rocks. "But you're in danger. This isn't the best time for a wander."

"My boat." His leg gave out, and he sank to the sand, bringing her with him. He groaned in obvious pain. "*Desculpa*," he gasped.

"We can't stop," Adi warned, hauling him back upright. He made a terrible noise, and she paused. After a moment, he gasped an affirmative sound. At least, what she interrupted as an affirmative sound. Either way, they couldn't stop, not in so open an area. "You either remember how to walk, or I'm leaving you." She wouldn't—she'd leave no one alone and exposed, especially when they were clearly in hiding.

"I remember how to walk," he insisted with a haughty sniff, one that was utterly at odds with his bedraggled appearance, stumbling gait, and breathless gasps of pain. "It's just proving somewhat difficult at the moment."

She believed it, and she started to ask about his boat when she realized another problem:

"We can't walk back up the cliffside."

Adi sighed. All she'd wanted was a walk on the beach in the storm. Well, she'd enjoyed that, screaming into the rain and wind, but apparently the storm had other thoughts on the matter.

The man (he hadn't offered a name, and frankly Adi did not need to know one) slowly turned his head. "No, probably not."

"You'll never make it," she added.

"Nope," he agreed in far too amenable a tone. "But I've no wish to meet the Frenchies, either."

Something in his tone told Adi he meant that, but wariness made the hairs on the back of her neck stand straight. Granted, she didn't wish to meet any Frenchies herself, but she hadn't much choice.

"I'm sorry to disappoint you," she said, breathing heavily, stumbling beside him in her wet gown as it dragged along the sand. "But they're everywhere. Right now, the only place even resembling shelter is crawling with French soldiers."

He rolled his head to the side and eyed her. In the cloudy night, the wind once more slamming into them, he looked confused. "That is hardly the hospitality I expected."

Adi snorted. "Are you drunk?"

"I never drink."

She frowned in disbelief. "Did you hit your head?"

"Oh, no doubt." He walked slower now, and she adjusted her grip.

"*Não, não, não.* No slowing down."

"I'm not." He paused. "I'm trying not to, but my legs have other ideas."

"You have two choices," she snapped. Or as much as her own breathless, tired state allowed. "Stay here for the French to discover you in the morning or walk faster."

"I like option two," he agreed. "Where's my bag?"

"You're holding it," she huffed, out of breath, struggling with this man, and yet amused.

"Oh." He nodded, then tilted forward. "Good," he added, straightening with another painful moan.

The household never laughed anymore, never teased or joked. They offered the French respectable entertainment: singing, music, meals on the *varanda* with the best views of the ocean. But amusement hovered on the surface only. Like what she could see of the ocean, only the very top of it, nothing beneath.

Yet this man, in a matter of minutes, had worried her, made

her chuckle, and reminded her that she did know how to smile. Perhaps all was not lost.

"Where are we?" he asked, voice slower and lower. Or perhaps that was the storm, whipping up again now that she'd found him.

"Along the coast," Adi hedged. She had no idea why she didn't tell him outright, but something stopped her. Just as she believed the storm had receded enough for her to find him, she listened to that niggling feeling in her stomach and didn't reveal everything.

"I thought as much." His tone, haughty and sardonic, once more made her lips tilt up into a small smile.

"The less you know the better," Adi huffed and finally, finally, spotted the cave entrance. She worried she'd miss it in the dark and rain, but she and her brother had grown up playing on this beach. Even on a wicked night like this, she knew where it lay.

The man slurred something, and she jerked him.

"What?" Breathing hard, she concentrated on placing one foot in front of the other and not tripping.

"I've put you in danger," he said, though she couldn't tell if that was what he'd originally uttered.

Adi grunted. "I'm in danger every day."

"Be that as it may, I'm not helping."

"No," she growled. "You aren't, and if we don't make it to the cave soon, I'm leaving you."

She probably wouldn't. But she had people depending on her, those she loved. Far too late, Adi realized the consequences of her actions.

Helping this man put her family in danger. Mélina, her brother's wife, and their young son, Rodrigo. Her mother-in-law —though that woman would no doubt outlive them all from sheer anger. Her own mother, who had taken them all in after Mateus's death, when the French drove farther and farther south. And her child, her beloved Gabriel.

"Where are we heading?"

Adi blinked and shook her head. Despite the danger, she couldn't leave him, and she knew it. "There's a cave ahead." She nodded, but all that did was cause them both to stumble in the wet sand. "It leads to a tunnel that will take us to the villa."

"And this villa is safe?" He wheezed out a short breath but continued on, leaning heavily on her now. "No, it's not, is it?"

"No," she agreed. "It's not."

"Why endanger yourself?" He paused, breathing heavily. "Endanger yourself more?"

"I can leave you," she offered, her own steps slowing. They both struggled, but Adi had a feeling this stranger was more injured than he let on. In addition to his struggling breath, he favored his left leg. With each step, he grew weaker, no matter how she tried to help.

"After all this?" He huffed a chuckle, and Adi wondered if he always showed such cheerfulness in the face of pain and danger. "I'm wounded."

"You are," she agreed.

"Not just in body." He gasped again, struggling, and she knew he'd injured his ribs. "Your words, they wound me."

"Keep talking and we'll both be wounded." She tried to track the villa's lanterns, which were once more dancing merrily in the wind. Did any venture closer? She didn't think so, but holding his weight meant she couldn't turn her head as far as she needed. "And stop pulling my hair."

"*Desculpa*," he said again. But the end of the word cut off in a gasp. "I say that a lot."

Aid swallowed her annoyance. It wasn't his fault. She paused, eyeing the lanterns, but still saw nothing out of the ordinary. Not his fault—but really, she didn't know that for sure. What was he doing on the beach in this storm? What had he said about a boat? She couldn't remember.

Not his fault for pulling her loose, wet hair. Definitely his fault for being caught in the storm.

Nothing she could do now. They still had another few minutes before they made it into the cave, longer given his rapidly weakening gait. She couldn't hear anything over the sound of the wind—or was that the frantic pounding of her heart?

"What's your name?" she asked for lack of anything else to say.

"Abreu," he slurred.

"You better stay awake." Her voice, sharper than she intended, jolted him. Good. She could not carry him across the wet sand and over the rocks that jutted up directly in front of the cave. "What were you doing in the storm?"

"Losing," he muttered, which she found more truthful than honest. "Didn't expect its viciousness. Didn't expect it at all." His head leaned heavy against her shoulder, only for him to jerk upright. "I'm not entirely certain this is proper."

"Me dragging you into a secret cave?" Adi huffed, her own strength lagging. "Or you leaning your head on my shoulder?"

"*Sim.*"

"I think, given the circumstances, we can dismiss propriety." Her lungs strained, and she swore the cave grew more distant with every step closer. "Though how anyone can mistake this for anything other than a rescue, I've no idea."

"Remind me to thank you later," Abreu mumbled.

She wondered what his first name was, and why he chose to offer only a surname. And why he evaded her questions. Of course, it was possible he didn't know, given his weakened state and clearly declining strength. Still, with all she'd suffered these last months, Adi found it difficult to trust.

Which didn't exactly explain why she was carrying this stranger from the shoreline to the cave. She needed to hide him somewhere, and this was the only location available.

"Finally." She breathed a short-lived sigh of relief as they stepped around the rocky barrier and into the relative sanctuary of the cave.

"Oh, good." His legs gave out again, and he sank to the ground. "I'm afraid I can't walk any farther."

Struggling to catch her own breath, Adi eyed him, a crumpled heap on the ground. She couldn't see his features, only the dark shape of his body on the sand beside her.

"All right," she conceded. "I can't carry you, and I'm not dragging you into the tunnels." Her arms and back ached, and she thought she twisted her knee when he stumbled the first time. "You stay here; I'll return in the morning with food."

"Why?"

She frowned. "Because we typically enjoy breakfast in the morning."

Abreu snorted what might be described as a laugh, but it ended on another agonized moan. "Yes, I, too, normally enjoy breakfast in the morning." He still seemed unable to catch his breath, yet he continued to speak. "I meant why are you helping me?"

"I've no idea."

Abreu laughed, a gasping, raw sound that echoed in the cave.

"Hush," Adi snapped, gesturing with her hands though even she couldn't see them in the darkness. "You'll give us away."

Probably not. They were well hidden, and the cave was half a mile from the villa. However, she had no idea which French patrols roamed the area. Or if anyone had, indeed, searched for her.

"I'm going to sit here," Abreu whispered in the loudest whisper she ever heard. "Possibly lie down."

"All right," she said to his now-prone body. Honestly, she had no idea if lying down was a good idea or not, but she hadn't any other response. "I'll return in a few hours with food."

"*Obrigado*," he muttered, but Adi doubted he even knew what he said.

"You're welcome," she whispered, and she hurried from the cave back along the beach. The rain had returned with a greater vengeance, but she didn't look back.

The cave wouldn't flood with the tide. She needn't worry about that. However, she did worry Abreu might wake and wander off before she returned. Well, if he did, he did. As long as he didn't wander toward the villa.

The wet sand slowed her steps, and now the storm hindered her, whereas before she'd reveled in its power. Eventually, the steps leading to her villa came into view, and she slowed, catching her breath.

"Thought the storm swept you to sea," Louis, the French guard, sneered.

"Not tonight." She breezed past him, ignoring the leer he offered, and stepped into the warm house she called home.

Two

Adi moved as quickly as her tired, sore legs could carry her, dripping rain and sand along her path. So much for sneaking in. The wet mess behind her was definitely noticeable. Adi ignored the sand between her toes that squelched uncomfortably.

Carefully placing her feet on the marble flooring so as not to slip, she glanced around the strangely silent hallway. She'd apologize to the maids for the mess she left in her wake. With any luck, the French colonel would slip on it and concuss himself.

Adi wasn't that lucky.

Especially since he was on the opposite side of the villa, listening to her sister-in-law's exquisite singing voice and exceptional pianoforte playing.

Inside her room, the one she now shared with Mélina and her son, her own son, her mother, *and* mother-in-law, when Inês graced them with her presence, Adi listened for telltale signs of their presence. But, despite the late hour, the area was as quiet as the hallway.

That quiet solitude was rare these days, and Adi wanted to

enjoy it. Except now that she had it, unease danced over her arms. She tried chalking it up to the chill the rain had left, or her soaked-through clothing, now heavy and uncomfortable. But she couldn't quite convince herself.

Glancing around the empty space, which was lit only by the candles, she listened for any sound. Though she trailed more wet sand across the floors as she did so, Adi quickly checked for spies. Soldiers lurking to overhear a stray word, servants where they shouldn't be.

Until tonight, Adi had held unshakable faith in her childhood household and their loyalty to the family. Now that she hid a stranger in the tunnels connecting the villa to the beach, all that had changed. She wasn't so certain about anything anymore. Then again, Adi couldn't separate her own secrets from the suspicion that had sunk deep into her bones the moment Napoleon sent his army across the border.

"Relax, Adelaida." Her admonishment did not quell her nervousness one bit.

She didn't know where any of her remaining family had disappeared to. As she'd crept across the halls, the rest of the villa hadn't echoed with their bickering. At the moment, it didn't matter. All she cared about was taking off her ruined gown and changing into something warm and dry.

The ties that held her bodice closed were, of course, sopping wet. They were also coated in a fine layer of sand, which made working the knots loose all but impossible. She tugged at them, but her fingers were cold and shaking from exhaustion and fear.

She was going to have to ring for her lady's maid's help.

Accepting defeat, Adi did so and moved to light more candles, stretching her fingers toward the warm flames. It wasn't Élea who arrived, but Mélina, looking cross and harried.

"What happened?" Adi whispered the moment Mélina closed the door.

"The colonel, he is in a foul mood." She looked behind her as if someone followed, a dark scowl over her beautiful lips. "He doesn't like the storms. Mama, she tried to soothe him but…" Mélina shook her head.

"Where's Élea?"

Mélina's scowl darkened even further. "She and the other servants were sent to the French wing to serve the colonel's special party."

A chill curled around Adi's heart. "Mélina…"

"Not that kind of party!" She looked horrified and glared once more at the closed door. "Lots of wine and food. Mama is helping in the kitchens. One of the men plays the lyre and is singing victory songs."

"Please help me with these ties." She motioned Mélina over. "I don't want to cut them if we can salvage the bodice."

Mélina clucked in disapproval and dug her finger into Adi's side. "With this tear? What were you doing? Climbing the rocks?"

She'd forgotten about the sound of rending cloth in the middle of the storm. What with the storm, the man, secreting him from the beach, and racing back to the house, her clothing was the last thing on her mind.

"In this storm?" She forced a small, weak laugh and shook her head. Her hair stuck to her neck and back, plastered there by the weight of the rain.

Mélina sighed and started on the knots. "Always going into the rain. You and Théo." She paused and breathed evenly for a moment. "You'll catch your death, Adi," she choked and stopped again.

"I needed the quiet," Adi murmured. She took Mélina's hand

and squeezed. "I promise I'm not going anywhere." The ties on her bodice finally slackened, and she laboriously tugged them loose. "Ah."

"Quiet?" Mélina sniffed hard, starting on her skirts. "In this storm?" She echoed Adi's own words back to her.

"Better than remaining in this house." Adi shook her head again, ignoring the river of water that slithered down her back. "I just needed to escape, even if only for a few moments."

Adi didn't bother to explain further. No one had ever understood her need for quiet, to be alone, away from others and with only herself for company. She loved the water, the constant crash of waves on the land, the vastness of the ocean. When she walked the beach, even when the fishermen pushed their *barca de pesca* into the water, a sense of peace hovered over everything. She loved that, craved it.

Walking her beloved beach in a storm? She could dance in that rain, laugh with her arms spread wide, let the storm wash away her emotions.

"Where's Inês?" Adi didn't particularly wish to know where her mother-in-law was currently stationed, but she asked anyway.

Her heavy skirts fell to the floor with a wet plop, and Adi grimaced. She pushed off the bodice and let that fall onto the pile of fabric as well. Mélina gave it a disapproving cluck and purposely eyed the trail of wetness Adi had left on the floor.

"The conservatory."

Again, Mélina meant. Or still, Adi supposed. Inês spent most of her time in the conservatory, looking over the rear gardens, playing the pianoforte or the mandolin. She rarely interacted with the rest of the household, and when she did, it was...less than pleasant.

Inês was less than pleasant, which Adi had discovered the hard way after two years of living with the woman. She'd only grown worse when her son died as part of the Portuguese resistance against the French.

Adi shivered and stared hard at the sparce candlelight, willing the images away. She hadn't seen the streets littered with bodies; the stories were terrible enough. Only a few survived the slaughter, and those who had whispered about it as if hell nipped on their heels.

She and Inês had fled in the dead of night, taking the servants who wished to leave and all the wealth they could carry south to Adi's childhood home on the coast. Far from the French, who occupied the Douro River. Far from the memory of Mateus, who had joined the Portuguese army when the French first marched into the country. Who had died alongside them.

Wiping her cheeks with suddenly hot fingers, Adi swallowed against the grief.

"*Irmã.*" Mélina reached for her, her hands warm and dry. "You'll catch your death, standing like this." She blinked down at Adi's legs. "You walked barefoot? Adelaida." She sighed, but there was a small smile lifting her lips.

"Any news from the village?"

"Nothing since your return yesterday." Mélina rang for the maid again. "Clean your feet, Adi."

"*Desculpa.*" Adi accepted the linen and dried her hair first, squeezing water from it until she was satisfied. She scrubbed her face, though that didn't ease the pain around her heart, closing her throat. Squeezing her eyes shut tight, Adi didn't know if the grief she carried was for her dead husband, her country, or for herself and what family remained.

"Does Mama have Gabriel?" She lowered her voice, though she remained fairly certain no one lurked about. Still, the walls had ears.

Mélina nodded silently, as if she, too, feared an eavesdropper.

They were both, no doubt, being unnecessarily paranoid. However, Adi took no chances with her son's safety. With any of their safety, given the French brutality and the current occupation of the villa.

No use dwelling on that now. She needed to show herself so no one searched the tunnels. As far as she knew, the French didn't yet know of them. It was one of her many constant fears, that the French would discover the tunnels between the house and the beach. That a member of the household would slip, someone from the village would snitch, or one of the more enterprising foot soldiers would explore a little too thoroughly and discover them.

Either way, she needed to move the stranger, and soon. And she'd need help, given his injuries.

"Where is Mama?" Adi finally asked. She sat on a chair and brushed sand from her legs and feet. She'd need to apologize to Élea for this mess, too. "The kitchens, you said?"

"I believe so, yes."

The kitchens were quite far from the conservatory, so her mother's location didn't exactly surprise Adi. They were also the one place Colonel Lambert had stationed guards, thereby providing much of the household an alibi. Apparently, he worried about being poisoned. With good reason. He'd stationed himself and his aide in the house of innocent civilians, utterly uninvited.

And unwanted.

Mélina helped her dress in a simple country gown. It made working around the house easier; she could move her arms much more freely. But it also allowed her small dagger to remain hidden in her bodice.

Adi had never used one in self-defense. But once they'd fled the invading French army, arming herself with even a small dagger seemed prudent, and she'd equipped the entire household. The world was dangerous enough without invading armies.

"*Obrigada*, Mélina." She squeezed her sister-in-law's hand. "Is Rodrigo with one of the maids?" Rodrigo was Mélina's son, Adi's nephew, and the heir to whatever would remain of the villa.

Mélina nodded. "He couldn't settle tonight, and with the colonel also in an upset, I thought it best they retire to the nursery." She paused and pressed her fingers to her eyes, looking as exhausted and worn-out as Adi felt.

"Find your rest, Mélina." She kissed her sister-in-law's cheek. "I have a feeling tomorrow will be another long day."

"All the days are long, Adi." She kissed her cheek and turned for the door. "Don't dawdle; we all need rest."

Élea entered then, looking exasperated but grateful. Adi stepped over the sodding pile of clothing and pulled the maid into a quick hug.

"You're unharmed?" She looked critically at Élea, who nodded. "The others are also? The soldiers didn't touch anyone?"

"None," Élea promised. "They were drinking and singing." Her lips twisted. "Very happy they were. They'll have drunk themselves into oblivion."

Good. Adi nodded and shooed Mélina from the room. "I'm sorry about the mess," she told Élea. "I'll make it up to you and the others. Get some rest, all of you," she said, and she repeated what she'd said to Mélina: "Tomorrow will be another long day."

Though Élea eyed her, she nonetheless bobbed quickly, gathered the wet gown, and disappeared from the room. Adi watched the closed door. She wouldn't risk any of their lives for her sudden good deed. Fear clenched her heart, making her fingers cold.

She'd placed the last members of her family in danger. Her

entire household. All because she couldn't leave an injured man to die on the beach.

Too late now, she thought and headed down the secret stairs toward the kitchens.

Karlotta Dos Santos blended into the kitchens as seamlessly as any cook. She stood chopping vegetables on a wide marble table. She didn't look up from her work when Adi entered, but tilted her head to the side where Gabriel, Adi's son, slept soundly.

Adi ignored the quiet, graceful dance of those in the kitchens. She also ignored the three guards stationed around the room as if they might know which spice was for flavor and which was poisonous. But their presence ensured Karlotta remained in their view and kept Gabriel safe.

After she thanked Joana, one of the scullery maids, for watching over him, Adi scooped Gabriel into her arms and held tight. His small, warm body stirred against her, but he didn't wake. Letting the comfort of holding her son steady her, Adi plastered on a smile and turned for the worktable.

"Mama." She kissed her mother's cheek but held back any words about the stranger in the tunnels.

Holding Gabriel, her mother beside her, Adi didn't want anyone else in the same danger in which she'd placed herself. Acting before she'd thought things through—how unusual for her. She was usually a planner, but Adi certainly hadn't done so tonight. Still, she couldn't have left the man in that storm, clearly injured, and with the French scouring every nook in search of rebels.

She kissed the top of Gabriel's head and sidled up to her mother. "How is Inês?"

"Bah." Karlotta waved her hand and frowned harder at the vegetables before her. Her fingers tightened around the knife. It was a wonder she hadn't already used it on the other woman. "No help."

"I know." Adi sighed and closed her eyes.

She only half listened as Karlotta grumbled about Inês. Inês had offered no help when they'd fled their villa along the Douro River, either. She hadn't complained about the rough cart ride or having to travel directly beside her servants, but she certainly hadn't helped. Upon arriving at the villa, she'd promptly taken Maya, her lady's maid, and hidden in her rooms.

When Colonel Lambert arrived and forced himself inside, she'd nearly caused herself a bout of apoplexy with her anger. It'd placed them all in danger, and Adi had beckoned a pair of footmen to carry her away. After that, Inês started locking herself in the conservatory.

Dismissing Inês and pushing those terrifying memories as far from her mind as possible, Adi assessed her current situation.

"She keeps out of the way," Adi offered, gently rocking Gabriel.

The stranger would need food. Soup perhaps, despite the heat that would return after the storm. Medicine, though there was precious little of anything left in the country. Perhaps cumin or anise in the vegetable soup. She'd assess his injuries before she decided on anything else.

"Bah," Mama spat again. "She's a leech."

"She mourns." It wasn't the first time Adi had said that, and it wouldn't be the last, she knew. Inês did mourn—her son, her husband, her vineyard, hundreds of years of family tradition. Her wealth, her place in society, her numerous servants.

They all mourned. And they had to move on if they wanted to stay alive. Inês had a choice, just as they all had. She could have left with the monarchy, the rich merchants, the cowardly government. She chose to stay, not out of duty but obstinance. Inês hadn't believed Napoleon would invade, and she hadn't believed he would be so brutal.

She was a fool.

"Bah," Karlotta snapped again. She slowly released the knife and leaned on the table. "How was the storm?"

"Beautiful." Adi sighed. "The lightning over the ocean made the sky look…" She shook her head.

"Like it might open up and swallow us?"

Huffing, she adjusted Gabriel in her arms. "You have no appreciation for storms over the water."

"I do," her mother corrected. "From inside, not for dancing around in them like a madwoman. That's Inês's position."

Karlotta was never one to let a dig at the other woman go. Adi merely grinned. "I enjoy the storms. They make me happy."

"God knows we have little enough of that around here." She picked up her knife and began chopping again.

Watching the kitchen staff go about their work, Adi waited until she and her mother shared a relatively private moment. "I need a small basket of food."

Karlotta eyed her sharply but didn't stop her chopping. "Why?"

"I can't tell you, Mama."

"Adelaida…" She trailed off in warning, but her mother's verbal threats hadn't had any effect on Adi since she was nine.

"Not so much they'll notice," Adi added. "They" being the French, of course. Or the staff—no sense inviting trouble. "Vegetables, figs, olives, and maybe a small pot of soup."

"We have little enough as it is, Adelaida," Karlotta hissed. "There better be a good reason."

"There is," she promised. At least, she hoped there was.

Helping was always a good reason. And helping a stranger who'd washed ashore seemed a good idea at the time. Even now, Adi didn't regret helping a man in obvious need.

She did have some concerns about the nature of his accident. Why had he thought traveling via boat in such a wicked storm might remotely be a good idea? But it'd been her mother who'd taught her to help in all situations. As the wealthiest family in the village, the Dos Santos family had an obligation to help those less fortunate.

Karlotta sighed and nodded, scraping the greens into a bowl and handing it off to the undercook. "Tonight?"

"Before breakfast is soon enough." She couldn't risk leaving the house again, not in this storm, not with the French scrutinizing her every move. Once, they might ignore, thinking her as mad as Inês. Twice in the same night? No.

Standing, careful not to jolt Gabriel, Adi kissed her mother's cheek. "It's late; I don't care what the colonel wants. Send everyone to bed. Dawn isn't far off."

Actually, she had no idea what time it was, but she didn't wish to accommodate Lambert one bit. Such small rebellions made every day a little easier.

Karlotta kissed Gabriel's cheek, resting her hand against the back of his head before kissing Adi's cheek. "You sleep, too, Adi, *anjinho*. I'll be along shortly."

Not that Adi slept much. Grief and anger kept her awake most nights, and rage and spite kept her going during the day. She'd not give the French—Colonel Lambert in particular—any reason to harm her people.

Even as she plotted his downfall. One way or another.

The house stood eerily quiet as she walked from the kitchens to the conservatory. As if it knew her destination and tried to warn her. Adi tried to laugh that off but still held

Gabriel tighter. He shifted and mumbled in his sleep but didn't wake.

Swallowing a nervousness she was unaccustomed to in her childhood home, she listened for boots echoing on the floors. Nothing. Even the soldiers left Inês alone. Just as well. Adi didn't know what the woman would do if one of them confronted her.

At the conservatory doors, she paused to listen. No sound emerged, and Adi debated entering. She should check on Inês, she knew that. See how her mother-in-law fared. At the very least ensure she ate.

But dread pooled in the pit of her stomach, and she tightened her arms around her son. She absolutely did not want to engage with Inês. The heaviness of the woman's grief weighed on the entire house. Not even the servants ventured here, only Maya. And Adi didn't blame them.

With one hand on the door handle, Adi waited. Still no sound. She doubted Inês had retired to their shared room. She hadn't been there in months, not since Lambert's arrival before Christmas.

The mandolin started up, and Adi dropped her hand. The mournful tune echoed along the empty hallway, wailing as Adi had not since leaving Évora.

She turned from the door and hurried through the villa, holding Gabriel tight as she climbed the stairs to their rooms. She didn't look at the soldiers who were guarding the staircase on the opposite end, the main living quarters, where the colonel and Bardot, his aide, now slept in blissful comfort. She barely dared breathe. Only in the silence and safety of her room did she allow herself a moment's weakness.

Not for her dead husband, who'd been foolish enough to believe any of them stood a chance against Napoleon's mighty army. Not for Inês, who hadn't wanted their marriage from the start, despite her husband's insistence. Not even for herself. She needed all her strength for tomorrow and the day after that. She needed to stand strong in the face of Lambert's sneering hatred and her not-unreasonable fear he'd slaughter them.

She collapsed into the chair by the cold fireplace and allowed herself a moment to mourn her own future.

"This was not how I envisioned our life, *amorzinho*." She pressed her lips into her little angel's downy hair. "Trapped in our villa, terrified that each day will be our last."

Angrily wiping her cheeks, Adi stood and carried Gabriel to what had once been the sitting room. It was now their bedroom, housing what few amenities they'd managed to keep from the French. The room was empty and quiet save for the rain beating against the tiled walls of the house. She stood before them and looked beyond the gardens and over the beach, but she could barely make out the ocean.

"Not today, *amorzinho*. I promise you, no matter what I have to do, we will survive."

She kissed the top of his head, set him in the bassinet beside the low bed they'd also rescued from Lambert's men, and quickly shed her own gown. She slipped her small dagger under her pillow. Just in case.

"What?" A lump was curled atop the blankets. "Lua?" Their Portuguese Water Dog blinked awake and woofed softly. "What are you doing here? Is this where you've been hiding all evening?"

Adi softly scratched behind Lua's ear as the dog sniffed the inside of her wrist. Normally, Lua followed Adi wherever she went, but since the arrival of the French, she'd taken to hiding. Apparently, the dog liked the colonel as much as the rest of the household did.

"Come on, you know you aren't allowed on the bed." Lua licked Adi's wrist and snuggled down, whining slightly. Huffing out a laugh, Adi shook her head. Poor Lua didn't like storms. "All right. One night."

Without another sound, Lua curled into a tight ball at Adi's side.

Adi turned toward the bassinet where Gabriel still slept soundly and closed her eyes. Reaching out, she rested her hand on Lua's side.

"I'll take you with me in the morning to the tunnels and the stranger," she whispered. It was no louder than a breath. "If nothing else, you can bite the man if he proves dangerous."

Three

Grayson Conrad opened his eyes to pitch blackness. "I'm blind?"

For one wild moment, he blinked rapidly, convincing himself his eyes were, indeed, open. He waved a hand in front of his face and barely made out its movement. All right. Alive and able to see. Good. In a very dark room then.

That's when the sound raging behind him finally registered. Grayson shook his head and immediately regretted it. The pain, as sharp as the one in his ribs, made the room tilt.

"Alive and still able to see, but holy hell, what a headache." The sound of his voice helped orient him, though it did little to dispel his headache. Or any of his aches.

Tilting his head carefully to one side, he breathed through the pain. He pressed his fingers to his temples and waited until the world steadied and the pounding eased—in his head, at least. He took a deep breath, tasted salt and sand on his lips, and listened.

Wind, he decided. Blowing like banshees he heard tales of as a child. Whipping at the opening of the...not room. Cave?

Oh, that made sense.

Shifting where he sat, he dropped one hand and, yes, he definitely sat on sand. As he brushed his hand against his thigh, he cataloged more uncomfortableness. Wet clothing. Wet, salty clothing. Grayson grimaced.

"Wonderful," he croaked around a scratchy throat.

He rubbed his sandy fingers against his wet trousers, but it did little to clean his hands. Sighing in resignation, Grayson pressed his fingers against his eyelids.

No, that did not ease his headache. Not even a little.

What had happened? Last he remembered, he'd been—oh. Right. The storm.

At least he wasn't in the pouring rain. For a bit there, as he'd sat against the rocks, his ribs screaming in competition with the wind, which whipped the rain against his body with a vengeance, he hadn't been certain he'd survive the night.

Standing on unsteady legs, Grayson groaned. One hand pressed to his ribs, though that did nothing to ease their pain. He stumbled, gasping for breath, and crashed backward against the cave wall.

"Still might not make it," he muttered.

Leaning against the wall as he struggled to regain his breath, Grayson gave himself a moment. Then another. One more, just to be certain his legs remembered how to hold him and his ribs weren't broken. His heart thundered in his chest at the simple movement.

"One step," he said. It was a saying his mother often used— you can only take one step at a time. Something her grandfather had told her. It made sense, of course. First step, then the second. But at the moment, Grayson's unsteady legs could barely accomplish that first step.

"You're not dead."

It took a moment for the words to make sense. Not because he couldn't understand Portuguese, but because no one had snuck up on him in nearly fifteen years.

"I debated even returning," the voice admitted, soft and lulling despite the storm outside.

"Thought you'd find a dead body?" Grayson stumbled toward the voice. He liked that voice, despite its insinuation. "Not a lot of faith in me."

His back and neck ached. His head pounded, and his ribs... well, he didn't want to think about his ribs. At least he didn't feel nauseous, which was a plus. He'd take any plus right then.

"What were you doing in that storm?"

"It came up far more swiftly than I anticipated," he admitted. "Stronger, too." The wind had gripped his sails in a vicious hold, dragging him toward land no matter how he fought. His lugger smashed against the rocky shoreline, and he washed ashore. "I remember swimming toward the only lights for miles around, a dozen lanterns bobbing in the wind." He snorted, which was a huge, painful mistake.

He struggled to catch his breath as his left side throbbed in screaming pain.

"Hoped I didn't walk—or swim—into a French trap," he finally managed. Whether he had was still up for debate, given he currently sat in a cave. "This isn't a French trap, is it?"

"I know nothing about you, Abreu. Not even your first name."

Ah. Well, yes, there'd been that. Grayson hadn't honestly thought about a pseudonym. He hadn't planned to stay on land long enough to make acquaintances. Or need help.

So much for that plan.

"I don't even know *your* name," he countered. His mind raced for a Portuguese name, but he wasn't exactly at his best.

He'd only used "Abreu" because one of their captains was Portuguese. Seemed fitting. John Abreu had also taught him the language, since Portugal was one of the countries his family's shipping business had ties to.

Grayson was eternally grateful to John for unknowingly saving his life.

The woman stopped before him, but in the darkness he couldn't make out anything about her. Except her voice, which he decided he adored. Soft, not merely quiet in the cave, but gentle. Lilting. The voice of an angel. When she'd spoken to him last night—

"How long have I been here?" he asked, peering around the cave for any source of light. "And how did you sneak up on me?"

He must've hit his head, addled his senses.

"It's just dawn now," the woman said, her voice flowing between them like a gentle river. "The fishermen are already out at sea."

Grayson grimaced. He was supposed to be on his way back to England by now. In and out—land, find his contact, exchange the food for information, and leave before dawn. It'd been a solid plan. Except for the storm. So maybe not that solid of a plan.

He'd piloted a small lugger from a larger vessel waiting beyond the French blockade. They'd wait for him, no matter how long he took. His sister and her husband were on that ship.

"I brought you food." She paused, and he thought she turned toward an opening. "Eat sparingly. This is all I could manage."

"Thank you." Grayson blinked, but the cave remained pitch-black. No, not exactly. Over the woman's shoulder, he saw a sliver of light, angled as if she'd dragged him around corners so he wouldn't be discovered.

"And again," he said as he realized the implications. "You saved my life."

She huffed a small laugh. "Don't make me regret it."

"In the last few minutes?" He grinned, though she couldn't see it. "How could I?"

"There are many ways," she said seriously. "These are not times for frivolousness."

"No," he agreed, equally serious. "They are not. And I do apologize for insinuating otherwise."

"What were you doing in the storm?"

Grayson accepted the still-warm pot of soup and fumbled with the string that held the cloth in place. Annoyed that his fingers had also forgotten how to work, he rolled his eyes and sighed. Finally, he released the covering and sniffed. Garlic and greens of some sort. He sipped right from the pot and let the warmth flow through him. "This is delicious, thank you."

"We have no meat," she admitted. "And very few vegetables."

"Thank you," he repeated. "It's more generous than I have a right to expect." Grayson paused and drank again, chewing the leafy greens. "Where am I?"

The moment the words left his mouth, he felt the woman shift. More alert, and even more still in the darkness. The sliver of light from around the corner backlit her, but all he could make out was the shape of her body.

"Where did you expect to be?" she asked, the words evenly spaced as she took a step away from him.

He didn't blame her, given Portugal's present troubles. He hated to heap anything onto her suspicion, especially since she'd saved his life. Still, he was reluctant to trust her. He didn't wish to set foot in any traps, nor did he wish to ensnare her in his own clandestine affairs.

"Carvalho."

"Why? What were you doing in that storm?" she asked for a third time.

He admired her tenacity, her bravery. Arguing with a stranger in a dark cave, where, if he were another sort of man, her body wouldn't be found for days, weeks.

Grayson finished the soup and set the pot back in the bag. His own oiled satchel still hung around his body, so at least that hadn't been lost.

"Given the current state of things," he allowed, "I don't think it's prudent of me to answer."

She huffed that breath of laughter again. Not exactly amused, Grayson acknowledged. More like a half snort. He shouldn't find it so endearing, but he did. Could be gratitude for his rescue. He doubted that. Not with the way her voice stretched between them, a caress that promised more.

"You could have left me for dead," he said, annoyed that his brain only now caught up with his circumstances. "Why didn't you?"

"I still can," she pointed out.

"True. Will you?"

He didn't need light to know she grimaced. "Probably not. Unless you turn out to be a French spy." Her voice was colder than the Atlantic he'd swum in last night. "If you are, I'll gut you myself."

Intrigued, he tilted his head, but he didn't question her further. "I'm not a French spy. Though I suppose I'd say that even if I were."

Alluring? Intriguing? Yes and yes. Grayson wanted to know all about his angelic savior. He sighed. Now probably wasn't the time for such thoughts.

"I'm not here to harm you, *senhora*."

"I suppose that remains to be seen, *senhor*."

"I suppose it does," he agreed, smiling wide. He liked her, definitely more than he ought to. "Paulo."

"Pardon?"

"My name," he lied. "It's Paulo." Well, his second name was Paul, after his father. Grayson Paul Robert Conrad.

"Well, Senhor Paulo Abreu, it's a pleasure to meet you." The rustle of skirts was the only indication she turned from him. "If you're still here at dusk, I'll return with more food."

He reached out and grabbed her arm to stop her exit, then immediately released it. He took a moment and tried to catch his beath. Damn ribs! "No," he managed through gritted teeth. "It's not necessary. No need to deplete your own stores."

In the oddly lit cave, he couldn't make out her gaze, but he felt its weight. Assessing, definitely curious. Still suspicious, too. "You're a strange man, Paulo Abreu."

"Am I?" He shrugged. Ow—that was a mistake he wouldn't be repeating. "Practical, perhaps."

"Don't venture beyond the shadows of the cave," she warned. "There are French patrols along the coast."

He knew that, which was why he sneaked—or tried to sneak—here on a cloudy night. Again, not his best plan. He was usually not a planner, but he'd needed to be for this mission.

So much for that.

"I still don't know your name."

She hesitated, her back facing him, her head turned just enough that the lightening sky bathed her profile. High cheekbones, a sharp nose, but he couldn't make out anything more. For reasons he'd rather not dwell upon, Grayson wanted to know her eye color. The deepest of browns? Blue like the sea? Or green like the lush vines he imagined Portugal sported in her numerous vineyards?

"Adelaida," she admitted.

"Adelaida." A beautiful name, one that rolled quite nicely off his tongue.

"Don't leave the cave," she rushed on. "If you do, I won't save you a second time."

Before he could agree or even comment on the beauty of her name, she hurried off, leaving only the briefest of shadows in her wake. And a titillating scent of...chocolate?

The moment she rounded one of the outcroppings, she disappeared from his sight. Grayson stepped forward but immediately stopped. He was in no shape to fight a single Frenchman, let alone an entire French patrol. He also didn't wish any trouble on Adelaida's head. She'd taken a great risk in rescuing him and bringing him food. Especially without knowing if he was, indeed, a French spy.

French? No. English? Yes.

Grayson walked around the cave, stretching the kinks from his neck and working the stiffness from his hips. Apparently, it'd been a rougher swim than he remembered. Or perhaps that had been the rocks along the shoreline he'd barely managed to escape. Or hadn't escaped, given his battered ribs.

He needed a new plan, and he had a feeling Angelic Adelaida was not going to like it.

***

Adi had very little to occupy her days. Physically, yes, there was much work—tending the gardens, cooking, helping with the washing, keeping the villa clean. Seeing to the day's *entertainment* for Colonel Lambert and Bardot. Staying out of the colonel's path.

However, her mind returned again and again to Paulo Abreu. That man carried secrets. She felt the burden of them deep in her bones. He'd offered no reason for having been in last night's storm, nor why he'd been at sea during such uncertain times. That alone didn't signify secrets, of course, but it added to her certainty that he carried them.

Stepping onto the balcony off the *salão*, Adi closed her eyes and tilted her face toward the sunlight. If she hadn't raced through last night's storm, she'd never have known it even passed through the village. This morning, the wind barely moved the trees, the sun shone from a cloudless sky, warming her cheeks, and the air smelled clean and fresh.

For a beautiful moment, Adi imagined she lived in a world of three years ago. Unmarried and free, racing along the beach as she wished. Her only responsibility creating beautiful, delicious chocolates that tempted the senses.

She blinked open her eyes, and reality closed in around her. That was unfair to Mateus. She'd cared for her husband, she had. Their families had known each other for decades. Their marriage had been arranged before Adi could walk. She hadn't minded the marriage, nor even the marriage bed. But she wondered, in the deepest part of her heart, what it would've been like to have married someone else. Anyone else.

"Stop being foolish," she snapped.

She spun from the view and stepped back inside. The dimness couldn't hide the soldiers stationed at the doors. Or their sly, curious looks. Adi swept past them, away from the view she once loved and the past she couldn't change.

"Ah, Senhora Machado." Colonel Lambert's smooth voice carried clearly along the hallway.

Adi froze. Plastering on a smile, she slowly turned and greeted the colonel. He looked refreshed, well-fed, well-rested. Damn the man. *Uma maldição* on all of them.

"Colonel Lambert." She nodded, watching his eyes narrow

slightly as she greeted him in French. Why were they all surprised the ladies of the villa spoke French?

"Enjoying the morning, I see." He nodded to the balcony.

Suddenly cold despite the late-July heat, Adi scrambled for anything civil. But Lambert made her skin crawl. Polite and courteous he might have been, but that was a thin veneer. Beneath his propriety lay the heart of a snake. Which was rude to the snake.

"'Tis a beautiful morning," she finally agreed. She almost commented on the view, but since the French anticipated a British invasion any day, she swallowed those words. "If you'll excuse me, Colonel, I'm needed in the kitchens."

Offering a sloppy curtsy Lambert hadn't earned and didn't warrant, Adi hurried down the main stairs. Her mother wasn't in the kitchens. Joana, the scullery maid turned nanny, rocked Gabriel, who slept awkwardly on her thin shoulder.

Adi kissed her son, whispering promises to both him and Joana that she'd protect them. Then she poured another pot of thin soup, ignored the guards, and left.

None of the kitchen staff would tattle. The French didn't need any information they didn't already have, and the household knew it. They had all lost loved ones in the invasion, and they loathed Lambert's presence in the villa.

Adi settled her headdress over her shoulders. Head high, eyes forward, she wandered the halls in a measured gait until she was certain no one followed her. No footsteps sounded on the floors; the sound of boots didn't echo throughout the hallways. She felt a little foolish carrying the pot of soup about the villa, but she didn't let that stop her.

Satisfied she was alone, she doubled back toward the cellar. The tunnels from the beach led to the wine cellar, an easy way of unloading the ships without a convenient port. Of course, the French had raided that first, even before they stole and slaughtered the farm animals. They'd threatened her mother at bayonet point for the key and had taken every bottle of wine the cellar stored.

They hadn't smashed the barrels filled with cacao, sugar, and the *pimenta moída* that gave their chocolates the bite no one else could claim. No, the soldiers knew what those barrels contained and kept them safe—for themselves.

Once more ensuring no soldier lurked in the now-emptied wine cellar, Adi adjusted her headdress and slipped through the hidden door. It closed softly behind her.

"You're still here," she said into the darkness.

Only Paulo's outline was visible in the midday sunlight. As she'd instructed, he hadn't wandered from the opening but stood just beyond the sun's reach. Not a fool, at least.

"I didn't exactly have anywhere to go." She didn't need to see his face to know he grinned. "You've returned early. I haven't a timepiece on me, but I know it's not dusk."

He confused her, with his easy wit and sardonic joking in the face of invasion. Confused, yes, but Adi liked it. His easy manner lessened the burden of living in an occupied home, terrified one wrong word might see them all killed. Her mother-in-law closed up in the conservatory, Mélina tasked with playing for the colonel and Bardot, her mother keeping their small stores of food rationed so everyone could eat.

No wonder she'd screamed into the storm last night. Adi wondered she didn't do so every night.

"I brought more soup." She skirted the small outcropping of rocks and held out the pot.

"I'm grateful." He coughed and shook his head. "I'm afraid I swallowed more water than I intended."

"How much did you intend to swallow?" She tilted her head as he accepted the pot, and she wondered if sitting would be too informal. She doubted there was any set etiquette for this sort of situation.

"None." His smile was again evident in his voice. She wanted to see that smile, wondered if it was as handsome as she imagined. Wide and boyish despite the warm masculinity in his tone. No, the man she'd half dragged from the beach was no boy. "That plan didn't exactly work out."

Adi giggled, only to immediately stifle it. A sharp thread of guilt wound through her—she shouldn't laugh when the entire household lay under the threat of death. However, even in the mere day since rescuing Paulo, Adi found herself lighter than she had been in years.

"Do most of your plans work out?"

"Eh." He made a movement with his hand she couldn't see between the deepening shadows and the bright sunlight. "Half and half, I'd say."

"Not exactly a resounding endorsement."

"I'm working on it." He paused, and she thought he sipped the soup. "Thank you for this, Adelaida. It's delicious."

"We have little meat." She hadn't meant to repeat herself, nor apologize for something beyond her control, but felt she owned Paulo an explanation. "The French colonel, he slaughtered our pigs for his own men."

"This is perfect, and I mean it. It's more than I expected."

He had an interesting way with words, and Adi frowned. "What did you expect?"

"Well, for a bit there, I expected to die on the beach." He sighed and shook his head, his gait slow and unsteady as he moved beside her. "That didn't happen, for which I am most grateful. My family would have been extremely displeased with me."

Something in his tone, just beneath the lightness of his

words, told her the truth of that. They'd have been devastated if he'd died on her beach. Without saying, he told of his closeness with them. Family? Wife? Children? He hadn't mentioned a wife. Hadn't mentioned anyone. Shifting on her rocky seat at that uncomfortable thought, she curled her hands into her skirts for lack of anywhere else to place them.

"Where are they?" Her voice had dropped, and she cleared the strange huskiness from her throat.

He paused, and though she couldn't see his eyes in the uncertain shadows, she felt him weigh his answer. "Safe."

"I'm glad." She laughed, bitterness choking her. "Jealous, but I'm glad someone is safe, at least."

"You shouldn't have come." He sighed and coughed again. He paused, breathing heavily, and when he spoke she knew he clenched his jaw against the pain. "You risk yourself and your household for me. Why?"

Adi had no idea. "You needed help." She laughed again, but this time the sound came out soft, as if she herself were amazed. She was, she supposed. "There you were, sitting on the beach. A pirate washed ashore."

"Pirate?"

"Have you a better term?"

"I'm—no, I suppose not. Pirate. Hmm, yes, I like it."

She smiled at the grin that was still in his voice. She knew that smile lit his face and felt herself jealous of the darkness, for only it could enjoy his smile. Ridiculous. "I didn't exactly pause to think, *Oh, this stranger might endanger me and my family. I shouldn't help him.*"

"You're a brave woman, Adelaida." He handed her the now-empty pot. "And I'm grateful for that."

"Your family is, too," she said, in what passed for a joking manner these days.

Paulo's laugh sounded rich and deep in the cave, and it sent shivers dancing over her arms. Stunned at her body's response, Adi gripped the pot harder and tried not to dwell on it. However, her body had other ideas, and that shiver raced from the top of her head down her spine. Arousal heated her blood as she sat on the rocks, speechless.

"I can't stay here," he said into the suddenly uncomfortable silence.

Perhaps it was uncomfortable only for her, her sudden and utterly preposterous longing for his hands on her bare skin. His mouth on hers. What would his kiss taste like? Salt and sand? Or the soup she'd brought?

"No." She licked her lips and shook her head. Arousal was not in her current plan. Or any plan. Survival, yes. Sleeping with this stranger? "I'm afraid the French will find you sooner or later."

She stumbled off the rock, her mind racing. How had she gone from listening to his laugh—his lovely, beautiful laugh—to thinking about sleeping with him?

Perhaps she had caught something in last night's storm.

Paulo sighed and moved, though she couldn't make it out. "I'll need a boat, but the French patrol the coastline."

"Of course—did you not see them last night?"

"In that storm?" He hummed. "They were smarter than me, I suppose. Stayed inside."

"Yes." She scrambled for the threads of this conversation. Shaking her head hard, Adi straightened and tried to meet his gaze, though she still couldn't see him clearly. "How are you at gardening?"

"Passable," Paulo said slowly. "Better with animals. But since the French took all of them, I can garden."

"I'll sneak you in—not into the villa but somewhere else.

Being outside is better than being in here." She sighed. Madness. What was she thinking?

"Why?"

"I can't think of a reason for a new male servant," she said before she realized that wasn't what he meant. "Oh. You meant why am I offering?"

"You've done enough, saved my life—I consider that huge, by the way. Definitely up there in my top three reasons for undying gratitude."

"Only the top three? I'd consider that the very top, at least." Her lips twitched. How did he manage that? Making her laugh even in the face of infinite danger and potential death?

"Forgive me, I misspoke. You're correct, of course. A definite number one reason for gratitude and appreciation."

"I don't know," Adi admitted, though her lips still twitched. "You needed help; you haven't tried to kill me."

"Not exactly a ringing endorsement." She heard his frown now, his displeasure sharp and clear. "Your standards are too low, I think."

"Mine are lately, I agree." Humor and witty banter? Perhaps she had caught fever in last night's storm.

"Still could be a French spy," Paulo said.

"Are you?" Adi asked carefully, easing the pot into one hand in case she needed her dagger.

"No, but I suppose all spies say that. I can't imagine any outright admit it."

"I suppose," she agreed warily. Her hand rested on her chest, where her heart beat faster. She felt the hilt of her small dagger but didn't grip it or pull it from its sheath. "Then who are you?"

"A man in your debt."

Still so secretive. Dropping her hand, she nodded; she could accept that for the moment. She believed he wasn't a spy, but something about his evasion warned her to tread carefully. "Keep an eye on the sun. The moment it sets, walk out of the cave and head south. There are stone steps that lead to the villa. Don't take them."

He snorted. "All right. No steps to the house."

"They're guarded by the French," she snapped. Part of her knew this was a terrible idea. She endangered her household, her mother, and her son. The other part couldn't leave anyone at the mercy of the French. The French showed no mercy. "Pass the steps, and there's a path. It's not well-kept anymore, but if you climb it, you'll emerge into the side gardens."

"This is a terrible idea," Paulo said, voice sharp.

At least he wasn't ignorant of the dangers. Adi nodded and licked her lips again. "I know, but unless you have a better one, this is the only idea we've got."

"I—well, no, I don't." Paulo sighed again. "All right, past the steps, up the cliff. I assume there are rosebushes or other thorny branches there?"

"Probably, but I've never climbed them." She shook her head. "No need." Her stomach jumped with nerves, but, for the first time in months, Adi didn't know if it was because of the invasion or something else. Or possibly both.

"As long as it keeps you out of danger," Paulo agreed. "I promise I'll blend in and disappear from any prying French gaze."

Adi didn't believe that for one moment. Something warned her that Paulo wasn't the sort of man who blended in or disappeared. Rather, he stood out in a crowd, commanded notice. He certainly commanded hers. She merely turned back for the tunnels.

Yes, she had a feeling she'd know where Paulo Abreu stood every waking moment.

Four

Grayson decided he'd better start thinking of himself as Paulo. Unless he planned on confessing to Angelic Adelaida, thereby placing them both in danger, Paulo he'd be for as long as he remained in Portugal.

He also needed to stop referring to her as Angelic Adelaida.

Sitting just inside the cave entrance as the sun began its long decline toward the horizon, he sorted through his oilskin satchel.

He didn't remember clenching it as he swam from the wreck of his lugger, but apparently he'd retained enough sense to do so. The crate of foodstuffs had sunk along with his ship. Considering the wreckage had no doubt washed ashore, he was lucky the French hadn't yet discovered him or Adelaida.

Then again, the current ran north to south, so with any luck —not that he'd experienced much on this voyage—the wreckage would wash ashore farther down the coast.

On his hip, his khanjar still sat in its sheath, held tight against his hip by his belt. "Currently all that I own in the world."

He'd definitely swallowed too much seawater. Grayson tugged the salt-and-sand-encrusted ties holding the flap closed.

His fingers fumbled, and it took him longer than expected to untie them. Finally, the carefully packaged supplies glinted in the sunlight. Setting them on the ground before him, he took inventory. The wrapped pomegranate root had survived the swim, and the tightly wrapped jars of mustard, linseed, ginger, and turmeric had likewise endured.

"Lucky." He looked around, expecting an answer, but of course no one sat with him in this hidden cave on the Portuguese coast. He'd sailed alone. Faster and easier that way.

He'd also promised he'd be careful. What if Adelaida hadn't found him in the storm?

What had she been doing in the storm? He'd been so grateful she *had* discovered him, he hadn't thought twice about why she'd been on the beach in the middle of a thunderstorm in the dead of night.

Was she his contact? No. She'd have mentioned it before now. Clearly, she hadn't been looking for him. So who had she been looking for? As he was fairly certain she wasn't his contact —no carefully crafted code words had been exchanged—she had to have another reason for wandering the beach.

At night. In a thunderstorm. With the French crawling all over the area. And apparently in her own villa.

It only brought more questions, none of which he'd find answers to in this cave.

Grayson repacked his jars and supplies, then carefully stood and steadied himself against the rocks. His left knee twinged but held his weight. That'd heal in another day. However, the ribs along his left side throbbed with each movement, every single breath. No help for it. He'd have to climb that cliff if he wanted to start his new charade as a gardener.

A bird landed just inside the cave opening. A tern, he thought, but he was hardly the expert. His younger brother,

Philip, could name dozens of species, but Grayson always thought many of them looked alike. Sounded alike, too, though Philip insisted otherwise.

"Hello, Philip," he greeted, though Grayson didn't know if the bird was male or female. He suddenly wished he'd paid more attention to Philip's ramblings.

The bird stilled and tilted its head. Grayson flicked his gaze to the opening but saw nothing. He didn't venture closer, not with the sun still shining so brightly over the beach. Curious though he was about the area, and confident in his own fighting skills, Grayson wasn't a fool. Well, perhaps he was, agreeing to slip through British and French patrols to the Portuguese coast for desperately needed information.

He'd have words with Lieutenant Colonel Marcus Hilton when he returned to England. Then again, he was the fool who agreed to this mad endeavor.

Waving that aside, Grayson smiled down at the bird but decided against bending over. His ribs hadn't yet forgiven him for the swim. "I'm afraid I don't have anything for you. I don't think mustard or ginger is good for birds, but I'm no expert."

Philip the bird continued watching him. "Oh, just taking a rest, are we? All right then; I can share my accommodations."

The bird hopped slightly, and Grayson wondered if that was a signal of some sort. No doubt he read entirely too much into this conversation, one-sided as it was. Easing onto one of the boulders, Grayson paused to catch his breath, then gestured to the rock beside him. "It's far too much space for one man. Please, enjoy yourself."

However, Philip the bird didn't seem to like the lodgings, and he took flight. Well. So much for hospitality. His mother would be disappointed in him; she strongly believed in helping others. Though perhaps not a bird.

Retreating back behind the cave walls, Grayson gathered his satchel, brushed his fingers over his khanjar, and eased down onto the ground. It wasn't as easy or as painless as he wished.

When he opened his eyes again, Grayson felt slightly more refreshed. He awkwardly pushed himself upright, teeth clenched around the stabbing hurt throbbing along his ribs.

"Great night for climbing," he muttered. Or tried to, given his breathless state. He slipped his khanjar from its sheath and crept to the cave opening.

Outside his sanctuary, the beach stretched for miles in both directions. The wind blew over the sand, lifting the fine grains against his face. Grayson didn't consider it a screaming banshee now, more like a constant breath.

In the starlit sky, the last fingers of the sun's rays having fully disappeared, all Grayson saw was the beach's beauty. The ocean calmly broke upon the shore in serene, constant waves that disappeared seamlessly into the horizon.

He took his time, paranoid on the open beach. No need to chance a run-in with some enterprising soldier.

He made his way easily enough to the stone steps Adelaida spoke of. Stepping just far enough from the cliff walls to look up them, he saw several lanterns lining the outside patio, and possibly three shadows. Grayson assumed those were soldiers and quickly stepped back against the safety of the cliff walls.

No voices traveled down the cliffside, and Grayson hurried across the base of the stairs to the path on the other side.

"Path." Grayson snorted. "Such a strong word."

It wasn't so much a path as it was an overgrown trail that wound precariously up the cliffside. And, yes, there were rosebushes. Of course there were. In the rapidly darkening night, he couldn't see how steep the path was, or how many more rosebushes grew in his way, but he hadn't much choice.

Grayson paused. He'd placed all his trust in a woman he didn't know. One with an angelic voice and curves that made him want to hide away with her for days on end. One who'd insisted he climb this path. He knew the French occupied the land and surrounded the coast. Why would anyone lie about French soldiers in her villa?

Unless Adelaida was a spy.

No help for it. He had two choices: stay here, exposed, and wait for Esme and Landon to rescue him, however long that might take. How embarrassing. Or he could climb upward to whatever relative safety that promised.

Grayson climbed.

He didn't cut the bushes with his khanjar, though he seriously considered it. He stepped carefully in the dark, easing his way upward, past the initial onslaught of thorns. No matter how judicious his step, he had a feeling he left a trail of destruction in his wake. One that even the laziest of soldiers could spot.

Halfway up the cliff, the rose thorns eased, but the path became steeper. Grayson gasped in pain as he leaned against a boulder jutting from the cliffside. His ribs most definitely did not appreciate this climb. Sheathing his dagger, he stepped slowly, but no matter how slow or careful he was, pain radiated from his ribs along his left side.

Teeth clenched, he tried to recite anything in an effort to focus his steps and keep his mind off his pain. The alphabet in every language he knew. The names of all the animals in his family's pens. His family's shipping company's ships and captains and their routes.

When he reached the top, sweating and gasping for breath, Grayson sank to his knees.

Oh, big mistake. That hurt, too.

Oh, did that hurt. What a bad idea this was, but now he was

there, struggling to breathe, ribs screaming, and quite unable to defend himself. He had no idea how he was going to stand again, let alone continue past the villa and into the gardens where Adelaida waited.

"You didn't tell me you were this injured," Adelaida snapped from beside him.

Annoyed with himself for not hearing her approach, *again*, Grayson blinked up at her. Once, just once, he'd like to see her in the sunlight. And perhaps not have her snapping at him.

"Just my ribs," he managed.

"Oh, only your ribs, of course." Adelaida sighed, a deep, long-suffering sound that made his lips twitch. At least that didn't hurt. "Men."

"I hear that often," Grayson conceded. "My oldest sister mutters it all the time."

If Esme could see him now, she'd be furious and would no doubt hit him for his recklessness. He'd probably deserve it, too.

"Left or right?" Adelaida asked, hovering over him.

"Left."

She moved in front of him and crouched down, easing her arm about his waist. "This is going to hurt."

It did. Dreadfully. Grayson clenched his teeth so hard, he thought he might've cracked one. Something in his jaw popped, but he didn't unclench his jaw for fear of making a sound. He didn't even want to know what happened to his ribs.

"I'll wrap them," Adelaida was saying when he found his breath again. "I don't know anything else for bruised ribs." She leaned back and peered at him. "They're not broken?"

Grayson's jaw was still clenched tight. He hadn't the strength to say anything. He hadn't the strength to shake his head, either, but he tried an abbreviated movement he hoped she saw and understood.

"Can you walk?"

He doubted it but saw no choice. He'd never been so grateful for help.

"Rosebushes," he managed. Breathing hurt, but he knew from experience that not taking deep breaths would only hurt his lungs in the end. Everything hurt, but, once again, his choices weren't really choices at all. "Lots of thorns."

"Are there?" Adelaida chuckled, a strained, breathless sound as they maneuvered along the dark side of the villa. Her body pressed warm against his, her hands steady as they held him upright. And, yes, her curves pressed lush and warm against him.

Shame he was in absolutely no condition to fully appreciate that.

"I'm afraid I haven't been down there in years. I'd forgotten…"

Something in her voice had him changing the subject. "Tell me a story?"

"A story?" Adelaida huffed. "Now?"

"Anything." Grayson paused. His ribs still ached, but his legs moved more freely now, and he thought he might be able to take a deep breath. Well, perhaps not that deep. "How much farther to the gardens?"

"We're there." She blew out a breath. "Sorry. I'll save the story for another day."

"I look forward to that." And he meant it. "Tell me about the household then. What do I need to know?"

"Colonel Lambert, Bardot, his aide, and a dozen foot soldiers occupy the villa. Another two dozen or so control the village."

"Where's the village?" Grayson stood straighter. His ribs still stung, but keeping upright helped.

"Where are you from?" Adelaida sounded suspicious again, and he cursed. "How do you not know what's happening here?"

"I do know," Grayson insisted quite truthfully. "But I don't know where we are. I had to swim ashore, and I'm disoriented."

He thought he might be close to his contact point. He'd planned on meeting the person in Carvalho, a village on the coast. Grayson had calculated his destination, but the storm made everything uncertain.

"What were you doing in that storm?" Adelaida asked again.

He hadn't the strength for any more lies, so he settled on the truth. No—that wouldn't do. No sense endangering her more than he already had. "I can't tell you."

Adelaida stilled. Her hands loosened from his waist and dropped his arm. "You can't," she repeated, words flat and suspicious.

"I've already placed you in danger, Adelaida." He paused, regulating his breathing. Perhaps his knee wasn't as healed as he'd hoped. "I don't wish to place you in more."

She offered a sardonic laugh that sent a chill down his spine. "I'm in danger every day. Every minute. A French colonel has taken over my home, and I don't know if he plans to kill my family, steal what little he hasn't already, or leave us alone. His soldiers trifle with my maids, and there's little I can do to protect them. Every moment, I'm terrified Lambert will realize I'm hiding you and kill someone I love."

Grayson opened his mouth but snapped it closed. "I'm sorry. You're right; my presence here places you in even more danger. But me telling you the truth won't help that." He slowly uncurled his hands from the painful fists he'd clenched them into. "Words don't adequately express my gratitude, they truly don't, Adelaida. You saved my life, and then you fed me and kept me alive."

"I'm starting to regret that," she mumbled.

His lips twitched. "I don't blame you, but I'll do whatever I can to keep you away from the French's wrath. I promise you that."

Grayson didn't need light to see her disbelieving look. "With bruised ribs? Little food? You can barely walk on your own."

"True," he conceded. "A week, and I'll be better." Perhaps two. Neither of them could afford longer than that. "They're not that badly bruised." They felt like it, but he hadn't a month or more to heal. Too much relied on his mobility. "But I do need to know where we are."

Adelaida sighed again, a mighty heave of breath. The crescent moon did little to illuminate her, and once more Grayson wished he could see her in daylight. "Villa Carvalho. The village Carvalho is just inland."

Well. Grayson blinked at her. He hadn't actually expected to wash ashore at his destination. That meant the storm hadn't blown him off course at all, just made it impossible to leave again. Suddenly, something she'd said a moment ago clicked.

"Your servants," he repeated. "Does that mean you're the mistress of this villa?" He made an aborted gesture at the house but didn't turn. He'd just got his breath back, no need for any sudden movements.

"You ask a lot of questions for a man who refuses to offer any answers of his own, Paulo."

"True," Grayson admitted. "But I promise you this: I'm no French spy. Whether you believe me or not, I'm not here to hurt you or your family." He paused, biting back his question.

Asking her if she was married probably wasn't ideal, given her mistrust. And their circumstances. And, for that matter, any bit of propriety.

"Can you walk on your own?" Adelaida tuned her back to him. "We've stayed too long."

Grayson turned around then, slowly shifting his entire body

until it faced the villa, but he saw no movement, no extra shadow. One colonel, one aide, a dozen or so soldiers, and who knew how many others in the household. He needed a new plan.

At the moment, all he could think of was lying down and resting his ribs.

"Are there other gardeners?" he asked as they walked a stone path toward a small cottage. His gait was slow and ponderous, but at least he walked on his own. Progress.

"Not anymore," Adelaida admitted. She unlocked the heavy door and pushed it open on hinges that screamed in protest. Wonderful. Wincing, she looked around the area, but seemed satisfied no one lurked about. He'd take care of the hinges—no sense alerting the household that someone stayed in what was clearly an unused cottage. "But you can't do anything, pretend garden or otherwise, until you heal. I'll return in the morning with food, and I'll wrap your ribs then."

"Once again, I'm in your debt." Grayson took her hand and kissed the back of it. Her palms were rough, used to hard work, and he wondered what she'd been forced to do since the French occupation. "Thank you, Adelaida."

"If I find out you are a spy, I'll gut you where you stand."

His lips twitched, but he only nodded seriously. "Understood."

Five

Adi had no idea what had possessed her to bring Paulo to the gardener's cottage. Or leave food for him there so he had more than the soup she'd brought that morning.

Madness, that's what it was.

Well, that, and a little defiance. Whether Paulo turned out to be nothing more than a fisherman or sailor...or a pirate, she amended with a twitch of her lips. Or maybe he was, indeed, some sort of spy, helping anyone against the French. The thought lit a fierce fire in her chest.

Helping Paulo sparked something in Adi she hadn't felt in nearly a year.

Maybe in forever.

Perhaps it was madness, but even the smallest treachery against Colonel Lambert lightened her step and made her grin in utter joy.

That grin stayed with her as she hurried back to the villa and slipped through the rear doors into the kitchens. A pair of soldiers stood guard, but they were chatting with each other and paid her no mind. They usually chatted with each other, as if whatever Colonel Lambert required of them here meant little.

Élea and Manuéla, the cook, shifted to block their view, though the soldiers didn't notice Adi's entrance and certainly didn't stop their conversations. She breathed a sigh of relief and stepped to the fire despite the sweltering day.

"Where were you?" her mother hissed, passing her Gabriel. He slept again, poor thing. Adi pressed a kiss against his soft cheek. She hated leaving him, especially when the hot stickiness of the summer made him feel poorly. She'd committed to keeping Paulo alive, yes, but Adi needed to balance rebellion and safety. She didn't know how to juggle all that, but for Gabriel's future, she would.

Doing what she could to disrupt what the colonel tried to accomplish here was one thing. Placing her beloved son in danger? Absolutely not.

"Best you don't know," she whispered back.

"Adi…" Karlotta's voice trailed off, and she glared, her lips pressed tightly together.

"Have they said anything?" Adi tilted her head toward the soldiers, who were relaxed, as if they stood in their own kitchens in whatever French village they came from. Anger choked her, the rage hotter than the noonday sun. This, this was why she helped Paulo. Why she traveled weekly to the village in search of information.

"Bah." Karlotta snorted and returned to the cutting table. "They drink your father's port and lose at cards."

Adi consciously loosened her grip around Gabriel so as not to wake him. She breathed out, but it did nothing to cool her raging anger.

Papa.

Her father, who they told everyone had died before the entire royal family fled to Brazil. Papa, who had *not* died but left with the rich merchants, abandoning wealth and the people on the wharves. Abandoning their country. He'd said he needed to ensure their sugar, cacao, and pepper reserves survived the war.

Adi believed him a coward. Given the acidic bite to her mother's words, she thought Karlotta believed him one as well.

Though Adi sometimes envied him. He didn't live beneath the same roof as the oppressors. He didn't wonder if each day might be his last. As she held her son in her arms, she renewed her vow, promising herself, Gabriel, her family, and the village that she'd persevere no matter what, so they all survived.

At least nothing had changed in the few hours she'd been missing. Adi kissed her mother's cheek and set Gabriel back in his bassinet. She stayed in the kitchens, helping prepare Lambert's elaborate dinners and desperately trying not to think about Paulo Abreu.

How his voice washed over her, calm and deep, like the ocean she so loved. She might've daydreamed about kissing him, though she didn't really know what he looked like. But he made her laugh, and though Adi held back her trust, he offered hope in her bleak, terrifying life.

Just after she returned from serving Lambert, Gabriel cried himself awake. She swooped him into her arms before the soldiers could so much as scowl. Élea followed her upstairs with a small tray, and Adi ate by the window.

Her window, which coincidently overlooked the gardener's cottage where Paulo slept.

"I hope this isn't a mistake," she whispered as Gabriel gnawed a small piece of orange. "I don't want you in danger, my little love." She kissed the top of his head as he grinned up at her, orange juice covering his face in a sticky mess. "I'd do anything to protect you."

"Mama." He slapped her face with his sticky hands, and Adi smiled down at him.

"I love you, too, *amorzinho*." She gave Gabriel another small piece of orange, which he gnawed with equal fervor. "But I couldn't leave someone on the beach in that storm. And I couldn't leave him to die, or, worse, be discovered by the French."

Gabriel nodded seriously, as if he understood. Dear God, Adi hoped he didn't. No, if there was one thing she planned on teaching her son, it was compassion.

"Compassion, Gabriel." She kissed his sticky cheek and smiled at her boy. "God knows there is little enough of it in this world."

After a restless night's sleep, one in a long line of them, Adi kissed Gabriel, promised not to be long, and left him playing with Joana. He was in enough danger simply living in the villa, but bringing him to Paulo? No. No matter how desperately Adi needed him with her, she couldn't do that.

Adi didn't think Lambert would murder her son for her sins. Though she firmly believed him a snake in army clothing, he seemed at least partly rational. A man who spent his days writing dispatches and listening to reports from the soldiers who occupied the village. He didn't take much interest in the household, as if his presence created enough obedience.

Which it did.

As the sun peeked over the horizon, Adi hurried along the path, listening for evidence of anyone following. Only the morning birdcalls filled the warm summer air. Still, she shivered as she dug the heavy ring of keys from her pocket and unlocked the cottage door.

It squeaked again, that horribly loud sound that no doubt woke the entire coast. Adi winced and glanced up and down the path, but no one had followed. She'd have to oil those hinges, but she had no idea what hinge oil might be, or even if they had any.

"Paulo?" she whispered.

"Still alive."

"Good. I'd hate to go to all this trouble only for you to have died in the middle of the night."

He offered a snorting laugh and appeared in front of her. His shadow, tall and slim, stood straight despite his ribs. That first night, in the rain, Adi hadn't noticed much about his body. Last night, helping him after he climbed up the cliffside, she'd been too concerned with hiding him in the shadows and moving him off the path.

Now, in the dark, musty cottage, unused for more than a year, Adi forcibly curled her fingers into tight fists. Reaching out and touching him might satisfy her curiosity, but it would only bring trouble.

More trouble than Lambert discovering them. Trouble to her heart.

"Can't get rid of me that easily, I'm afraid." He let out a grunt and a slow, painful breath. "Not with these ribs."

"How did you sleep?" Adi closed her eyes. Oh, that was not what she'd wanted to ask. "I mean, did you have a rough night?" She felt her cheeks heat and was absurdly grateful for the dim interior. "With your ribs?"

"Eh, well enough." She heard the amusement in his voice, but he didn't mention anything about her fumbling questions. "This isn't the first time I've bruised my ribs." He made a small humming sound in the back of his throat, one Adi found fascinating.

She moved to the large wooden table, which was barely visible in the growing dawn. "No?" she prompted when he didn't continue.

"No." He drew out the word. "I was going to say it's the first time my bruised ribs are my own fault."

Adi paused at the table and turned, curious. "You don't sound certain."

Oh, she wished she could see his face. The way his lips formed that amused hum. Adi thought he'd moved his hands along his ribs, and she wanted very much to see those hands. And his ribs, preferably naked. When he'd kissed her fingers last night, his had curled strong and warm around hers. Confident, secure. Yes, she very much wanted to feel that again.

Flushed from thoughts she most certainly should not have been thinking, she rubbed her fingers against her skirts, tingling now with awareness. What sort of fool was she? Hiding Paulo in her gardener's cottage until he healed was one thing. Lusting after him was quite another.

Paulo stood a respectable distance away and made no untoward move whatsoever. The distance didn't stop her wayward thoughts.

But, oh, that awareness heating her blood felt good. Alive. Yes, that was the word—*alive*. Adi shook her head, but it did nothing to shake free this new awareness tingling along her skin. She grasped at their conversation, trying to bring her mind back to the present.

"I think," Paulo was saying slowly, "that my previous bruised ribs were also my fault." He laughed, a short, breathless sound tinged with pain. "Don't tell my mother. I swore to her I never had any choice."

"Other times?" She tilted her head, fascinated with his statement. "How many other times?"

"Trouble follows us." He sighed. "It's a family trait."

Adi laughed. She couldn't help it; the sound erupted from her in a burst of joy. She'd forgotten what that felt like. It had been so long—long before the French invasion, she'd wager, if she were a gambling woman.

Laughter was a scarce commodity in her household. A dead one. Or perhaps not quite so dead.

"I promise." She stifled her giggles, shocked at her behavior. She covered her mouth, but it did nothing to stop the sound. "I'd say swimming for your life in a raging thunderstorm counts as not having a choice. Well, you did have a choice, I suppose," she added. "But the other choice was to drown."

"Aye, maybe, but just in case." If the sunlight had dented the room, Adi swore she'd have seen him wink. "Don't mention that part."

She laughed again. "Your secret is safe with me."

Given the chances of her ever meeting his mother, Adi waved it off. But the way he spoke, as if she might, as if she held his safety in her hands, made her smile. Adi had a feeling that smile would remain the rest of the day.

"Bread," she said, rather too abruptly. She cleared her throat and tried again. This was not a rendezvous, though he was her secret. And nothing between them spoke of courtship, though she tried desperately not to think of what kissing him might be like.

She'd imagined it all through her restless night—she'd no need for more imagining. Like how his lips would move against hers, or the way his hands would cup her face. The feel of those strong, calloused hands on her skin.

No, that thought definitely did not send shivers down her spine.

"I brought bread, warmed in the ovens. No olive oil, I'm afraid." Her fingers tangled together, a nervous gesture Adi hadn't performed in a decade. She'd forced herself out of that particular nervousness, unwilling to show anyone her innermost feelings. Shocked she'd reverted, she lifted her chin and folded her hands primly in front of her.

"I appreciate anything you can spare," Paulo said in a warm, sincere tone that raced over her bare arms. "You've been most generous."

"Yes, well, you're welcome." She swallowed, stepping slightly to the side as the sunlight struggled through the smudged windows. "I'll be back with something later, probably at dusk."

"Adelaida." Paulo reached out and took her hands, held them in his for a silent moment. He breathed shallowly, and only then did she remember the bandages she'd brought.

"I should wrap your ribs." She licked her lips; her throat was dry. How was it that a single touch affected her at all, let alone blanked her mind and made her senses run wild? Her fingers tightened around his even as she told herself to release his hand. She didn't, but she knew she ought to. "We have no lavender, I'm afraid."

"Just as well. I'm sensitive to lavender."

Adi blinked. "I've never heard of such a thing. I didn't know that was even possible. Who's averse to lavender?"

He chuckled again, that short, breathless sound that said more about his pain than he admitted. "My father is the same. Gives him awful sneezing fits."

"How strange." The room had brightened with the dawn but didn't show Paulo clearly enough for Adi's burning curiosity. A vague outline, one she already knew. He was taller than she was by a decent amount, and he had broad shoulders—which she desperately wanted to feel without helping him walk.

"*Láudano*?" She shook her head as the offer slipped out. "The French took most of that, but we hid a little."

"No. Never use the stuff." Something in his voice gave her pause. He didn't elaborate, merely held her hand. Adi feared she could grow all too used to that hand-holding.

"Cloves?" Her voice rose embarrassingly, and Adi coughed to clear it. "I can crush some in a soup."

"Thank you." His hands tightened around hers.

Adi wondered if he could hear her pounding heart. She'd never had a schoolgirl crush like her sister or friends. She'd always known she'd marry Mateus, so she hadn't bothered with anyone else. What had it mattered? Their families signed the contract before Adi could walk. Mateus, however, for all his flattery and professions of love, had never made her heart race like this.

"You should return," Paulo whispered. He didn't release her, nor did he step back. His hand suddenly tightened around hers, and before Adi realized it, he'd pushed her behind him and pulled a dagger from his side. He'd grunted in pain but didn't move, and she had no idea what was happening.

Heart racing, she listened for whatever Paulo had heard. The French? Had Colonel Lambert followed her, or one of his soldiers? Did they suspect Adi's treachery despite her careful sneaking about?

The scratch came from the door, followed by a plaintive whimper.

"Lua." All her breath rushed from her in a knee-weakening moment.

"Who?" Paulo asked. He was half-turned toward her, his dagger still at the ready.

She had questions. Despite his injured ribs, he moved gracefully, swiftly. He'd pushed her aside and drawn his knife in an immediate and smooth move. Perhaps he truly was a pirate.

"My dog." Adi swallowed her questions and her pounding fear. "Stay in the shadows, in case someone followed her."

Adi waited only long enough for him to obey before opening the squeaky door. If that sound didn't attract curious soldiers, she doubted anything would. "I need to fix that," she muttered in the moment before Lua leaped at her legs.

"What are you doing here?" Crouching down, she rubbed the dog's ears, accepting her kisses as she sniffed suspiciously at Adi's clothing. "Are you alone?"

The sun had fully risen now, casting the pathway in dappling shadows beneath the oak trees the area was named after. Over the sound of her heart racing in her ears, all Adi could hear was happy birdsong.

She saw nothing out of the ordinary, but then no one walked this path anymore. No one had a reason to. Except her. And Lua, it seemed.

Turning back to Paulo, she eased the door closed, but that didn't stop the horrid squeaking. "I'll find something to oil that," she promised.

"Who is this?" Paulo, breathing hard and clutching his ribs, now sat on the floor, holding out one hand for Lua to suspiciously sniff. "Yes, you're a beauty, you are. What's your name?"

Stunned at the scene before her, Adi offered, "Lua. She's my dog. I brought her from Douro. She seems to like the coast more."

"Douro?" His head shot up. "You're from the river? I thought you said you were mistress here."

The sun backlit him, making a halo around his dark head. Too dark on the beach, and in the cave too light with the morning sunlight backlighting him. One day she'd see him in the perfect amount of light.

Stepping back from the door, Adi skirted a sunbeam and sat on the bed. She wrinkled her nose at the musty scent and the dust that curled up around her. She stared at Lua, who now lay on her back, letting Paulo scratch her belly.

"Yes." Adi licked her lips, her fingers cold despite the warm summer morning. The memories chilled her, froze her blood even as her anger ran red-hot. "I grew up here," she whispered, watching Lua rather than Paulo. "This was my home, before my marriage."

Paulo's hands stilled before they resumed scratching. He didn't say anything, only watched her from the floor.

"We lived along the river, a vineyard that had been in my husband's family for generations. When the French came…" Her voice hitched, and she pressed her lips together to stop the sob. "We left. Me, my mother-in-law, Lua, my son Gabriel, and any servant who wished to."

"Your husband?" Paulo's voice, soft and concerned, barely reached her.

"He had already joined the army. So many did. Friends, servants, acquaintances, employees. They thought they could stop the mighty French army."

"I'm sorry." He stood, a slow, obviously painful movement. Gasping for breath, he walked the few feet over to her and held out his hand.

Adi looked up at him and took it, refusing to let her tears fall.

"It's all right to cry," he said as she stood. Paulo wrapped his right arm around her, holding her close. Adi stilled, confused, but she accepted his comfort after a short moment. His shirt, dry with saltwater and sand, scratched her cheek, but Adi didn't move from the comfort of his embrace. "Crying isn't a weakness, but a show of compassion."

"Perhaps," she agreed. Sniffing hard, she stepped back and met his gaze. A lovely blue-green, she saw. His eyes were the color of the ocean she so loved. "But until the French occupiers are dead or banished from my country, I'm afraid I'm out of compassion."

"Maybe." Paulo brushed her cheek, leaving a trail of pleasure in his finger's wake. How did he do that? Offer kindness and thrill in the same movement? "But you saved me when you could've left me on that beach."

The words she spoke to Gabriel last night echoed in her head now. Adi nodded. "I promised Gabriel I'd teach him compassion," she admitted. "God knows there's little enough of it in this world."

Six

Clearly abandoned, musty, mildewy, and dusty, the gardener's cottage didn't exactly offer the ideal healing sanctuary.

Still, sanctuary it was.

No nosy servants or curious villagers he couldn't fend off. No worry about French soldiers he was clearly in no shape to fight—not too much worry, he amended as he breathed through the pain of simply breathing. He slept on the floor, propped against the single pillow Adelaida had smuggled in. It helped ease the discomfort of sleeping awkwardly between the wall and the table leg.

That, at least, was better than the bed. The bed that was surely a home for bedbugs and who knew what else growing inside.

His ribs ached with every breath, every movement, every thought. Carefully sitting up, using stomach muscles that protested mightily, he breathed deeply through the pain.

Breathe in. Accept the beauty of another day. Breathe out. Release all pain.

Grayson sat on the floor, letting the throbbing ache in his left side recede to a dull constant. He'd need to heal more quickly than time allowed if he still wanted to meet his contact, deliver the requested herbs, and—and what? Leave on a ship that no longer existed?

So much for his return voyage to England. Now he'd need to wait for Esme and Landon to mount a rescue. And, oh, the teasing might never end. But better rescued than dead at the bottom of the ocean.

They wouldn't immediately search for him. And Grayson had no idea what was happening on the ocean. For all he knew, they'd managed to entangle themselves in a battle with a French ship.

Keeping his torso straight and still, he shifted his legs beneath him. *Breathe in, hold, breathe out, release the pain.* He carefully pushed off the floor with only his legs until he stood upright. It wasn't as easy as he'd imagined, and he leaned against the table, once more gasping for breath.

His forced immobility had at least given him confidence to begin his exercises. Only perhaps not just yet, while he tried to catch his breath. Several choice curses escaped, but speaking only added to his pain.

The sun had only just risen, casting the cottage in strange, pink rays that were severely obscured by the filthy windows. Despite his aversion to dust and mold, and the sneezing fits they gave him, Grayson wouldn't clean them. No reason to alert the rest of the household that someone was here. No, the more this cottage stayed the same, the less danger he placed Adelaida in.

Breathing far too heavily for any sort of healing, he moved carefully toward the table, where the remnants of last night's meal lay. Bread and soup with vegetables and cloves. The cloves helped, or perhaps the soup did. Either way, he devoured the remains of the meal and silently thanked Adelaida's household for their unknowing sacrifice.

As the morning slowly brightened with the sunrise, Grayson listened for telltale signs of Adelaida's arrival. He worked through abbreviated versions of his usual exercises, and some his father had taught him to counter bruised ribs.

Trouble and bruised ribs followed the family. He hadn't lied when he told Adelaida that. Or perhaps the family found trouble. Also a possibility.

The morning continued to brighten, and still no sign of Adelaida. Worry gnawed through him. Had the French colonel discovered her deception? He'd placed her and her entire household in even more danger. Had one of the household betrayed her? A foot soldier followed her?

He eyed the door and debated the merits of sneaking about in his condition. No. That would only betray her trust, and he refused to do that when she'd risked everything for a stranger.

Then, the slight clink of metal against metal, a key against the strike plate of the lock. The sun was higher now. Midmorning, at least.

Grayson stepped for the far corner and drew his khanjar. Just in case.

Adelaida stepped into the cottage, backlit by the sun and utterly stunning. Grayson's heart skipped when he saw her clearly for the first time.

"Paulo?" she whispered, then said something softer to Lua, who happily trotted inside.

"I'm here." Grayson stepped from the shadows and drank her in.

Her hair, a stunning mass of red-brown, sat about her head

in intricate braids. Her eyes, the same deep brown he'd envisioned, watched him carefully from the doorway. Her sharp nose twitched, but she smiled.

"You look exhausted." He skirted the sunlight that was streaming in from the doorway and took the pot of soup and the bread. "Come inside. I can't offer you much, but there's a fairly uncomfortable chair by the table."

Grayson glanced outside, but the path looked deserted. A lone bird hopped along the path. Philip? He grinned but had no idea. Just in case, he tossed a breadcrumb, an offering of friendship.

He closed the door and guided Adelaida to the table and the single chair the cottage boasted. It'd been cleaned out of all essentials, except for the disgusting mattress and that one chair. He had a feeling the long wooden table that stretched the length of the house had been built first, then the walls of the cottage around it.

"I'm all right." She sighed gratefully as she sat. "Gabriel was up all night." She shifted on the chair and frowned. "This is horribly uncomfortable."

"Better than the bed. I don't think that thing's been aired out in a decade, at least."

Adelaida chuckled, a soft, tired sound. "I'm sure you're right."

"What about Gabriel?" He peered down at her, but she'd closed her eyes. In the brightening room, she looked as if she slept sitting upright. "Is he ill?"

"No, just growing." She stood and shook out her skirts as if shaking herself awake. "He's teething and fussy. Plus, he's outgrown his bassinet, but I'm afraid we have nowhere else for him to sleep. The bed is crowded enough with—" She cut herself off. "Every other bed is taken, and Lambert shipped several of our finer ones to Lisbon."

"For Junot?" Grayson frowned and leaned against the table. How many slept in a bed? As many as possible, he'd wager, especially if Lambert had taken all the others. He broke off a chunk of bread and offered her the rest.

"That's for you," she insisted. "It's all I can afford to bring. Eat while you can."

Accepting that for the truth it was, he chewed and tried to understand why Colonel Lambert would ship beds from Carvalho to Lisbon. Other than to inconvenience the people here. They'd looted everything, the bastards.

That question, its strangeness, only reinforced the fact that time was ticking.

Sooner rather than later, the French would discover his presence. Or they would simply kill the villagers here, as they had in so many other places. He'd offer transportation for Adelaida and her family if she wished. Safety in England, a new start until she could return home.

But he couldn't do that from the cottage. And there was the small matter of procuring a ship, of course.

One step at a time.

"Let me wrap your ribs." She produced a length of bandage and beckoned him forward.

"That's not necessary," he protested. But, unfortunately for him, his screaming ribs drowned out his weak protests.

Adelaida made a stern throat-clearing sound. Lips twitching, he nodded—one of the least painful movements—and stepped forward.

"You'll, ah…ahem. You'll need to take your shirt off."

As much as that sounded sensual—scandalous, even—the

very thought of lifting his arms made Grayson pause. What a blow to his pride. Still, he was stubborn. Arrogant, even. But stupid?

No. Kaya Conrad didn't raise stupid children.

"Right. Yes. I don't think I can manage that."

"Sit." Adelaida pushed him into the chair and carefully gathered the material in her hand. "I'll wash this," she offered, her voice low and calm. Except he heard the hitch in her breath, the slight catch as her fingertips brushed along his sides. "Your trousers, too, if you wish." Her breath blew out all at once. "I'm certain they're covered in salt and sand also."

"Thank you." Grayson pushed the words past his lips. No matter how uncomfortable, the pain in his ribs couldn't drown out the arousal in his cock. "I appreciate that."

He cleared his throat and tried for something else. Anything to keep his mind—and his body—off the way Adelaida's fingers felt on his skin. Their soft brush like a gentle breeze. The heat from her touch burning through him.

"All right." She cleared her throat again, and he heard her step back. "You can stand. I'll need you to raise your arms."

"This is why I never have my ribs wrapped." But he dutifully did as she told. Jaw clenched, Grayson tried to remember how to breathe, but the pain sucked it from him.

"I understand." She slowly moved the bandage over his torso, keeping the material tight. "But it's all I know for bruised ribs. And even this, I had to ask Manuéla."

He looked down at her askance, trying not to fantasize about her lips on his chest. "What did she say to that?"

"Nothing. Manuéla has worked in the kitchens since my father was a child. She won't breathe a word of this."

"Good," he gasped as she pulled the bandage tight. "That's good." He gasped again. "Too tight. I need to breathe."

"Sorry. But my understanding is that the wrap needs to be tight to prevent movement."

"Yes, I'm sure, but breathing too shallowly will only make my recovery longer."

"How so?" Even in the dimness, he saw her head tilt. Grayson wanted to reach out and touch her cheek, feel her lean into his palm.

He cleared his throat. "Restricting my breathing will make my lungs weaker. Not too much; it's temporary, but we best not chance it, given the circumstances."

"Are you certain? Manuéla was most specific."

"I didn't exaggerate when I said I've had bruised ribs before." He shook his head as she loosened the wrap, even if she couldn't see him in the uncertain light. "A consequence of standing up for myself."

Standing up for his family, too. Friends like Landon. The village kids who couldn't defend themselves. He remembered how the nurse at school had wrapped them despite his protests. And how Landon had cut the wrappings away the moment they returned to their rooms.

"A consequence." She hummed and tucked in one end. "Perhaps, and a painful one. But standing up for yourself—did you do that often?"

"Often enough." He slowly lowered his arms. "I'm only going to be able to stand this for a couple of days."

"Did you find fights often? Even at school?"

"Yes. It's how I met my best friend." He offered a weak chuckle as he got used to the wrap. "Some of the older boys were harassing him about his family." Landon's parents courted scandal the way most courted favor with the royal court. "I didn't like that. He brushed off the taunting—apparently, he was used to it. But I couldn't; it wasn't right."

Grayson also remembered the horrible words the school nurse had muttered about sons of merchants not knowing their station. But the bruised ribs incident at Eton had brought his best friend into his life, so he'd ignored that woman. Ignorant people rarely accepted change. And being friends with Landon, who was now the Marquess of Strachan and his brother-in-law, more than made up for such malicious comments.

Adelaida smoothed her hands over his chest, and Grayson forgot Landon and Eton. All that mattered was her touch.

"I'm afraid I haven't any clothing with me. I'll bring it later."

"Thank you." He caught her hand and kissed her fingertips. He absolutely adored the way her breath caught at their touch.

"Paulo..." His fake name settled between them.

Grayson very much wanted to kiss her, but he cleared his throat and stepped back instead. "Have you a large gardening hat?" he managed in an effort to break the tension.

"Pardon?" Adelaida blinked up at him, those beautiful eyes tired even in the low light.

Grayson wanted to reach out, feel the softness of her cheek, brush his fingertips along her jaw. Instead, he grinned and lifted the pot of soup. He drank slowly, letting the heat and the bite of the cloves warm him. It did nothing to ease his need to touch Adelaida.

Lua let out a soft woof, and Grayson looked down at her sharply. He couldn't say if that quiet, muffled sound was a warning that others approached or that he ought to tread carefully around her mistress.

"A hat," he repeated, bringing his mind back to the matter at hand. He finished the soup and set the pot on the table, breaking off another chunk of bread. "I'll need new trousers, too, if you can spare them."

He gestured to his left leg, where a hole in his trousers clearly showed his scraped knee. It'd healed nicely, far more quickly than his ribs would. Grayson ignored the half dozen other rips and tears from his climb last night. Lua sniffed his leg and curled between him and Adelaida, her rear on his bare foot, her head toward her mistress.

"I—yes. Though you're a fair bit taller than my father, I'm sure we can work something out." She crouched down, absently scratching Lua while she examined his knee. "You can move it easily enough?"

"Yes." He demonstrated by shifting his weight to his right leg and bending his left. It made odd pulling motions on the muscles around his ribs, but the knee itself didn't hurt. Much.

She straightened, coming up to his chest. Tilting her head, she met his gaze and watched him silently for a long moment.

He wondered what she thought. Wondered what she'd do if he drew her close and kissed her.

"How are you with a needle and thread?" Her lips twitched as if she thought she knew the answer. But if there was one thing his parents had imparted on him, it was the need to know.

"I'm no seamstress, but I've a fair hand." He settled against the table, still close enough to reach for her, and opted for the truth. "I mentioned trouble follows us, yes?"

Adelaida hummed, and she sat back in the chair. She looked as if she might fall over, but she held herself straight as she settled against the spindles of the chairback. Grayson swore they were bent purposely, so as to elicit maximum discomfort.

"You did," she allowed.

"My parents insisted on teaching us how to survive. I have three younger siblings and an older sister, and they taught us all how to defend ourselves with a dagger." He brushed the khanjar at his side, which was safely sheathed and ready should he need it.

"We also learned to cook, sew a wound—or a pair of trousers—and find our way by the stars."

"The stars?" She nodded and leaned forward. "You know the names of the constellations?"

"Oh, yes." He shifted against the table and grunted. "My sister Esme and I used to sit outside for hours and watch them." Grayson closed his eyes and so easily saw him and Esme, sitting in the fields, watching the night sky bright with a thousand stars.

When they were older, Landon and his valet would join them. But for a long time, it was only he and Esme. They'd roam the land, as carefree as anything, swimming in the lake, wading the river, climbing over the ruins that dotted the property. They'd race with the neighbor children, but always, always, they spent nights staring at the sky.

"We'd pick out the constellations and make up stories about them."

"I used to love looking up at the sky," Adelaida admitted. "Watching the stars over the ocean, imagining what they looked like up close. Once, my brother Théo and I even took one of the *barca de pesca* out and floated on the water, just staring up at the sky."

She closed her eyes and sighed. There was a smile on her face he hadn't seen before. He'd seen her frown and scowl, an angry turn of her lips and a scared one. Even though he'd heard her laugh, this was the first time he'd seen her face when she'd done so. The sheer joy of remembrance shone so brightly, the sunlight had nothing on her.

Once more, Grayson wanted to reach out, touch her as if he could feel her joy with his fingers. He folded his arms across his chest and held himself still. No touching. Instead, he grinned in return, enjoying this moment with her.

"I'd like to take you onto the ocean," he said before his brain caught up with his mouth. "Take you far from shore so we can stare at the stars, no one around for miles."

"I'd like that." Her smile softened. It no longer held the sheer joy of memory, but a softer acceptance that didn't diminish her happiness.

Adelaida took his hand and held it a moment. Her fingers were cool around his, firm.

He leaned closer, drawn to her as he had been since the night she rescued him. Long before he'd seen her in the light, when all he knew of her was the power of her stubbornness that had kept him alive in the driving rain and wet, shifting sand.

His ribs protested, and Grayson sucked in a breath. He almost cursed, but the words were lost in the breathless pain of his side.

"I should return." Adelaida dropped his hand as if it burned and quickly scooted from him.

She tripped over a snoozing Lua, and Grayson reached forward to steady her. Pain exploded over his left side, but he held her tight.

"You shouldn't move like that," she scolded.

"Right." He nodded. His eyes clenched closed as his ribs forcibly reminded him of their current state. "Yes. Next time, I'll let you fall over Lua."

Adelaida offered a breathless laugh but didn't move from his embrace, such as it was. Grayson slowly removed his hands from her waist and breathed carefully through the pain. The shallow breaths didn't help, but he doubted anything would right then.

"I have a bit of *láudano*." Adelaida's voice came soft and concerned through the pain screaming over his body and yelling into his brain. Grayson forced his eyes open. "I know you said you didn't want any, but you're in such pain. Are you certain? I can fetch it if you want."

Slowly, in small movements, Grayson shook his head. "No." He cleared his throat and tried again. "*Não obrigado.*"

"You're in pain," she insisted, skimming her hand over his side but not touching him. "Don't be stubborn."

Grayson shook his head again, those same small movements that did little to diminish his agony. "I'll be all right." At the moment, that was a lie, but he definitely didn't want any laudanum.

"You are a stubborn man, Paulo Abreu." Adelaida sighed and stepped back, careful of a once-more sleeping Lua.

Her use of his pseudonym shocked him, and he blinked down at her. Kissing her? He shook his head. A fool.

"Perhaps," he offered in a lighter tone, though he doubted he could move his left arm at all. So much for protecting her. "You're not the first person to tell me that."

Adelaida pressed her lips together and huffed a very unlady-like snort. "Of that, I am positive."

Grayson grinned as the pain eased. He continued his shallow breaths, trying not to sneeze or cough or yawn.

"I should return; I've been here too long." She whistled for Lua, who stretched slowly and shook herself. "I'll return at dusk with the trousers. You'll have to patch your clothing yourself." She stopped at the door. "It'll bring too much scrutiny if we do it."

"Understandable. Bring what you can, and I'll make do." Grayson stepped forward, just short of the sunlight doing its best to stream in through the grimy window. "Is the gardening shed around here? Close to the cottage?"

Adelaida eyed him curiously but nodded. "*Sim.* Around back."

"Be careful, Adelaida." He glanced out the window but

could see very little. Stepping through the sunbeam, he took her hand and raised it to his lips. "I'm in your debt."

"I'll return at dusk."

Grayson watched her hurry from the cottage, the door squeaking obnoxiously on its hinges as she departed. He waited another moment, listening for any sound other than his strained breathing and the constant cheerfulness of the birds. Nothing.

He desperately wanted to venture outside, see the area. Explore his surroundings and gauge where the French might be stationed—how many, if they'd mounted canons along the seawall, anything. He had no idea how far the village was, nor if his contact had even stayed in the area.

It'd been several days now, and he wasn't certain the man lingered. Not that Grayson blamed him. Whether or not he greeted this Sebastião, he needed information. And a ship.

One step at a time.

Grayson needed patience. Not his strong suit.

Rushing ahead into danger? No problem. Waiting while his body healed so he didn't put others in danger? He could manage that, but not the boredom. And he'd forgotten to ask Adelaida for a book. Not that he could read Portuguese so well. He knew the bare minimum, but he doubted the household had books in English or German or Egyptian. Still, anything was better than sitting in this dusty, forgotten cottage, waiting for Adelaida's return.

"It's going to be a long day."

Slowly lowering himself back onto the floor, he eyed the table but then dismissed it. It sat too high, and if someone happened past the windows and chanced a look inside, they'd see a body lying atop it. Instead, he moved beneath it. At least there he'd be hidden from prying eyes.

"I hate doing nothing," he grumbled, propped against the

wall, head pillowed uncomfortably on his salt-and-sand-covered coat.

Closing his eyes, Grayson easily envisioned Adelaida's face when she spoke of watching the stars, and his own lips turned upward in a smile as he drifted back to sleep.

Seven

Ten days. For ten days, Grayson cursed his idea of sleeping beneath the table, though it remained the safest place. It sounded all well and good when he'd wanted to hide from potential prying eyes—less so when he had to get out from beneath it without further injuring his ribs, his knee, or banging his head.

He'd become quite the expert on leaning awkwardly between wall and table, propped almost upright. The table leg dug into his back, but moving the mattress proved too disgusting—no wonder the French hadn't taken it. Grayson had nearly perfected shifting onto his left side, keeping his body straight as a board, and pushing up with his right arm. His uninjured side bore the brunt of movement, though it was far from painless.

The sun had long since set—not that he enjoyed sleep anymore. His enforced rest had wreaked havoc on his sleeping cycle. Unlike his younger sister, Yara, Grayson preferred mornings, waking with the sun and enjoying a quiet start to the day, no matter how busy that day might prove to be.

Now, stretching carefully, his head pounding, he catalogued

his recovery. Such as it was. He was desperately thirsty, and every joint moved stiffly. Restless as he waited for Adelaida's arrival, he worked on his exercises, slowly going through the stretching movements until his ribs twinged a bit more than was comfortable.

"Ten days," he muttered. He'd also taken to speaking aloud, talking to himself. Or the birds.

Adelaida never stayed as long as he'd have liked. Which, the more time passed, was quite a while. He enjoyed talking with her, listening to the events of her day. In a way, her life sounded as monotonous as his, the same thing over and over. Yet she never made it sound so. Grayson envied her way of storytelling. She made him laugh over Lua and Gabriel's antics, shared her fears of the soldiers, her worry and anger at how her mother-in-law closed herself off from everyone—and refused to help with any of the household chores.

She never spoke of Colonel Lambert. Though anger and uncertainty coated her every move, every word, she never spoke of him directly. Grayson had the sense he terrified her.

He stilled when he heard the tap of the key against the strike plate. Adelaida's signal that she'd arrived. Though the room was cast in shadows, he moved to the corner, his fingers gripping his khanjar.

"Paulo?" Adelaida's breathless voice echoed from the doorway.

"I'm here." His lips twitched as he reached out to rest his hand on her arm. "Where did you think I'd wander off to?"

She laughed but struggled to regain her breath. He waited, frowning. Ushering her inside, he closed the door, which was no longer squeaky. A week ago, she'd snuck out olive oil, the only grease either could find, and they'd spent the hour before dawn greasing the hinges. Such a waste, but effective.

"What's wrong?" he whispered, closing the door behind her. "And where's Lua?"

"She's with my mother," Adelaida admitted. "Mélina..." She sighed, regaining her breath. "Mélina is suspicious. So is the colonel." She shook her head. "He was unusually chatty tonight."

A chill raced down Grayson's spine, and he looked out the window. It was a reflex—he couldn't see anything, of course, not through the grime and the darkness.

"What did the colonel say?"

"Nothing." She waved a hand, but her breath hadn't eased. "Nothing out of the ordinary. He doesn't need to say anything. He asks, we jump. What else are we to do if we are to protect our people?"

Her family. All those she had left in this world.

"I don't want you sneaking down here anymore," he said. He wished he could see her clearly. "You're already in danger; coming here isn't helping."

He hated how his mere presence endangered her more than having to live in the same house as the enemy. Still, he was grateful for the company, food, and bandages.

The glimpses he'd caught of her in the sunlight tempted him. Her wit and humor in the face of this occupation wound around his heart. He wanted to help—he wanted to kiss her. He tried to remind himself he had a duty to his mission, but Adelaida was the reason for that mission.

"I'm fine." She paused and moved to the table. The room remained empty enough that neither needed to worry about tripping over anything in the dark. "Lambert is bored, I believe."

"A bored colonel is never good." He sighed and leaned against the table as she took the chair. He chose his next words carefully. "What did he want from you?"

She laughed, a short, mirthless sound. The soup pot scraped against the wooden tabletop, followed by another sound. Intrigued, Grayson looked down but couldn't see more than a vague outline. The household couldn't afford to feed him even the small amount of soup and bread Adelaida secreted out.

"He rediscovered his love of chocolate." She sighed, a drawn-out, weary sound that emanated from her toes.

Grayson reached out and found her hand, cool despite the evening's heat. Her fingers were always cool. "Chocolate?"

"Yes, we are chocolatiers." She paused, her fingers relaxing in his hold. "Or were, before the war knocked on our door. The very finest in all of Portugal." Her voice calmed, now confident and proud. "We were the chocolatiers to the Crown."

"Truly?" Grayson blinked, but of course he couldn't see her. Pity, that. "I wasn't aware there was such a thing."

He stopped before he spoke too boldly, gave too much away. He was Paulo, the Portuguese sailor who crashed his ship along the coast. Not Grayson Conrad, part-time spy from Hertford-shire, England.

"I brought you a small pot, still warm. Our secret recipe." Adelaida's tone told him what her words did not. That no matter the circumstances, she was proud of her heritage. That, Grayson understood all too well.

"I love chocolate." He reluctantly released her hand and lifted the first pot.

"That's the soup." Her hand rested on his. "I'm sure you're tired of soup and vegetables, but—"

"It's delicious." He rushed to cut her off. "I savor every bit of it. And the company." He grinned, lifting the pot in salute. "The company is a definite addition."

"I'll be sure to tell Lua that." She laughed again, and Grayson thought he could listen to that laugh for years. He wondered if her eyes sparkled, wanted desperately to watch her mouth stretch into a smile when she found the slightest bit of joy. "I'm sure she'll be most pleased."

"Dogs are the best company; I can't disagree there." He chuckled and sipped the warm soup. "And they do make me laugh." He took another sip. It eased his thirst, and though he wanted a flask of water or juice to cool the stickiness in this closed-in room, he didn't want to place Adelaida in any more danger.

"She is a comfort," Adelaida said softly. "I'm not sure how good of a guard dog she is, but she's protective of me and Gabriel, and she does not like the French."

"Not many do these days," he agreed. He finished the soup and let the warmth flow through him despite the heat. "Tell me more of the colonel. And Mélina's suspicions."

"What's there to tell?" She huffed in annoyance and stood, pacing toward the rear of the cottage and back again. Grayson admired her form, though he could only see it in shadow. "Colonels like him populate the coast, waiting for Junot or Napoleon to order them about. He writes dispatches here and there, sends his men to the village or Lisbon."

"Why the village?" Grayson frowned into the dark bottom of his soup pot. He had a feeling the colonel suspected traitors. But then, according to the French, all of Portugal were traitors to Napoleon's Continental System. "I mean, why there specifically? Wouldn't he be more worried about securing the coastline?"

"He worries about that, too," Adelaida said. "He and Bardot speak frequently of that. But there are rumblings in the village about English spies and..." She sighed. "Never mind. It's silly."

"Silly enough for Lambert to believe it," Grayson pointed out.

She didn't say anything, and he let it go. English spies, he believed, of course, given the Portuguese chose to honor the Anglo-Portuguese Treaty instead of caving to Napoleon, which had caused this invasion. And he wasn't fool enough to believe he was the only spy in the country. Even this far south.

Lieutenant Colonel Marcus Hilton of His Majesty's secret spy network, for whom Grayson had agreed to this small incursion, had hinted at a multitude of British spies already in Portugal. But they'd needed someone willing to slip in and out, run Napoleon's blockade and return with information on troop movements.

Look what agreement had gotten him.

Still, he could name a hundred worse ways to spend his time than conversing with Adelaida.

Could've done without the bruised ribs.

If British spies were in Carvalho, was one of them his contact? He and Hilton had assumed it was a Portuguese citizen, one who was furious with the French occupation and willing to risk his life for the now-sunken crate of food and the medicine Grayson still hid in his satchel. He figured that by now the person would've left, figured no one was coming or run afoul of either the storm or the French.

"I'm still puzzled by the beds," he said instead of pushing. Whatever Adelaida hadn't told him—her silly piece of information—could wait. "It's one thing for Lambert to want a nice bed to sleep in, but quite another for him to care if his troops have one, too."

"I think he took them to punish us," Adelaida whispered then sighed. "Or for his own villa in France."

"Both reasons are possible." He frowned. "But why? Other than he's the invading army and wishes to make your lives as miserable as possible." Grayson paused, eying the bedding he hadn't touched since stumbling into this cottage. No one had touched that bed, and once more he wondered why it'd been abandoned when everything else had been looted. "Is that why he wanted a chocolate tasting?"

He looked at the forgotten pot of chocolate on the table. He lifted it, untied the string, and held the cloth covering secure. The scent hit him first, delicious, rich, warm. A bite of spice, too.

"We also make *pastelaria*, but the French stole all our port and food, including the almonds." Her voice held the bitter tone it often did when she spoke of Lambert and his soldiers, but there was something different about it tonight. Resignation. Or perhaps she was just too tired to do anything about it.

She walked back to him, her footsteps silent, the slight swish of her skirts the only sound of her movement. Adelaida leaned closer, as if she could point out anything in the darkness. "Blending the chocolate requires a gentle touch; it cannot be rushed."

"My aunt, she loves chocolate." He sniffed the temptation and knew he'd have to share Adelaida's incredible concoction with Aunt Nadia when he returned to England—*if*, not *when*. "Each morning, she used to savor a pot at the start of her day."

"Take a sip," Adelaida whispered, voice low and enticing. A tempting promise. "Just a small one. Let the chocolate sit on your tongue." Grayson let the lilting enticement wash over him. "It's still warm yet, a mixture of our very best beans and sugar."

He paused. "And the workers on your sugar plantation?"

Grayson didn't need to see Adelaida to feel her momentary confusion, just like he didn't need sunlight to see her smile. "My father, he went to Brazil with the monarchy." Her voice dropped, still enticing but firm. "We told the French he died last year; we told everyone that. The entire village believes he died of fever. But he escaped to Brazil with the royal fleet to ensure our workers are treated properly."

Once more, she sighed in bone-weary resignation. "He got it into his head that someone needed to protect our assets there. That if he wasn't there to do so, we'd not have any business after the war. No one could talk him out of it, and Théo, my brother, refused to abandon the people here." Her voice dropped again, and that bitter anger coated every breath. "I know he oversees our people there, and I'm grateful he cares, but everyone needs help."

Surprised, Grayson nodded. "Good man, your father." Odd that he would abandon his family. Unless he had a second family in Brazil? Mere speculation on Grayson's part. "Not many bother with their workers in the Americas."

"I know, which is why I understand. Most days." Her voice dropped again. "Several years ago, he and Théo traveled to Brazil to inspect the crops. The overseers did not treat the workers well—they whipped them and starved them, stole their wages. Papa said Théo was so furious, he tore the whip from one of the overseer's hands and turned it on him." Adelaida let out a small, soft laugh. "It's not a laughing matter, but knowing he stood up for those who provide for us makes me proud."

"You should be proud," Grayson agreed. "Showing compassion is never a weakness. And those who work for you should be treated with the same respect as those you consider equals."

In the dark, empty cottage, he swore he saw Adelaida's head tilt in curiosity. Or perhaps in understanding. Their entire acquaintance had been conducted in the dark hours, and no matter how he wished otherwise, he couldn't imagine her features with any certainty.

"You're a strange man, Paulo Abreu."

Her use of his fake name always stilled Grayson, but he tried to brush it away. That name kept them both safe. "For seeing people as equals? You aren't the first person to tell me that."

"Sip the chocolate, Paulo, before it cools too much."

He sipped the chocolate.

It exploded over his tongue, a glorious sensation of rich darkness with a hint of sugary sweetness. He wasn't used to sugar—his family boycotted anything from Britain's colonies or the Americas, where slaves were used to line the pockets of the rich.

The chocolate slid down his throat, a lovely, warm sensation that left the most pleasant of aftertastes. A little pepper, he thought.

"It's amazing," he agreed, taking another sip. "I've tasted my share of chocolate, and this far exceeds them all. What's that spiciness?"

"The *pimenta moída* is native to the land. Wait until you taste my candies and *pastelarias*," she promised.

Adelaida must've realized how suggestive that sounded at the same time he did, because she stepped back and cleared her throat.

Scrambling for anything that would put her at ease, Grayson set the chocolate on the table and grabbed her hands. They curled around his, cool and solid.

"I should return," she whispered, but she didn't release his hands nor walk for the door. "I've already stayed too long."

"I know." He tightened his hold on her fingers. "I don't mean to keep you here. Is Gabriel all right? Your mother? Mélina?"

"*Sim, sim,* they are well, thank you." She paused and shook her head. "Inês, she still plays the pianoforte all night."

Meaning she still didn't help with the chores. Grayson glanced at the table, where his satchel was carefully hidden in the far corner, out of the way. He had herbs there, ones he dared not use in his own soup. They were for his mysterious contact, a promise he'd made to help them in exchange for information.

Torn, Grayson squeezed Adelaida's hands before releasing them. "About that gardener's hat we spoke of."

"Hat?" She paused and cleared her throat. "What about it?"

"My ribs are less tender; it's time I earned my keep."

"Paulo." She drew out his name in exasperation.

"Dressing as a gardener will draw little attention." Even if whoever his contact was had information on troop movements, Grayson could spend his restless nights wandering the back of the villa, well away from the gardens. Well away from the night guards. "If any of Lambert's men even notice, just tell them you hired me from the village. I needed work."

"If anyone sees you, they'll know you aren't from the village."

True, but he didn't have any other ideas. He had no ideas at all. No idea how to slip into the village when his ribs still ached and would hinder any self-defense he might need. No idea how to get through the French blockade. The ship still awaited him, that much he knew. Esme and Landon wouldn't abandon him. But he had no idea how to get there.

The small fishing boats wouldn't work. Actually, he wasn't sure about that. How many wished to leave, and how many would they need for all the villagers?

"All right," he conceded. "If—and that's a big if—anyone questions you about me, tell them I came from the north looking for food and work."

"That's the same story," she pointed out. "Just a different location."

"True." He grinned. "But it will work."

She shook her head and hummed in amusement. He liked that, the soft sound of pleasure she often made when she didn't want to laugh outright. "Do you even know how to garden?"

"No, but it can't be too difficult." He paused. "I can tell a weed from a vegetable. Mostly."

"And your ribs?" She crossed her arms in front of her, and if there'd been even a smidgen of sunlight, Grayson knew he'd have seen her smirking at him.

"Healed enough. I promise not to engage in any fisticuffs." Though he was confident in his abilities against any soldier, healed ribs or not, Grayson didn't wish to chance anything. Not with Adelaida's life in the balance.

"I was thinking of bending over. Kneeling in the dirt."

"Ah, yes, that as well. I promise I'll bend and kneel carefully."

"You're mad."

"In here? With nothing to read? No one to talk to except you for only several moments every day?" Grayson nodded, the loneliness and isolation of the last ten days tumbling out. "Yes. Yes, I am."

"I'm sorry." She took his hand, her fingers stroking his knuckles. "I wish I could stay all day. Or bring Gabriel. I'm sure he'd love wandering the gardens. But I'm afraid to bring him out too much."

Afraid of the attention she might bring down on him, she meant. Grayson cursed himself and his selfishness. For as trapped as he was in this cottage, she was even more so in the villa. The size of the house didn't matter.

The only difference was, he could leave. Thank her for her hospitality, leave her the herbs he'd brought for his contact, and disappear before the French knew he'd been here. Grayson paused. He could, but until that moment, he hadn't thought to do so. In fact, thinking on it now, he immediately dismissed the idea.

No, he wouldn't leave Adelaida until he could guarantee her safety. One way or another.

"One step at a time," Grayson said aloud. "My mother says that. We can't take our second step without completing the first."

"Wise woman, your mother."

"You two have a lot in common." He chuckled and brushed his fingertips over her cheek. They were as soft as he remembered, and the feel of her skin rushed through him. "Except I want to kiss you."

Eight

Adi's breath stopped. "Oh."

Ah, yes, brilliant, Adi. A man professes he wants to kiss you and what do you say? Oh. Perfect. She wanted to say more, but all her breath left in that one word, and her mind utterly blanked.

"You sound surprised," Paulo whispered, his fingers still stroking her cheek.

She quite liked that feeling. Mateus had rarely touched her so, though from what she'd discerned about the marriage bed, he'd been a generous lover. But stroking her cheek as if he adored the feel of her skin? Adi doubted that had ever occurred to him.

"I'm...well, yes, I am surprised," she admitted.

She was blushing, and she knew it. Could he feel the heat of her skin against his fingertip? Oh, but she wanted to kiss Paulo, wanted to know the taste of him, the feel of his lips against hers. How his hands might feel against her skin. They had seen work, were calloused from the ship, she'd guess. How would they feel against her thighs?

Faced with the sudden reality of his confession, she floundered.

"Why?" His fingers brushed along her jaw, over her chin, just shy of her lips.

"Why am I surprised?" She laughed, a breathless sort of sound. "You hardly know me."

"I know you very well, Adelaida."

She loved how he said her name. That admission rushed through her like the storm on the night she'd found him. Wild and untamed, making her heart pound and her blood heat.

"How so?"

"I know you treasure your solitude more than you admit." His thumb grazed her lower lip. "And I know you will protect Gabriel until your last breath." His fingers brushed along her throat, light as a feather over the skin left exposed by her simple gown. "I know you'd protect Inês from the French even though you dislike her, and you would die for your mother, sister-in-law, and servants."

"That should be obvious." Her breath came faster, but she remained rooted in place. "Who wouldn't die for her son?"

Paulo dismissed that with an impatient snort. "I can name a few. But your love for Gabriel is obvious. You're strong, resilient, caring, kind, and smart. You care for this household and the village above yourself."

Adi wanted to utter a witty remark about why he'd listed smart last, but his thumb had returned to her lower lip. She couldn't form words. She swallowed, her gaze held by his even in the dusty, uncertain light.

"And you care," he repeated.

"I care about my people," she countered. "I care about Portugal and Carvalho and—"

"You *care*," he said more firmly. "You rescued me from that storm not knowing who I was or why I was on that beach."

"I still don't know who you are or why you were on that beach." It was a weak argument, and though she wanted answers, she also wanted his kiss.

What had he said? One step at a time. This felt like she was about to leap from the cliffs overlooking the beach without any safety net beneath her.

"Are you going to kiss me?" Where that boldness came from, Adi didn't know, but she embraced it.

Paulo laughed and leaned in. "As much and as often as you wish."

Adi refused to answer that—she hadn't an answer. Her skin tingled with every brush of his fingers, and she craved more. Heat pooled between her legs. She wanted Paulo's touch there, too.

His mouth pressed softly against hers, and Adi instantly knew she didn't want him to stop. Ever. His mouth was firm, warm, sure.

Perfect.

Hesitant, tentative, she kissed him back. Felt his beard along her skin and shuddered. Her hands no longer curled into the skirts she hadn't realized she was gripping, but now gripped his shirt. Pulling him closer. Or holding tight as the maelstrom of that kiss raced through her like a beautiful storm.

He smiled against her lips, his hands cupping her face. Heart racing, breathing heavy, she pulled back and watched his eyes blink open. Adi wanted to see them clearly in sunlight as they watched her.

"Adelaida?"

"Kiss me again."

Adi didn't know where that command came from. All she

knew was she wanted more. More of his kiss, more of that wonderful rush of need. That ache of wanting.

This kiss was rough, just short of desperate, and Adi reveled in it. Paulo stirred a fire in her she'd thought long dead, and she burned with his touch, hot and bright and all-consuming. He backed her against the table, and she had a wild thought about making love to him right there, on the table in the gardener's cottage.

Shocked at her mind for jumping from kissing to making love, Adi pulled back. On the table? In the middle of the day? Scandalous. Tempting.

Breathing hard, mind whirling, she tried to grab whatever sense she retained. It proved elusive.

"Paulo."

He cursed. Not the reaction she'd expected. He cursed a rather impressive litany in at least two languages that weren't Portuguese.

Adi paused, not at his cursing itself, though that shocked her. No, at the intense look in his eyes when they met hers again. Everything in her stilled, and she knew something had changed. Had she truly brought in a madman from the beach, offered him food and shelter, *and kissed him*?

She scooted around him, no longer trapped between his strong, hard body and the table. The door lay only a few steps behind her. If need be, she could always shout for help—even for French help. Claim she'd discovered this stranger in her cottage.

"Adelaida." His voice caught her. "Please stop. I won't hurt you." He offered a small sound of resignation and shook his head. "I'm still the same man who kissed you."

"You aren't though. What's changed?"

"I—my name isn't Paulo." He sounded accepting now, as if

he knew this was the moment everything would change. "It's Grayson, Grayson Conrad."

"Grayson Conrad," she repeated. Her hand inched upward, toward the dagger hidden in her bodice.

At the time, it'd seemed an ideal hiding place, but now that she actually needed it, Adi realized the disadvantage. She'd need a pocket, or perhaps to simply keep it at her waist, like Paulo—or Grayson Conrad, or whomever he claimed to be.

"Yes, I'm here. Well, it sounds far more fantastical than it is." He hadn't moved, and he kept his hands out so Adi could see them. She was not reassured. "We received a letter."

"We," she repeated, not at all certain where he was headed or where she expected him to. "Who is we, what letter, and what does this have to do with me?"

"I—it's a long story," he hedged.

She slipped her dagger free of her bodice and held it before her. She was under no illusion she could do much damage, especially given his own at his hip. Paulo—Grayson—eyed it in the uncertain light but didn't acknowledge it. Nor did he draw his own. "Talk. Fast."

"Would you care to sit?"

"Or I can call for the soldiers."

His lips twisted into a funny half smile, half grimace. "That's understandable. All right. I'm friends with a man who works for the Crown. His superior is a spymaster, one who focuses on Napoleon's activities in the Americas."

A chill raced down her spine. Spies—*porra*, she knew it. Spies, no, in the Americas?

Cold now, Adi stilled. Papa lived in Brazil; had Napoleon somehow found him? Or attacked Rio de Janeiro? Papa had planned to visit their sugar and cocoa estates before settling in the capital.

No. None of that explained Grayson's presence here.

"If he's focused on the Americas, why are you in Carvalho?"

"I—I'm getting there."

"Talk faster."

He cleared his throat and nodded. Yes, she clearly saw his smile and wanted to punch it off his face. She'd slapped Théo once, but that was a decade ago at least.

"Hilton—the spymaster—intercepted a letter from this area to the British. In it, the writer claimed to know French troop movements, size, locations, and artillery placements. In exchange for this information, he wanted food and medicine."

Adi nodded. It sounded plausible. Completely believable, even. But it didn't explain why he'd lied. "All right. Say I believe you. What happened?"

"That storm." He scowled, the same expression she'd grown to like but now made her shiver in apprehension. "I hadn't expected it. I'd been led to believe there was very little rain along the southern coast during the summer."

"You were caught unawares," she said, repeating what she'd already gleaned from their conversations of the previous two weeks. "What happened to this mysterious contact?"

"I don't know. I couldn't venture out; I know my limits." He pressed his hand to his left side, where his ribs were still healing. He'd said that before, or words to that effect. That he wouldn't put anyone in danger because he couldn't take care of himself.

"All right," she repeated. "Why confess now?"

Paulo—Grayson—paused. It wasn't a long hesitation, but enough to make her wonder what he truly thought. What he'd planned on saying before he stopped and changed his mind.

"It didn't seem right, you kissing Paulo."

That made very little sense from a man professing to be a spy, but Adi ignored it. No doubt she'd fuss over it later, as she lay in her bed wide awake and restless. But right then, she pushed it aside.

"Where did you come up with Paulo?" She lowered her dagger. She didn't return it to its sheath in her bodice, but she didn't hold it before her, either.

"It's my middle name. Paul. Named for my father."

"For an Englishman, you speak excellent Portuguese."

"Oh." He grinned; it was there and gone in a heartbeat. She wanted to smack him for his arrogance. "Thank you. I learned from a native speaker."

Adi nodded, then felt foolish for doing so. What did it matter? Now she was harboring a British spy. Not simply a fellow countryman injured and hiding from the French. Oh, no. A spy.

"Who is this person you're supposed to meet?" Adi paused and sighed. "It's been two weeks; are you certain they're still waiting?" She narrowed her eyes. "You brought food? You smuggled in *food*, and I've *fed* you?"

"No." Grayson held up his hands, shaking his head. "No, not food. I lost that in the storm. I swear, I wouldn't have taken from you if I had other means. I did retain the herbs, but I figured my contact needed them more than I did."

She glared for another moment, then nodded. She believed him, though after the revelations of the last quarter hour, she didn't know why. "All right. This contact?" she prompted, impatient.

"I was to meet him in Carvalho, goes by Sebastian. Sebastião," he added in proper Portuguese.

Adi stopped. Sebastião? Then she laughed. She laughed and laughed and wondered if perhaps she'd broken down like Inês. This wasn't the joyful sound she reveled in with Gabriel, or even those few times Paulo—Grayson, *porra*—had made her laugh. No, this bordered on hysterical.

"Adelaida?" Grayson asked, inching closer. She didn't even bother to raise her dagger. "Everything all right?"

"Sebastião." She shook her head and wiped her cheeks. "*Caralho*," she cursed. "Of course."

"Does the name mean something to you?"

"Have you ever heard of Rei Sebastião?" He shook his head, which didn't surprise her. "He died a few hundred years ago, but there are those who believe that in Portugal's hour of need"—she rolled her eyes—"he'll return from the dead and save us all."

"Ah." Grayson—and that name sounded so strange—nodded. "I see."

"Do you?" Adi sighed and slipped her dagger back into its sheath.

"Someone used his name not only to conceal their own, but also to bring hope."

"Hope?" Her laugh tasted bitter on her tongue. Just moments before, she'd kissed Grayson and wanted more. Now, the hopelessness and despair she'd carried with her for months crashed back down upon her. "We have no hope. Someone plans to take credit for Portugal's salvation. There've been dozens who claim to be him, returned from the dead. None of them are real." She glared at Grayson once more. "No one can return from the dead."

"This is true. But I didn't mean it that way, though I see how you believe so." She wondered what he meant by that but hadn't the strength to ask. "I mean using the legend of Sebastião as a beacon of hope to sustain the people."

"Food sustains us," she snapped. When had she grown so acrimonious? "As does the British promise to route the French from our lands."

"And that promise still stands," Grayson insisted. This name unsettled her. His real name, according to him, though he'd made a good case for Paulo Abreu, so she had no idea what to believe. "My understanding is that British troop arrival is imminent."

She watched him, uncertain whether she believed that or not. She wanted to; God knew she wanted to believe every word. Not only because she found him attractive. She enjoyed his company, wanted more time together, and definitely wanted more kisses. But she wanted the truth in his words because she desperately wanted her country free from French invaders.

"Is that how you planned to return home?"

"No. Well, not immediately." He sighed and leaned against the table, looking tired and defeated in the darkening night. "I'd planned on slipping in, finding Sebastião, exchanging information for food and herbs, and leaving the same night."

"How?"

"There's a ship waiting beyond the French blockade. We towed my lugger as close as we could to evade detection. Then I sailed past the French ships and toward shore."

Adi nodded. She didn't have a reply. It hadn't worked, and they both knew that. No use rehashing what happened after that. No use bringing it up at all.

"And now?"

"I'd prefer to leave before the British invade." He paused, and even in the darkness she knew his gaze never left hers. "I'd prefer to bring you back with me. You, Gabriel, your whole family. Lua, of course."

She heard the smile in his voice at the mention of her dog. She appreciated the addition but couldn't quite return the smile. Her insides had frozen.

"Your entire household, if they want."

Her mouth went dry. Leave Portugal? Leave her home? Abandon her people as the monarchy, *her father*, the entire government had? Adi wanted to snap at him, sneer that she'd never. But her responsibilities loomed larger than even her love of this land.

All of them? The household, even the villagers?

"You make bold promises, Grayson Conrad." Arrogance? Or confidence? She had no idea.

"I never make a promise I can't keep." She swore he was grinning again. He had a habit of doing so at the oddest of times. Before tonight, Adi found it endearing. Now, she wanted to slap him. He stirred a violence in her she hadn't realized she had. "It's a failing, I'm told, but we Conrads take our oaths seriously."

"I, too, take my oaths and responsibilities seriously. The Dos Santoses have lived here for generations. We can trace our family back to before Tariq ibn Ziyad invaded, before cacao made its way to our shores. Always, the village relied on us, and always we ensured they had food, protection, opportunities."

Adi licked her lips and folded her hands in front of her. Grayson tempted her. Tempted her mind with his wit, her heart with his laughter, her body with his kiss. He brought her joy when she thought she'd lost it all, and he made her laugh in the face of oppression and occupation and such seething anger, she wondered the entire countryside hadn't already exploded.

She'd wanted more, wanted to see where this might lead. Now, she had no idea, and she refused to take one more step with him until she regained her footing.

"You're a good family," Grayson said, and suddenly she found him closer. He didn't reach for her, which was just as well, since Adi couldn't guarantee she *wouldn't* slap him. "Any family that puts their people over themselves deserves protection as well. Not many do."

She only nodded. Inês hadn't, not really. She cared for the money that the vineyard brought in, that the workers ensured her. But as for them themselves? Adi hadn't ever seen it. Mateus cared, from what she'd seen of his interactions, but those were few and far between.

"What do you want from me?" The moment the words left her mouth, Adi wanted to snatch them back and stuff them deep inside.

After that kiss? She closed her eyes and hoped the floor might open up and swallow her. As she'd never seen that happen, and figured if it could, it would've the moment Colonel Lambert entered the village, Adi merely sighed.

"I want a great many things." Grayson's voice flowed over her, smooth and strong like the chocolate she loved working with. "Right now, I want you safe."

"How?" She swallowed. "How would you transport all of us back to England?"

The thought tempted her, called to her in a way she didn't understand and hadn't even wondered about. Leave Portugal? They had no means, no ship, no help. Even if—*when*—the British army arrived, they'd never offer her one of their own ships. Except...now. Maybe.

"Leave the details to me." He sounded so confident. Or perhaps egotistical. "Right now, we need to find this Sebastião and see what he knows."

Information in exchange for food. What had Grayson transported? Pigs? Cattle? Vegetables and fruits? That seemed the most likely. "Where are the herbs?" She'd forgotten about them, but, as he said, they were important. "Which ones?"

"They're in my satchel." He must've gestured to the floor and the bag she'd also forgotten about. She'd not even bothered to search it, oh, no, but had left him with his secrets. Adi sighed. No sense berating herself over the past. It couldn't be changed.

"Pomegranate root, mustard, linseed, ginger, and turmeric."

Her eyebrows shot up. "You managed to save all that while swimming through the ocean in that storm?" She shook her head, annoyed that he'd managed to impress her.

"Would you like them now?"

Yes. Adi paused and swallowed the agreement. She could take them, add them to the kitchens and ignore the surprise when the cook found the extra herbs. It'd be harder to hide them from the soldiers there, tasked with ensuring they didn't poison Lambert. For all their nonchalance about the cooking itself, they often conducted random inspections of the food. And if they discovered the additional herbs, they'd have more questions—at the end of their bayonets.

As limited as food in the villa was, the village had even less. They needed the medicinal herbs more. She could always bring them into Carvalho during their weekly supervised visit.

"No. They'll hold for another couple days until we figure out how to go about finding this Sebastião."

"You should return, Adelaida." She really shouldn't like the way he said her name as much as she did. Now, with his deception revealed, she really didn't want to like the low warmth he injected into the word. "It's late."

"What are you planning?" She narrowed her eyes though she barely made out his still form.

"Another night of exercise," he admitted. "But I think tomorrow I might need that gardener's hat after all."

Nine

The next morning, just as the sun peeked over the horizon, Adi returned to the cottage with a wide-brimmed gardener's hat, a basket of gardening tools they'd taken when Pedro, their gardener, died in a fruitless stand against the French, and a pair of gloves that had seen better days.

"*Aqui*." She set the basket on the table as Lua followed her in and presented herself for her morning rubdown from Paulo. Grayson.

Adi still hadn't figured out how to wrap her head around how foolish she'd been, how easily he'd duped her. She'd been suspicious of anyone who didn't speak Portuguese, but he had, and quite fluently, too. She should've been more suspicious of his appearance on her beach during the storm. Or even of the storm's sudden lessening so she might hear his call.

But she'd been too caught up in keeping him alive and away from prying French eyes. She'd let her hatred of the French, and her desire to keep her countryman alive, blind her. She hadn't asked enough questions, or perhaps not the right ones.

Now, as Grayson quietly thanked her for the vegetable soup

and olives and settled the too-large hat on his head, she saw he moved easier. Two weeks must've helped him heal. Good. The sooner he left, the safer all of them would be.

"I don't care how good you are with that dagger." She nodded to his side though the sunlight hadn't yet reached the cottage and she barely saw his outline. "If you bring any harm on my family or this village, I'll gut you myself."

"I understand." He sighed, setting the empty pot on the table. "I don't blame you."

She probably wouldn't turn him over to the French. Last night, as she watched Gabriel sleep and listened to her mother's restless movements, Adi knew she wouldn't let the French learn of his presence. That'd only bring their anger down on her loved ones. She refused to allow any more harm to come to the people under her care.

And no matter how angry she was over Grayson's betrayal, she also couldn't blame him for keeping his secrets. He knew as little of her as she did of him. It hadn't lessened the hurt that cut through her, but, intellectually, she understood it.

"When Lambert and his men forced open our doors and marched themselves inside," Adi said, not entirely certain why she was telling Grayson these things, "I promised my people and my village they'd be safe. That promise didn't stop their angry resentment, nor their whispers of rebellion. We're a proud people, and we don't agree with what our government has become."

"Are you worried what the British might think with Lambert in your villa?"

"Bah," she spat, a fine imitation of her mother. Adi even waved her hand the way Karlotta did. "No. All that matters is our people know the truth, and they do. In these past months, I've managed to keep everyone calm enough to gather information against the invaders instead of haphazardly rising up, only to be slaughtered."

Adi hadn't expected a British spy to wash up on her beach.

Fortuitous, indeed.

"I promised my people safety." Adi still wasn't certain whether Grayson was trustworthy. She tried to control her anger —at herself for wanting him, for believing his story, for trusting him when everything around her had told her otherwise. It still burned through her, hot and vicious, threatening to scorch her.

"I've chosen to believe you." She hadn't meant to announce it like she stood in front of an audience in the Palace of Queluz, but she couldn't relax around him now. In front of Paulo, she'd grown at ease, reckless in her trust. Her daydreams. With Grayson, she couldn't afford that same carelessness. "Because of your stated reasons for being here, though you must understand I find it difficult to trust you again."

Porra. She hadn't meant *again.* That had slipped out.

Grayson held himself still in the rapidly brightening day but nodded. She had a feeling it wasn't his ribs that pained him, but her words.

Confused, Adi plunged on. "You didn't know the story of Sebastião or what it means to many here." She licked her lips and hated that she'd done so, showed him the slightest unease.

"You don't believe the legend. About Sebastião." Grayson nodded again. "I don't blame you." She had a feeling he meant her mistrust, but she couldn't bring herself to ask. "It's fantastical, I agree. However, I think it's the hope the story brings that makes it meaningful."

"Hope is the hardest, and last, bit to release. Hope is all we have left, but it's slowly dwindling. I don't know what you know of our government, and I'm not here for a political lesson."

She'd hashed that out enough with Mama and Mélina in

those early days. After Papa's escape to Brazil and the family's fury over his desertion. And then again, after Théo's death.

"I know your government made a deal with mine," Grayson said softly. "I take it you don't agree?"

He phrased it as a question, but Adi heard the flatness in his tone. No, she did not agree, and she heard the disagreement in his voice also. She tried not to latch on to that, but it settled in her heart.

"Take the richest and flee, leaving the rest of the country to fend for themselves?" She offered a mocking laugh, her fingers tight in the folds of her skirts in the vain hope of holding back her tirade. "No," she ground out. "I do not agree."

"That's because you care, Adelaida." He shifted closer, though she didn't think him foolish enough to touch her.

No matter how she burned for that touch. A repeat of last night's kiss. She was the foolish one, foolish to want, hope, believe. Desire.

"You care about your household and your people, the village you grew up in." The low chuckle, a warmth she hadn't expected, drifted across the slight space between them. "I've met a lot of landowners who don't—most of them don't. They care about profits and gathering wealth like a dragon of old, and they don't care how they accomplish that."

"*Merda*," she muttered. "I don't want to agree with you."

Grayson laughed, the same sound that initially won her over, that made her think all was not lost. Adi didn't know whether she ought to punch him, for the sake of doing so, or kiss him again. She settled on bunching her skirts tighter so she didn't reach for him at all.

Why had she spoken? What was her point? Ah, yes, that silly myth.

"I'll help you find Sebastião, or your version of him." She

pressed her lips together, but the words burst forth, and no matter how she tried, she was unable to hold them back. "Did you mean it? About taking us all away?"

"Yes." He agreed so quickly, Adi didn't know if he meant it. "Anyone who wishes to leave."

She nodded, a slow movement. Damn this man for tempting her so. Safety for her family, her Gabriel. For the villagers who had remained loyal. "We'll find Sebastião and your information. You find us transport."

"What changed your mind?" He paused, then stepped carefully closer. "I don't mean about leaving; I mean about me. Believing me."

"I'm not sure I do," she began. "But you didn't know the story of Sebastião, only that you were meeting a man by that name. It's not an uncommon name, but the story is unique. I'm not certain the French know it, but if someone were to use it as a ploy, they'd have been familiar with at least the basics of Sebastião's life. Well, death, in this case."

"Where did he die?" Lua nudged Grayson's leg, and he crouched down, still that slow, careful movement, with one hand pressed against his ribs. "Sebastião, I mean. Yes, you're a good girl," he purred to Lua.

Adi refused to let his low, soothing voice—directed at her *dog*—sway her. Until last night's confession, she had very much wanted that tone directed at her. Had seriously considered an affair with a stranger. Now, she wasn't certain what she wanted. But she hated the jealousy that stabbed her heart at his tone with Lua.

"Morocco," she said flatly. "He wanted to reprise some great Portuguese empire."

"You disagree with that?" Once more, his tone told Adi he, too, disagreed. Intriguing.

"I disagree with leaving behind your responsibilities in a misguided attempt to regain something that was never yours. He had a country to administer, people who depended on him." Adi packed up the empty pot and pushed the basket of gardening tools across the table. It made a horrible screech that had Lua growling and on her feet in an instant.

"I disagree with putting your own ambitions over feeding your people."

Without another word, she called to Lua and left the cottage. "I'm a fool, Lua," she muttered as they hurried back to the villa. "A stupid, stupid fool."

Grayson stepped for the door right before it slammed closed. He didn't follow Adelaida out. Through the grimy window, he watched her and Lua hurry from the cottage and down the deserted path before disappearing around a corner that led back to the main house. The rising sun glinted off her hair, deepening the browns that reminded him of melted chocolate.

He didn't blame her for her anger, the resentment she held for Sebastião—the king, not Grayson's contact—and for the current monarchy.

Turning for the table, he picked up the basket of gardening tools and slipped out the door. He paused for a long moment outside in the fresh air. Two weeks might not seem long, but until then he'd spent the majority of his days outdoors, on the farm, in the stables or animal pens, or simply walking the grounds. Later, on his beloved ships.

He closed his eyes and took a moment he didn't have to simply enjoy the morning. The birds, his constant companions these last weeks, chirped cheerfully, as if they were happy to finally greet him in daylight. Grayson looked into the trees and grinned, nodding at them.

"Good morning to you, too," he said and turned for the gardens.

He'd long since scouted out the lay of the land. The gardens, the soldiers, the villa's doors. There was the gardener's cottage he used and a smaller shed that still housed the tools. A few other small structures, all beautifully tiled, dotted the rear of the property, but he saw nothing out of the ordinary for a villa this size.

Head down, hunched slightly, he purposely limped slowly along the path. He took the long way around the house, admiring the intricate tilework and small, wrought iron enclosed balconies. No sense in running into a French soldier.

Though it was no doubt his imagination, Grayson swore the fresh scent of the ocean teased him, tempting him to abandon his plan and sneak down to the beach.

Not today. Today would hopefully bring a glimpse of Adelaida. And his new job.

The gardens were a sight, all right. He hadn't been able to discern the various clumps during his nighttime walks. He'd been more concerned with locating the soldiers and each and every entrance to the villa. In daylight, he saw everything clearly. Weeds choked what looked like a fertile garden, masking the vegetables beneath. Patches of well-tended vegetables lay around the edges of the expansive area. Farther to the north, the once ornamental gardens also lay choked beneath a tangled mess of overgrown vines and weeds.

He set the basket on the ground, then dug out the pillow and knelt on it. His ribs still twinged with the movement, but it didn't steal his breath or make the world spin. Grayson considered that a win.

Early morning passed quickly, with him adding to a growing

pile of weeds. The faint but constant noise from the kitchens kept him company in the increasingly hot day. No French—all the voices spoke Portuguese. From his evening scouting, he knew two guards stood by the outer door, with a third by the one that connected kitchens to the rest of the house.

He knew the moment Adelaida spotted him. He'd positioned himself facing the villa, and when she stepped from the doorway she stole his breath. Her hair was, indeed, the color of chocolate, rich and dark and alluring. From this distance and with her hair tightly braided, he couldn't see the red streaks he remembered from before. Pity. Her eyes, that same beautiful deep brown, widened. Her mouth opened, only to snap shut as she stalked from the kitchens.

"What are you doing?" she hissed, the words low and angry as they scraped along the space between them. "I thought you were going to the village to look for your contact."

"No. I mean, yes, that's my plan." Actually, it hadn't even occurred to him that he might immediately leave for the village. He'd wanted a glimpse of her. Wanted to see her standing in the sunlight as he tackled the overgrown garden. "You need more food and have limited workers. It's the least I can do."

Grayson almost laughed at himself. He'd been so focused on seeing Adelaida in the sunlight, on watching her for more than a few stolen moments at dawn and dusk, that he hadn't quite thought that through. Nor had he realized that, despite her gift of gardening tools, she hadn't expected him in her gardens. She constantly surprised him.

"What did you think I needed the tools and hat for?"

"A disguise," she muttered, side-eying the villa. He, too, looked in that direction but saw nothing amiss. "You couldn't very well waltz into the village looking like a waterlogged pirate."

"A pirate?" He chuckled, careful to keep his voice low. She'd called him that before, and he'd laughed then. He liked it. "A gardener pirate. Doesn't quite have the ring I'd hoped for."

Her lips twitched, that beautiful movement that told him she didn't want to smile. The tension in her shoulders eased, and she pinched the bridge of her nose. Before she could comment, Lua trotted up and nudged his leg. Grayson obediently scratched behind her ears but didn't take his gaze from Adelaida.

"Your vegetable garden is overrun."

She stared at him in silent disbelief. "Yes, I'm quite aware."

Grayson chuckled. "Are the soldiers still in the kitchens?"

"Yes, the two on day shift. Two more are stationed at the front entrance, and there are more down the drive."

He nodded. She'd told him this before, of course, during one of her visits. "Nothing's changed; Lambert is complacent."

"Why shouldn't he be?" she asked bitterly. "He's murdered a quarter of the area already."

His head jerked up, precariously tilting the ill-fitting hat. "What?" She hadn't told him that. But the set look on her face, angry and determined and so very furious, told him this wasn't a new incident. "When?"

The beautiful summer morning suddenly dimmed, the air colder now. Adelaida rubbed her arms as if she, too, felt the chill.

"In the spring," she whispered. "Before I could convince—" she broke off and shook her head.

Before she could convince the townspeople to wait and watch and plan.

"All right." He wouldn't make her repeat that.

She was tightly coiled, and Grayson wondered she didn't explode. But then she lifted her head and glared down her nose at him. He didn't smile. No matter how he might normally try to lighten the moment, he had nothing.

Because he didn't want to hurt her or make light of her situation. He knew the French occupied the village, her villa—indeed, the entire coastline. He knew they massacred any who stood in their way. Anyone they wished. That bands of soldiers roved the countryside looting, raping, and murdering anyone they pleased. He knew they'd cut a swath through Spain and Portugal to teach the Portuguese a lesson and subjugate them.

And he knew the French would never subjugate the people of this villa.

"Can you get away this afternoon?" he asked instead, his mind racing for a plan. "The sooner we discover Sebastião, the better for everyone, I think."

"Come with you into the village?" Once more, Adelaida paused and glanced toward the villa, but still no one exited. "Tomorrow morning. I need to make my weekly visit anyway."

"Weekly visit?" he repeated, suddenly feeling several steps behind her. "What weekly visit?"

She glanced at him, then turned for the kitchens. "It's our responsibility to ensure the village has what they need. I do so by visiting weekly. We'll be accompanied by a pair of guards. Don't bring your herbs."

"All right."

Adelaida stopped at the edge of the plot he'd finished clearing. She sighed and shook her head. "I'll tell them I need you to drive the donkey."

"Will they believe that?"

"If it means they won't argue over which one has to, they'll accept anything."

Grayson nodded, though she couldn't see him, and watched her disappear into the villa, Lua walking beside her. There was much to this area he didn't know. Much Adelaida kept from him for the sake of her people.

He admired that, her taking care of them in the face of

horror and terror. With her own family quite literally held at musket point. It was time he put his sneaking-about skills to good use.

Standing, Grayson stretched. He swallowed the moan of discomfort when the movement tugged at his ribs.

Healing, yes, but still tender. No help for it. He needed to risk his own discomfort for the sake of this entire village. Grayson's gaze strayed to the open doors of the kitchen. For the sake of Adelaida.

Ten

Adi didn't know what she expected. Sneaking her pirate into the village beneath the French's noses? Letting him wander and ask whatever questions he might ask to discover this Sebastião?

Madness.

She also really needed to stop referring to him as her pirate. Or hers at all.

Except her lips still tingled with that remembered kiss. And her skin heated with the memory of his touch, sure and confident and so very warm on her arms, her shoulders. Adi tried—and failed—not to think about his touch on other parts of her. Those parts burned for more.

"Mademoiselle." Louis, her guard for the day, smirked. He took exceptional pains to leer at her whenever he was near, which made Adi want to either vomit or punch him. Or both.

No wonder she had such rage in her that she'd seriously considered resorting to violence.

His presence dispelled any thought of lust she felt for her

pirate—still not a pirate, and definitely not hers. Truly, she needed to remember that.

However, the pair of French soldiers hadn't even blinked when she said her gardener would drive Rémy. Rémy, who disliked anyone and everyone, who only moved when he wished, and then not very far or fast. Rémy, the only animal left at the villa they could claim. Besides Lua.

"Well?" Louis demanded.

Grayson stiffened but gave Rémy one more gentle pat. Adi couldn't hear what he'd said to the donkey, but the gentleness with which he'd greeted him told her more than words could. The guards didn't much care—for the people, the land, or the animals.

Of course, they also didn't care or understand why she made her weekly trips into the village and complained. Loud and long. At least Lambert understood the responsibilities of the villa and agreed. One thing in his favor. The only thing.

The French guards might not understand Rémy, but Grayson did. He had said he was better with animals than gardening. The proof lay in Rémy's displeased snort when Grayson stopped petting him.

Grayson helped her up the step and onto the cart's seat, then he limped around Rémy. The soldiers didn't help, of course. Just watched with undisguised smirks as Grayson awkwardly climbed onto the cart and took the reins.

She didn't help him, couldn't if they both wanted to survive this charade. From the corner of her eye, she saw his pained grimace as he hauled himself up the step and into the seat. Adi bit her lip, purposefully ignoring the soldiers' snickers.

Grayson breathed heavily beside her. He was slightly hunched over, though they both knew that wouldn't help the pain in his ribs. He'd wrapped an arm about his torso, eyes closed, breathing through the pain.

"*Dama*." He grinned from beneath his filthy, rumpled hat, his blue-green eyes bright against his shadowed face. Beautiful eyes that sparkled in the sunlight.

"Paulo." She forced her gaze from his and stared ahead, nodding regally.

Everything since waking this morning had been an act, and she played her part to perfection. From slipping out before the sun rose and bringing Grayson food to insisting Mélina and Mama stay home today. They'd been suspiciously quiet when she told them she'd travel to Carvalho with the new gardener she'd hired.

Neither had asked about this gardener, not with so many ears about. Adi knew the moment she returned, they'd bombard her with questions. She had no idea what she'd say, but figured she'd think of something by the time she and Grayson returned from the village. Probably. Hopefully.

Her nuisance guards had climbed into their own cart, their wagon drawn by a pair of horses that once belonged to the household's stables. When she'd told Grayson the French had taken everything, she meant it.

Lambert only allowed them to visit the village once a week because he didn't want another uprising. Not because he cared what happened to her people. Because he didn't want his own comfort disrupted. If he slaughtered the household, who would serve his meals?

Leering Louis and his friend climbed into the second cart and slapped the horses with a harsh rein. Grayson muttered in a language she didn't know. From the angry scowl on his face, Adi assumed he cursed the French soldiers, and she didn't blame him. They had no appreciation for anything.

Grayson clucked his tongue and gently tapped the reins on Rémy's back. The donkey balked and glared over his shoulder, but Grayson waited patiently. Stubborn meets stubborn.

Behind them, Louis shouted, "Stupid cripple! Stick to your flowers and leave the driving to us."

"Rémy," Grayson said, his voice low and enticing. Adi tried not to wonder how he'd sound the next time they kissed.

Not that there would be a next time. Still, a woman could hope.

"If you ignore them now and do everything I say, I promise you I'll let you bite them." He paused and leaned over, sucking in a breath at the pained movement. "In the balls," he promised.

Adi snorted. No doubt she should be offended at the language. Scandalized. Shocked, at the very least. She covered her mouth and stifled a laugh, trying in vain to turn it into a cough.

Rémy, who clearly understood Grayson's promise, snorted and started off, plodding along at his own pace. Louis hated the slowness and when forced to drive the cart whipped the poor donkey until he—Louis, not Rémy—frothed at the mouth. Grayson merely let the donkey walk along. He hummed a tune and ignored the rather vulgar grumbling from the cart behind them.

For the first time in months, Adi relaxed. She released the anger and fear she'd held since Lambert arrived at the end of last year. For the first time in far, far too long, she breathed in hope. Her shoulders sagged with a release of the tension she thought she'd never be rid of.

"Can I watch?" Oh, that wasn't what she'd wanted to ask.

"Watch?" Grayson stopped humming and grinned. He didn't turn his head, gave nothing away as they traipsed along the well-worn path between villa and village. "Rémy bite the soldiers?"

He chuckled, and Adi smiled, something else in her tightening. He had a lovely chuckle, different from his laugh when it'd echoed off the cave walls. Or his cocky assurance in the cottage. This sound, a low promise of...something, wound through her and settled between her legs.

Oh, heavens, what a mess.

"They deserve nothing less." She swallowed and hoped her voice didn't sound as breathless as she feared. "And a great deal more," Adi added. "They're horrible people who care nothing for the village or the countryside." She paused and loosened her fingers from the basket she held on her lap. "And they beat Rémy."

"No wonder he doesn't like them." Grayson clucked at the donkey, who ignored everything but taking one step and then another. "Twice," he promised Rémy. "I'll let you bite them all twice."

Adi stifled another laugh.

"Anyone who abuses an animal is no better than the dirt on my boot." Grayson half turned, then stopped. She saw his jaw clench and his hands tighten on the reins. "Still behind us?"

Adi shifted slowly, as if checking the bread and vegetables gathered behind her. "Yes. They're arguing; I can't hear what they're saying, though."

"No matter." He flicked a hand in dismissal. "Yara, my younger sister, she'd have skinned them both alive if she knew what they'd done to poor Rémy."

"Truly?" Adi suddenly felt the weight of her dagger between her breasts. "She knows how to use a knife?" She made an aborted motion toward the dagger at his hip, only then realizing he wasn't wearing it.

"My parents, they taught us all." He sighed. "The world is a dangerous place, and this was the only way they knew to protect us. Making sure we could protect ourselves and those who needed it."

"I see they passed that down to their son." Her lips twitched, and she settled back onto the bench, secure in the knowledge that nothing said between them would leave this cart. "Finding trouble."

"I'm afraid it's a Conrad failing, Adelaida." And he sounded so sorrowful, Adi choked on another laugh.

"Tell me of your sister."

Anything, tell me anything about anyone, she wanted to beg. Any story, any piece of knowledge that would turn her thoughts from the heavy burden of daily survival. And if her heart fluttered slightly in knowing more of Grayson Conrad, well, no one but she would know.

"Yara is fierce, young. But so very smart." He shook his head, his hands once more relaxed on Rémy's reins. "My mother, she started a business for the women of the county. Those who needed food, shelter, income."

"I like your mother," Adi whispered. "She's a smart, responsible woman."

"She's brilliant, yes. But not as brilliant as Yara."

His pride in his mother and sister shone so clearly, Adi thought she could reach out and touch it. Cup the precious words in her hands and hold them close to her heart. He meant it. Not merely the words. He meant the emotion behind those words. He loved his family and was fiercely proud of them.

Had anyone ever spoken of her with such passion? Never to her face.

"Yara loves animals. Bird with a broken wing? She's rescued hundreds. Livestock birth gone wrong? Call for Yara. She's read every article the Odiham Agricultural Society has put out, and

I'd wager she knows more about animal husbandry than all those stuffy men combined."

Awed, Adi merely stared ahead. "A woman? Able to use her knowledge without shame?"

Envy settled in her heart at Yara Conrad's freedom. The support her parents had given to cultivate such interest and knowledge. The confidence with which to use it. The pride in Grayson's voice as he spoke of his sister, clearly so beloved and fawned over.

"Before I could walk, my parents drew up my marriage contract." The words came out before she realized they'd even bubbled to the surface. She tried to swallow them down, but they'd escaped. No putting them back in the box now. "My grandfather knew his father through shipping and thought it a good match. My entire life, I knew I'd marry Mateus and join our chocolatier with his vineyards."

She gestured to the side, where a large building lay amongst the oak trees. Grayson glanced at it before turning back with a frown.

"Our chocolate house, the kitchens where we used to make our creations. Closed off now." Even if they opened again, the French wouldn't pay. They'd steal the chocolate as they had their livestock and vegetables. "I've debated opening it again, simply so I have more frequent access to the village and their information."

"Is that what you want?"

She didn't know what she wanted. Had never thought of her own wants. Dreams? She pushed them aside—for the family, the business, the village, the people, the land.

Rather than the bread and olive oil she'd enjoyed for breakfast, Adi tasted the bitterness of a life only half lived. She'd walked through those years the way Rémy now plodded along the path. Alive but never truly living.

"I don't know what I want."

Grayson wrapped the reins around his hands and closed his fists tight around the leather. He didn't worry about Rémy, who knew this path better than any of them. None of them could afford him reaching for Adelaida and pulling her into his arms. Soothing the angry, acidic words that tumbled from her lips.

She didn't say; she didn't need to. No, she hadn't wanted the marriage.

A thousand questions tumbled around his head, but Grayson settled on, "Did you love him?"

"Not really. No." She sighed, a deep breath of resignation. "I cared for him. I mourned his death."

"Do you miss him?"

"No." She broke off on a sob. Her shoulders quivered just once. "I'm a terrible person, going to hell for certain."

"You're not," he tried to assure her, but she had already closed herself off, hidden away the parts that had only just started to blossom. "No one is punished for being forced into an unhappy marriage."

"It wasn't unhappy," she tried, the words thick and choked. "He was a wonderful man, strong, supportive. He cared about his workers and saw I wanted nothing." She furtively swiped at her cheeks, her back straight as she stared ahead, toward the village. "He was generous with his coin and in bed."

A deep blush crept up her throat and stained her cheeks. Grayson stared as her lips opened and closed, only to press together hard. Damn the French for following them. He held the reins tighter.

He absolutely could not touch her.

Not here, not with those idiot soldiers following them. No matter how badly he wanted to take her into his arms and comfort her.

"I shouldn't have said that."

"I've never married myself," Grayson started, hoping his confession would ease her embarrassment and pain. "However, in my observation, just because a man is kind and generous, and even passionate, doesn't mean the marriage is a good fit."

Beside him, Adelaida jerked. "So I've heard," she murmured. He scrambled for a change in subject, but she beat him to it. "Why haven't you married? Too busy spying on innocent Portuguese?"

He snorted and shook his head. "I'm not spying on you, Adelaida." He stretched his legs out before him and winced at the tug on his ribs. "I'm spying on the French. They just happen to be in Portugal."

"Bah." She harrumphed. "The French want Portuguese wine and gold. The English want French gold. Everyone wants land and power. No one cares about the people." Her voice lowered. "Not even our government. They left so fast, they didn't even bother with half their wealth."

"I agree with that. But I care. Otherwise, I wouldn't have agreed to this little adventure." He paused. Now wasn't the time for cynicism. "Wars are fought over lands, resources. It's the people who are always caught in the middle." Grayson stretched again, but only a slight tug pulled at the muscles around his ribs.

"Is that why you're here? To protect us?" Her tone dismissed that outright. "You know nothing about what it's like here."

"That's true," he allowed. "I've spent my time here hiding and healing. And I'm grateful for that, more than words can convey. I had the means and opportunity; not many can say the same. You saved me." He stopped, frowning. "How did you?"

"What do you mean?" Adi cleared her throat from the emotion coating her words.

"I mean on the beach in that storm, how did you know I was there? Where I was," he clarified.

"I heard your call." She sounded as confused as he.

"I didn't. I didn't call out. I wouldn't have put myself in danger." A quick glance showed her confusion matched his. How had she found him in so vicious a storm when he knew, *knew*, he hadn't made a sound. Not consciously, though he supposed a gasp of pain might've escaped his lips.

But one loud enough for Adelaida to hear? No.

Brushing that aside—he had no answers and doubted he'd find them—Grayson changed the subject. "It's also why I'm here. Britain will invade no matter what. Giving them what little information Sebastião can offer about the French, or whatever else I can uncover here, will hopefully shorten the war."

"Do you really believe that?" Adelaida half turned on the bench, but he didn't dare meet her gaze. Not when he was dressed as a servant under the watchful glare of the guards behind them. "That the French, currently the greatest army in the world, will be so easily defeated?"

"Easily, no." He gave an aborted shake of his head. "But they will be. Everyone is eventually."

The air was warm and heavy, the weather a sharp contrast to the night he'd washed ashore. The sun shone unrelentingly overhead, bouncing off everything despite his battered gardener's hat. Grayson squinted past Rémy into the distance and could only just make out the village.

"Nothing worthwhile is ever easy," he admitted.

"No." He couldn't hear anything behind that word. No sharpness, no bitterness, not even any weariness. A simple, flat agreement. "Where were you supposed to meet Sebastião?"

"Just at the village's edge. There's a road that leads from the beach, I understand."

"Yes, parallel to this one. This is the only direct road from the villa to Carvalho." She settled on the bench again, her head tilted so he couldn't see her face around her headscarf. "But there are others, of course. The one you needed travels straight to the water. The fishermen use it to bring their catches to the market." She paused. "Used it. Now they deliver directly to the French quartermaster that Lambert has stationed at the shoreline every morning."

"How does the village survive?"

"Spite," she whispered. "Tenacity."

"I can appreciate that." He'd lived his life that way. Showing the world he didn't care what they thought about an upstart merchant's son being better than the nobility or gentry.

"I'll need an excuse," he said, watching the village grow steadily closer no matter Rémy's plodding gait. At least he was steady. "A reason I'm there and not following you."

Adelaida gave a small, contained wave from where she'd folded her hands in her lap. Just enough to convey her dismissal, not nearly extravagant enough to catch the attention of the guards. "Wander off. They'll think you're fetching something for me or the household. No one in the village will question that."

She paused, a slightly longer one than he'd expected.

"You don't trust the village?"

"Grayson Conrad," she said on a weary sigh. Not nearly the sigh he wanted her to use when saying his name. "I don't trust anyone."

He snorted in amused understanding. "I appreciate that." He did, but his mind raced with ways to earn her trust. "Anyone in particular I should avoid?"

Another small, bitter laugh. "Anyone calling themselves

Sebastião." But she shook her head. "Forgive me, I don't mean to sound resentful. If this Sebastião truly is able to help end a war that hasn't yet begun, I'm thrilled. We can't afford any more damage to our land or our people."

"You don't believe in Sebastião." He hummed, keeping his head still in case the French watched. He doubted it. He heard the rise and fall of their voices.

"I don't believe the myth has returned, no. Do I believe someone has information?" Another small wave of her hand. "Yes. There's always information to be had, to barter. It's been nearly two weeks since you've landed. If Sebastião still waits, his information is old."

"I'll have to return tonight," Grayson agreed. Annoyed with himself for not healing sooner, he tugged on the reins. Rémy snorted and stopped. "Sorry, Rémy."

He sighed and gently tapped the donkey, but Rémy refused any further movement. Doubly annoyed now, Grayson muttered several curses and climbed from the cart. He landed awkwardly on his left leg. It gave out, and his ribs reminded him he wasn't as fully healed as he wished.

As a show for the French soldiers now cursing him, Grayson thought it a spectacular display. As a means to ensure his ribs healed enough to protect himself, Sebastião if necessary, and Adelaida definitely, it was less than spectacular.

"Come on, Rémy, be a good boy. I'm sorry for jerking the reins, but you're not the only one unhappy with his current position." Grayson rubbed his hand down Rémy's neck, promising apples, carrots, sweet potatoes, squash. As much hay as he wished.

"A ship voyage away from the French," Grayson added just as one of the soldiers stomped up.

"Move that donkey, old man. We don't have time for his laziness."

"*Sim, sim, senhor.*" Grayson kept his voice low and soft. He supposed he should've added a creaky quality but thought of that too late. He was too busy not stabbing the man with the khanjar he had hidden in his boot.

"Now, old man. If he doesn't want to be shipped to a glue factory." The soldier's sneer was enough to upset Rémy, who clearly understood the tone, if not the words.

Oops. Grayson wasn't supposed to understand, either. He merely nodded frantically, muttering in Portuguese. So much for covert spying.

Finally, Rémy started again, moving forward with that same plodding gait as before. He was just fast enough that Grayson almost missed his chance to climb into the cart. He did so, swinging upward as the guards behind him resumed their argument.

"What did you promise Rémy?" Adelaida asked, amusement back in her tone. "Apples and what else?"

"Anything," Grayson gasped, jaw clenched around the pain. "Anything to get him away from the French. He doesn't much care for them."

"I think you'll find no one does," she said. "Can you hear which village girl they're arguing over?"

"Amelia." He choked out the word around clenched teeth, breathing shallowly. "I think we ought to find her before they do."

She grinned, a bright, fierce smile that showed such passion, such fire, his heart skipped. "I heartily agree."

Eleven

A di accepted Grayson's hand as she stepped down the cart's single step and onto the block. Shame. She'd have liked his hands on her waist. Which would've given them both away to the French and anyone else watching.

Still, Adi couldn't help but imagine his touch. That single kiss still made her lips tingle.

"Gr—Paulo?" She watched him breathe hard, his jaw clenched tight.

His face looked pale beneath the hat he kept tipped, hiding his eyes if not his beard. Beneath both hat and beard, he looked about to pass out, either from pain or the heat. As they'd pulled into town, she'd asked after his ribs, but he'd dismissed her concern with a wink and a smile.

She wasn't fooled.

"I can walk," he promised before she could utter another word. Adi eyed him disbelievingly. "I can." Now there was more humor in his tone. "Walking is easy. Breathing?" He gave a furtive shake of his head. "That's harder."

"If you aren't as healed as you say—" she began, but he cut her off.

"I am." She huffed in disbelief. "All right, I'm not," he amended. "But neither of us have any more time."

"No," she agreed. "We do not." She took one of the baskets from the cart and slung it over her arm. "Help me unload then. One of the guards will stay while the other delivers their provisions. Then you can walk the market; there isn't much, but it will offer you an excuse to disappear into the crowd."

"I'm not leaving you, Adelaida."

She eyed him. "I don't understand." Louis, the leering French guard, glared at her slowness but didn't offer any help. The guards never did. She tilted her chin and calmly met his gaze.

"I believe the garrison waits for you?" she offered in her best lady-of-the-villa voice. She'd spoken in French, which always seemed to displease him.

Adi had no idea why. He leered at her even now, and Adi wondered if he drooled. Disgusted, she turned back to Grayson and her own cart. Grayson looked murderous. Alarmed, she quickly stepped in front of him and blocked Louis's view. After another moment, Louis moved off while Anton, clearly the loser of the coin toss, stood at the head of the street and guarded her.

People fled from the cart's path with their eyes lowered and their heads bowed. The show of deference only puffed up the French's chests. But Adi saw something different than deference.

"They're going to explode." Grayson's hard, calm voice came from beside her.

Her head jerked in his direction, but he kept that ridiculous hat pulled low over his brow. "Yes."

She hesitated, but at this point both of them were in too deep. She'd gone from wading through Carvalho's anger and deception to swimming right into the current. His hand brushed hers, there and gone before she could blink.

Perhaps she wasn't swimming alone.

"It's one thing, I think, to understand that no one wants invaders taking over their lives." He turned and stood at the rear of the cart, his posture slightly stooped. She couldn't tell if it was for show or because of the pain. "I can write memos to every captain, colonel, and general I know, even the Duke of York and Albany himself, and still not convey the fear and anger here with any justice."

Adi wondered if he knew this duke but didn't ask. It wasn't that important.

"I'm not certain I can, either," she whispered though they stood alone. "We've lived with such fear and anger for so long, the constant burden waiting for *something* to happen. It's become normal. The fear and waiting. Bubbling up but never quite overflowing."

The French cart disappeared around the corner, and the square held its breath. A moment, then another. As if in one long exhale, they resumed their motions. Adi watched them, as she had once a week every week for months now.

"Not yet," she added.

"They're waiting," Grayson said from beside her.

He was far closer than he'd been a moment ago. His hand brushed hers again, no more than a whisper. Then he held her hand, and Adi's world rightened. How strange to feel this way when she'd known him mere days. Two weeks, and even then only snatches of time spent together.

No one had ever promised her salvation from the French. No one had ever made her heart race, her blood heat, pooling low between her legs and tempting her to touch herself. Even her daily exhaustion couldn't quell that burning need.

"I thought you wanted to find Sebastião." Her voice cracked, and she stepped from his touch no matter how she longed for more. For his hands on her bare legs, his mouth on hers. "Find him and discover his information."

"I did. I do. And I will." He watched her a moment, though Adi couldn't see his gaze. Those beautiful blue-green eyes she dreamt about. Grayson grunted as he lifted one of the crates of olives off the back of the cart. "Where do you want this, *dama*?"

His voice had changed from strong and confident, the voice she heard in her dreams, to a quiet, subtle Portuguese. It set her off guard, and she stumbled on the uneven cobblestone. Grayson easily caught her, his strong, sure grip belying the false voice he used whenever anyone drew near.

Adi merely nodded toward the small chapel behind him, where Padre Lucio stood waiting.

One eye on the seemingly disinterested guard, Grayson unlatched the cart while Adelaida and the priest talked. The other man nodded once, then completely ignored him, which suited Grayson just fine. The fewer people who noticed him, the better.

He hated the step back into the cart; it pulled on his barely healed ribs. Nonetheless, he climbed in and shifted the remaining crates closer to the opening for easier distribution. Breathing hard, his left side throbbing in vicious anger at the movement, Grayson half slid, half jumped from the cart back to the cobblestone road.

He tipped his hat to Adelaida. Was he supposed to do that? He had no idea. He held her gaze another moment, then turned and wandered through the growing crowd toward what remained of the market square.

He'd leave the gossip, the information gathering, and the food distribution to Adelaida and Padre Lucio. He had his own information to gather.

Not many walked the market. Most flocked to the church and the food Adelaida offered. While he appreciated her generosity, Grayson knew she needed the food—and the medicinal herbs he'd brought—as well. Hell, the entire country needed it, stripped bare as they were by Junot and his army. When he returned to England, he'd organize a smuggling operation back here—food, medicines, anything the people needed.

Lips twitching at Adelaida's nickname for him, Grayson kept to the sidewalk, away from the square proper. He supposed he would become her pirate. *Her* pirate? Shaking his head, he hunched his shoulders and limped his way along the cobblestones. Hers?

Where had such a thought come from? Madness. While he was happy he could help in any way possible, he hadn't planned on becoming involved with the people. In and out, that was his plan.

Except it hadn't worked out like that, and now he was invested. Invested in her life, her struggles. Her happiness.

Humming a tune his mother used to sing, Grayson tried to push all that aside. Adelaida consumed enough of his thoughts, and right then he needed to stay focused on blending in.

Making his slow way down the main street, he kept his head down and his eyes focused on his surroundings. No cart traveled these roads, and the few people who walked them gave him a wide berth. Grayson didn't blame them. He was a stranger, though he'd arrived with Dama Adelaida.

As the midmorning sun rose high overhead and its heat baked the village, Grayson stepped into the square, where only a handful of stalls remained open. From here, he saw the secondary road from the beach and the two that led out of the village.

A pair of guards stood at each, one facing the village, the other the road. A half dozen more stood at various points along the square. Grayson wondered what they searched for, why so many had garrisoned this small village on the coast.

But then, he knew why. Junot, and by default Lambert, expected the British to land here, at Carvalho or close enough, and they expected to see them any day now. Odd, that. He'd have wagered on Lisbon for obvious, capital-of-Portugal reasons. Then again, Hilton believed so strongly in that mysterious letter promising troop movements that Grayson had agreed to land here, over a hundred miles south of Lisbon.

Still didn't explain the mattress hoarding. Then again, Grayson had heard that Junot was irrational, so demanding all the villa's best mattresses wasn't that surprising. Maybe Lambert was courting favor with Junot. Or even Napoleon. Most likely, he sent them back to his own villa—the spoils of war at the expense of the village.

It didn't matter. The mattresses were gone, as was the majority of their food.

Turning from the street before the soldiers could do more than glare, he limped his way along the market, which sat atop a small hill. He watched a smattering of fishmongers and coster-mongers hawk their wares.

No one stood out as Sebastião, either by dint of standing out or by sneaking about and hiding. Grayson hadn't expected to find the man. Not after two weeks, and not in the square in the middle of the day. He needed the lay of the land, now that he was on land and not in the ocean.

He turned about the square again, but other than the layer of fear permeating those few who walked the market, Grayson might have stood in the market square of his own village.

Ah.

Idiot. Therein lay the problem. *He* was the stranger here, the suspicion that stood out. He walked the market, looking for anyone who might seem either questionable or his contact, when he knew no one and nothing here. Slowly turning, Grayson made his laborious way back to the church.

Annoyed with himself, he dismissed asking Adelaida for help. She'd done far more than he had any right to ask for, and she'd done so at great risk to herself and her family.

The church came into view, a large structure that spoke of the wealth of the family and the village. Grayson wasn't surprised to see the line snaking down the street. He hadn't seen the second cart, the one driven by Louis, since it disappeared. Where was the garrison stationed? He planned to return tonight and search.

The wind carried a hint of the sea, and he breathed deeply as he watched the crowd. Leaning against the wall of the church, Grayson didn't need to search for Adelaida—she stood out as if she towered over the group.

Commanding as she handed out food, graceful as she listened to each person who bobbed in respect. He couldn't hear what she said, but the majority of those villagers who received her gifts left smiling. She spoke with each person, listened to whatever they said and—

Grayson nearly laughed.

This was how she gathered her information. Impressive. Right beneath French noses. If he hadn't seen her reaction first-hand, Grayson would've sworn Adelaida was his contact, this Sebastião. She gathered information better than anyone he'd ever seen. If she wasn't this Sebastião, then who was? One of the villagers? Adelaida hadn't mentioned anyone specific.

Children played at the end of the street, laughing loudly as they kicked a ball of some sort. A pair stood slightly apart, so slight anyone who wasn't searching for a modicum of suspicion might not notice. But Grayson noticed, and he applauded the lookouts.

They were right beneath Anton's nose. Anton, who watched the line with thinly disguised annoyance and a great deal of arrogance.

He couldn't hear the roll of wagon wheels over cobblestones, but he didn't need to. The children-watch moved like the tide, sweeping backward onto the street, still playing, still laughing. A smooth wave of moment that clearly alerted the village.

Adelaida and the padre handed out food more quickly now. A few villagers lingered—those with information, he presumed —but most left as soon as they received their basket.

Pushing off the wall, Grayson hurried to the cart, mindful of his own role in their charade. He climbed in and hunched over, cursing his ribs as he watched the road, waiting for the French cart to roll into view.

A woman, dressed much like the others, lingered along the wall by the church. She wore a headdress, as all the women did, but she partially hid her face with its ends. She didn't seem to be in any rush despite the inexorable movement of the French. Curious, Grayson eyed her, but she watched Adelaida and the padre. Just when it was her turn for food and information, the woman looked directly at him.

"Paulo."

Adelaida's voice jerked him back to the moment, to the sound of the French cart. The woman lingered, which was odd, given everyone else had fled. She hadn't taken any food, either.

"Are you ready?" He tore his gaze from the woman and watched Adelaida scramble into the cart.

"Yes, I—" She broke off and frowned. "Maya?"

Grayson followed her gaze to the woman at the corner of the church. Something in Adelaida's voice told him she wasn't one of her regulars.

"She's not waiting for food?"

"She's Inês's lady's maid." Adelaida shook her head, but before he could respond, Maya had disappeared. Then Louis appeared, looking as unpleasant as ever. Anton leaped into the cart with a scowl for both Louis and Adelaida.

Surly man.

"Your mother-in-law?" Grayson flicked the reins, and Rémy, who seemed to understand his job, trod forward.

"Yes. I mean, yes, Maya is Inês's lady's maid." Adelaida blew out a breath and shook her head. She looked around, but carefully, so as not to draw attention from the French, who once more trailed them. "But she shouldn't be here. There's no reason for her to have left the villa."

"She doesn't know anyone in the village? A lover, a friend?" Grayson doubted it but had no other suggestions.

"They know no one here." Adelaida frowned, looking straight ahead. "And I'd rather not think of Maya and a lover, thank you. She's as vicious and conniving as Inês." His lips twitched, but he masterfully held in his snort of amusement. Adelaida didn't look amused. "Damn them both for being so careless."

"Are you certain it's her?"

"No." But her lips pressed tight together. "Not entirely. Did you see her clearly?"

"She hid her face," he admitted. "I'll find her around the villa and confirm." He paused, but something told him Adelaida already believed the woman was Maya. "If she's caught outside the villa without permission, will Lambert take it out on you as well?"

"I don't know." She gave an aborted shake of her head. "We've all followed his orders. Well, followed them as far as the French know." She scowled, and a low, angry sound rumbled from her throat. "At least, I thought we had. Maya wouldn't have left the villa without Inês knowing. Without her blessing."

"Then we either have a spy on our hands, or something else is happening." Grayson couldn't shake the sudden chill that made his ribs throb. "Either way, it doesn't bode well."

"Nothing bodes well," she snapped. Sighing, she rubbed her forehead. "I'm sorry."

"Don't apologize." He stretched his left side, trying to breathe normally. "Why are you apologizing?"

"I don't know," she admitted with a choked laugh. "I feel like I apologize daily. To Mama, Mélina, Gabriel. Especially Gabriel. How will you enter the villa?"

"I managed to sneak in and out of my own home quite often as a child." Grayson grinned and winked at her. "Trust me."

"For reasons I do not understand and cannot begin to, I do trust you."

The honesty in her voice settled around Grayson's heart. Her trust ignited something inside him he had no words to explain.

"Maya, or even Inês, aren't our worst problem." Her voice had dropped, and she sat straight, staring at Rémy, who moved like a snail.

"What happened?"

"Padre Lucio took in refugees. People claiming to have crossed the border from Spain." She swallowed, and her fingers clasped tightly together until her knuckles whitened. "They said the British had, indeed, invaded. North of Lisbon. Two sisters from Évora were among them."

"Évora? Where's that?" He didn't think it sounded familiar, not on the coast or near Lisbon, at least.

"Near the Spanish border, almost a hundred miles from Lisbon, I think. I've never been." Adelaida stopped and pressed a hand to her chest, as if her next words physically pained her. Cold settled in Grayson's bones. "They said…" She stopped again, lips pressed together. "The sisters, they said they fled a massacre."

"Massacre?" His hands tightened around Rémy's reins. "In Évora?"

"*Sim*," she whispered, barely nodding. "The city, they rose up against the French."

"I'm sorry." Grayson didn't need to hear the rest. He knew what had happened after that. Junot had received his reinforcements in the spring; there were more than enough seasoned soldiers to quell an uprising. "I'm so sorry, Adelaida."

"This is what I strive to prevent. What I feared might happen here."

"You've kept them safe," he assured her, though he didn't know if his words had any effect. She looked pale beneath her headdress. Battered, yes, but not broken.

"If we know of this, Lambert and Bardot do as well." She slowly uncurled her hands but didn't look at him. "The village already knows. I could barely get them to keep their promise to me."

Admiration welled within him. She'd single-handedly managed to keep safe this entire village of, what, five hundred people? A thousand? She'd managed to gather information and promise a plan of rebellion, and all beneath Lambert's nose.

"You're a remarkable woman, Adelaida," he whispered as

they passed beneath the oak and olive trees. "And I promise you, I'll do whatever it takes to prevent a massacre here."

She nodded, her head turning just enough to watch him. "Once again, I believe you, Grayson Conrad. Don't disappoint me."

"Never," he swore, and he felt that vow deep in his soul.

Oh, he was in trouble.

Twelve

di watched Gabriel sleep, counting the minutes until she needed to leave the safe cocoon they'd created in the single room they shared. She heard Rodrigo giggling about whatever Mélina had whispered, the sweet innocence of a child.

Brushing Gabriel's dark hair from his forehead, Adi replayed the conversation she and Grayson had on their ride back from the village. All night, she'd remembered the words she promised him. That she trusted him.

How was it she trusted him more than anyone else in her life, those she'd known forever?

"Are you going to lie there all day?" Her mother's voice, soft so as not to wake Gabriel but nonetheless firm, startled Adi.

A quick glance at the window showed her the sun was already lighting the sky. "I didn't realize the time." She kissed Gabriel's cheek and stood to start her day.

Always the same, and Adi wondered if this was what it would have been like had Mateus not died, had the French not invaded. Had Grayson not washed up on her beach.

The maids arrived, looking wan and tired, and Adi sat still as one of them pinned up her hair.

"Is the colonel awake?" she whispered.

"No, *dama*. He and Bardot sleep yet. No midnight couriers arrived."

Good. That meant she could slip in and see Grayson first before serving the colonel his breakfast. Lambert took unholy joy in making the women of the house serve him.

The morning air was cool as she hurried from the kitchens toward the cottage. The birds chirped along her path, and for the first time in a long, long while, Adi took a moment. She stopped and simply enjoyed the sound, the calmness of the morning.

But the shadows quickly disappeared, and she hadn't much time. Soon. One way or another, she promised herself, she'd soon spend the entire morning listening to birdsong. Sipping her *café* on the balcony and simply enjoying the moment.

The cottage door opened before she could insert the key. Grayson stood there, looking as tired as she felt. His beard had filled in, and she was sorry she couldn't see his face. Just as well. At least it helped disguise him.

"Everything all right?" he asked, closing the door behind her.

"I miss the quiet," she admitted before she could stop the words. "I want to sit on my balcony and look over the ocean and sip my *café* and—yes." She swallowed and handed him the small pot of soup and chunk of bread dipped in olive oil. "Yes, everything is all right."

Grayson laughed, a quiet, understanding sound that made her think perhaps he knew what she meant. All right was not truly so, but at the moment, she couldn't remedy that.

He pulled her toward the table. "Did you used to do that? Sit outside and watch the ocean?"

"No." A bitter regret in a long line of them. "I always rushed.

There was much that needed doing—the chocolate needed stirring, the pastries needed rolling. The village needed help in one way or another, and though we employed all we could, there were still those in need. The old, the sick, the widows and orphans."

She sat in the chair, but she really wanted to rest her head on the table and close her eyes. Just for a moment. However, she still hadn't the time.

"Always running, yes?" He nodded and broke off a bit of bread, dunking it in the thick vegetable soup. "My father, he has a saying for that. Apparently in his youth he felt the same, running either to something new or from something else."

His voice held a quality she couldn't quite decipher. As if his father ran for reasons not as noble as seeing to an entire village's well-being. But she couldn't ignore the warmth with which he spoke of his father. Paul, wasn't it? He'd said his middle name was Paul, named after his father.

"He said that there was nothing like taking a moment and breathing in a new day." Grayson shook his head and finished the pot of soup, then set it on the table. "There was a time when he didn't believe he'd see a new day."

"And you?"

"I never thought about it. Always had the time." His voice softened, a thread of something mysterious there. Longing? Regret? "I love the mornings. Waking with the dawn, taking time to drink my coffee, listening to the birds." He shook his head and stared at his soup. "I took that for granted. That I could, that I had the right to take that time."

That's what it was. Regret. She'd heard the arrogance of his pride before. The way he spoke of procuring a ship, of returning to England. Even of taking them all with him. Now, that arrogance cracked. What had caused that change?

"I know." She shook her head and stretched her legs before

her. Though the cottage remained dark, she watched the shadows as she rotated her ankles. "Not about your father, I mean. But I know what it's like to face such uncertainty that you aren't sure tomorrow will ever come." Her voice trembled, and she hated that.

"It will." He crouched before her, as graceful a movement as she'd ever seen from him. Taking her hands, he kissed her knuckles and watched her, though the room remained as dim as always. "I promise you, Adelaida. Tomorrow will come for all of you."

She wasn't as certain.

"What do you do all day?" she asked. "Watch the birds?"

"No." He grinned, that smile that made her heart flip. "I usually sleep during the day, after you visit."

"Oh. And at night then?"

"Wander the villa. Louis and his friend—Anton, I think— they are most put out that Amelia has disappeared." He stretched slightly, grimacing, but he didn't seem to be in as much pain as even yesterday. "Where did you send her?"

"Nowhere." Adi grinned. Her fierce satisfaction of having outmaneuvered the guards welled within her. "Nowhere they'd look, at least. She's helping Padre Lucio." Grayson chuckled and finished the bread. "What else did you overhear?"

"Bardot is annoyed that there isn't more action, though Lambert is quite content here. He doesn't believe the British will honor their word, and he says if they do, they won't land here. Not with any force, at least. A token show for their promise."

Anger surged through Adi, and she shot up. The chair scraped against the floor, hitting the table, but she ignored it. Hands clenched at her sides, she glared at Grayson, though he obviously had nothing to do with Lambert's actions. "He eats us out of house and home, drinks our wine, sends our livestock to his troops in the village, and leaves precious few vegetables for the rest of us."

"I know." He caught her hands, holding her still but not stopping her. "I know, Adelaida."

"Why do you call me that?" she demanded, unable to control her temper, her tongue, or her traitorous body.

Oh, but she wanted his hands on more than her wrists.

"What?" Even in the darkness, she heard his frown. He was clearly as taken aback by her question as she. "Adelaida? Isn't that your name?"

"Yes." He had her all muddled, and Adi didn't know what she wanted. "It is. Adelaida. But everyone calls me Adi."

"Adi," he said slowly, his thumbs doing magnificent things to her inner wrists. The sensation shot up her arms, tingling through her. "Adelaida." Her name was softer now, a caress as tender as his fingers. "I prefer Adelaida."

She preferred he say her full name as well, but she couldn't find the breath to tell him so.

"Adelaida."

It wound through her as soft as silk, as inexorable as iron. His hands pulled her closer, and she didn't resist.

"Grayson."

"I like the way you say my name when I'm about to kiss you." He pressed a gentle kiss to the corner of her mouth. His beard scratched her lightly, sending sparks of pleasure along her nerves.

"Oh." Adi wished she had more, but anticipation sucked the breath right from her.

"I like that even better."

Before she could think of any reply, he was kissing her, and Adi decided no reply was necessary.

He pulled her tight against him, kissing her deeply, as if his very soul depended on it. As if his continued existence did. Maybe that was true. Or maybe she'd longed for such passion her entire life, and now it exploded within her.

He kissed her, his tongue sweeping over hers, the taste of the soup light on his tongue, along with something so very Grayson that Adi wanted more. He pressed her against the table, leaning over her, hands braced on the worn wood.

She'd never felt so wanted.

One hand cupped his cheek even as his kisses blanked her mind. Her fingers combed through his hair, cupped the back of his head, played over the shell of his ear.

"Adelaida."

His voice washed over her, warm and wanting. Her knees weakened, even as her fingers tightened around the nape of his neck.

"I—" She swallowed and tried to grasp for words. "I should leave."

Adi didn't even grab the basket. She raced from the cottage, leaving the door wide open. Tripping over the uneven and overgrown path, she didn't stop. Couldn't, because she knew if she did, she'd turn right back around and find Grayson again.

Just outside the kitchens, she gasped for breath. What had she been thinking?

Oh, but she'd craved that kiss since he'd first kissed her. A need that even now burned through her, tempting her. *Go back. Return to Grayson's arms and embrace that pleasure.*

"Adi?" Mélina's voice jerked her away from the sheer pleasure of Grayson's arms around her, his mouth kissing her in such sinful ways she nearly combusted right there. "What's wrong?"

Mélina stepped from the kitchens, concern heavy in her quiet voice. Her brow creased, and her lips pulled down. Remorse stabbed Adi through the heart, but she forced a smile.

"Nothing, Mélina," she promised. Taking her sister-in-law's hand, she squeezed it, though she doubted that conveyed much of anything. "No need to worry."

Mélina's eyebrows shot upward. "Worry?" She barked a sharp, cynical laugh. "I worry about everyone, *irmã*. Rodrigo, Gabriel, Mama. Even Inês, though she doesn't deserve it. The villa, the village. You."

Her eyes narrowed, dark and assessing. Adi went cold and dropped Mélina's hand. She didn't need her sister-in-law worrying about her. Not with the secrets Adi carried. Or, worse, worrying so much she investigated Adi's wanderings.

"You hired a gardener no one knows about. What do you pay him?"

"Pay?" Adi swallowed a laugh. It hadn't even occurred to her. "I pay him in what little vegetables and bread we can spare. Olive oil and soup. And whatever thin protection we offer here." Adi hadn't meant the words to sound snappish, and she tried to moderate her tone, her breathing.

Grayson's kiss thundered through her like the storm on the night they met, just as wild and passionate. Licking her lips, she shook her head and looked toward the gardens rather than the cottage.

"He does a decent job clearing the weeds." She waved a hand in at the gardens. "And he drives Rémy without much fuss. I don't have to sit beside the guards and listen as they threaten and flirt."

She hadn't told Grayson that, and only now did Adi realize it was because she hadn't wanted his anger to explode. Not when so many depended on her discretion. Adi pressed her lips together and tasted his kiss. So much for discretion.

"Does Louis still bother you?" Mélina's voice lowered. "You told me he'd stopped."

"He did." In a way. Adi didn't know why Louis's sneering innuendos had stopped, only that they had. He still leered at her, but though his comments bordered on inappropriate, they didn't outright cross over.

Perhaps Lambert had more control over his men than Adi gave him credit him for. In all fairness, she gave that man no credit.

"Mélina, what's brought this on?"

"You've changed."

The bluntness from her normally kind and understanding sister-in-law surprised her. Even with the invasion and occupation, the death of Théo, everything they'd endured this last year, Mélina was understanding and thoughtful.

Blinking in confusion, Adi shook her head, as if that might clear the passion of Grayson's kiss. "How so?"

"Since the storm. You're...I don't know. More relaxed. Happier."

Her eyebrows shot up. "Happier?"

More scared. Terrified, even. That someone might discover her secret. *Secrets*, she supposed, the pleasure of that kiss still dancing over her skin.

"Maybe not happier." Mélina glanced over her shoulder, but neither of the guards were watching them. "More relaxed?" She shook her head. "I'm not sure. Different."

Adi opened her mouth, then snapped it closed. She had no idea what to say; she wasn't sure she had anything appropriate. Not the truth, that was for certain.

"I'm not." It was a weak insistence. "I'm—" She shook her head. "I don't know."

"Is it the gardener?"

Once more, she blinked in surprise. "Paulo?"

"Is that his name?" Mélina eyed her suspiciously. Perhaps

knowingly was more apt. "You've told us nothing about him. Not where he came from, who he is." She paused and scowled. "Not even his name. Is he not as old as he pretends?"

Old? What? Adi had lost the thread of the conversation. "I don't know what you're talking about, Mélina. What about him? He's from the north, came in search of food and work." She swallowed a smile at that—it was the exact story she'd insisted no one would believe. Now she fervently hoped Mélina believed her.

"Does he make you happy? Is that why you smile more at Gabriel? Why you tease Rodrigo like you used to?"

Had she? Did she? Adi had tried, really she had. Tried not to show the hope that blossomed in her chest at Grayson's promises. Or the passion that made her feel so alive she could sing. Or the pull he held over her. She wouldn't, not unless she wanted the entire countryside to flee in horror. But she felt it. She constantly searched for a simple glimpse of him. Just one during the day.

She wanted that joy she felt in his presence. The way he made her laugh. She wanted that always, not in snatches in the predawn and dusk. Always.

Oh, she was in trouble.

"Best we not speak of him," Adi managed, frantically trying not to drown in the reality that had now smacked her in the face.

Or the heart.

"No sense letting the guards know of his presence. They ignore most of the staff; it's safer for everyone that way."

"Adelaida." Mélina shook her head. She sounded resigned but also concerned. "What trouble have you brought down upon us?"

"None," she insisted more strongly. She was confident in that, at least. "I'll protect this family, this household, and this village until my last breath."

"I know, I've never doubted that." Mélina leaned up and kissed her cheek. "What about you?"

"Me?" she asked somewhat numbly.

She drowned in need, in happiness. In want. Fool that she was.

"I want you happy, *irmã*. You deserve it."

"I want us all to survive this occupation and the coming war."

She kissed Mélina's cheek in return, then stepped around her and started her day. She'd need to serve Lambert and Bardot. She'd need to ensure no one bothered Grayson. Paulo. And she probably should figure out how to seamlessly integrate him into the staff without any of them snitching.

"*Dama*," Manuéla whispered with a side-eye toward the guards. "The colonel, he waits for his breakfast."

Porro. She was late. Between Grayson's magnificent kisses that had left her weak and Mélina's worry that did little to dampen the happiness singing through her veins, Adi had lost all track of time.

"*Obrigada*, Manuéla." She nodded and took the cart, wheeling it out of the kitchens.

Colonel Lambert took breakfast on the balcony with Bardot as they read over the morning dispatches. Adi dreaded this meeting every single day. She almost didn't mind the degradation of having to serve him; she'd rather do it herself than one of the maids, who had less protection.

Lambert insisted it be her, Mélina, or Mama, and Adi knew, deep in her soul, that it was a show of strength over the household. Bastard that he was. Mélina sang and played the pianoforte for them, so Adi served them their meals.

Outside his door, she straightened, tucked in the few strands of hair that had escaped her tight braids, and smiled. This was the part she played, and she'd do it until he was gone. One way or another.

Adi knew as surely as she knew the taste of Grayson's kiss that they'd all leave. She'd ensure that. Lambert might think he controlled Carvalho, but Adi knew she did.

She knocked. "*Sinto muito*, Colonel," she said with her fake smile. Switching to French, she added, "*Je suis terriblement désolé*, Colonel." Adi offered a deep curtsy and pushed the cart toward the balcony.

Lambert and Bardot already sat there, the most recent dispatches in a small pile on the table. The letters came twice a day, just at dawn and midafternoon, unless a special courier arrived during the night. Which seldom happened. Adi knew the route; the courier always took the same way. Sloppy. Complacent.

"It's a beautiful morning. Would you like me to pour?"

"*Non, non.*" Lambert waved her away. "You're late."

"*Toutes mes excuses.*" Adi kept her gaze down, fire flaring in her chest.

She'd wished for *something*. Not hope—that had seemed too large, too out of her reach. Adi had prayed for deliverance from the French, and now that it lay, quite literally, in her gardener's cottage, she had shied from it.

No more.

Grayson's kisses might have made her feel truly alive, but his promise of escape now pushed her forward. She hadn't wanted to leave Carvalho. Her home, her heritage, her people.

The conceited, supercilious quality in Lambert's voice snapped everything into place.

They'd leave. All of them. But first, they'd stop Lambert and his plans.

Thirteen

Temper boiling, jaw clenched against inappropriate and no doubt deathly words, Adi left Lambert and Bardot. She slipped from the room—her father's room—and quietly back into the kitchens. Head high, she nodded to the guards watching her with suspicious expressions. They usually were after her return from serving breakfast, but, as Lambert still very much lived, they had nothing to do but scowl.

"Thank you, Joana." She smiled at the girl, rested a hand on her thin shoulder. "I'll watch Gabriel for a while."

"*Sim, dama.*" Joana bobbed a curtsy and quickly left.

Adi scooped up her son, bouncing him on her hip until he laughed and laughed. The entire kitchen stilled. Adi ignored them all—the guards now shifting uncomfortably, her mother staring at her open-mouthed, the staff's incredulous looks. All that mattered was Gabriel as he giggled and babbled.

His safety, his future, his happiness.

She couldn't have said what made her snap. What changed her mind about the steady plan she'd enacted months ago. What pushed her forward before she thought she was ready.

Grayson? He promised a way out of this hell, and, God help her, Adi believed him.

Not that she had any idea how he planned to keep his promise. But she knew he would. He'd said all Conrads kept their word, but Adi had heard many things from many people. Grayson was the first person she believed. Truly, completely believed.

All that mattered was disrupting the French lines and helping her family escape. Even Inês, she supposed.

Grinning at Gabriel as he demanded more bounces, she turned and caught her mother's gaze. Karlotta's face softened as she watched her grandson. This was what mattered. This was all that mattered.

"Mama." She kissed Karlotta's cheek.

"I'd forgotten what his laugh sounds like," she whispered. "It's been so long."

Yes. Too long. Adi understood that as well as anyone. Gabriel had grown, changed since the French invasion. He didn't remember Mateus, probably not Inês, either. But he knew her, and he knew how to laugh.

"We're leaving."

Karlotta twitched back in shock. "*Perdoe?*" she hissed. "Now?"

"Not now," Adi rushed in assurance. "By the quarter moon." Maybe the new moon. She had absolutely no idea, but she couldn't hedge. Her mother would never believe her then.

"Adi, have you lost your mind?"

"Not at all," she said confidently. But she kept her voice low, ensuring the soldiers heard nothing. That none of the staff did. Not yet. They needed discretion, needed to move with prudence. Adi didn't want anyone to slip up in front of the soldiers because of excitement or nervousness.

"What use is preserving a thousand years of our heritage if none of us are alive to carry it on?" Gabriel reached for Karlotta, who took him without a second thought.

Would he reach for Grayson like that? How would Grayson react if he did? She banished those thoughts. No sense dwelling on nonsense what-ifs. Not now. Still, the idea took root in her heart, and she had no idea how to dislodge it.

"Adi, you're mad."

"Mad?" She swallowed a laugh that would have most assuredly reinforced that thought in her mother's mind. "No, Mama. I am determined. They've taken enough. No more."

Karlotta opened her mouth but merely shook her head. "Why now?"

"I've had enough."

"Is this about your gardener?"

Adi swallowed another laugh and the automatic denial that he wasn't her gardener. Pirate, maybe. Her lips twitched at the thought. "No, Mama. It's about us. The French took our people, our food, our home. They massacred us in Évora. They looted our wine, our heritage, our mattresses. But I refuse to allow them a single thing more."

"Another Évora?" Karlotta snapped. "Adi..."

"No." She eyed the soldiers, who watched them carefully. Smiling, she took Gabriel and bounced him on her hip again until he laughed once more. She smiled down at him and cooed, as if speaking to her son rather than plotting an overthrow. "I will protect our people as we swore. It's about freedom. It's about living another day so that there is always a Carvalho."

Kissing her mother's cheek, she breezed past the soldiers and out the door. She had plans to make, ideas about vandalizing the French's fortifications. She'd insisted no villagers move until she had more information. For months, they had listened.

What changed? her mother had asked.

Adi honestly didn't know. She only knew that now was the time. They'd massacred Évora. The British had, indeed, invaded as promised. She'd not squander another moment.

Perhaps that was it. Her conversation with Grayson about enjoying the mornings.

Perhaps. Somehow, it all came back round to him.

"Adi?" Mélina and Rodrigo sat on a bench beneath one of the oak trees. Rodrigo scratched numbers on a chalkboard, carefully copying those Mélina had written.

"I'm enjoying the morning," Adi said.

Closing her eyes, she tilted her head upward and spun in a circle. Gabriel laughed again, clutching her in fearless joy. Confident she'd never let him fall.

"It's been so long since I have," she admitted. "So long since laughter filled this villa."

Filled her heart. She didn't say that; she'd never admitted how unhappy she was in her marriage. "Unhappy" perhaps wasn't the right word, but Adi hadn't another. Discontent? Still not correct.

"What's changed?" Mélina asked, standing and looking at Adi as if she belonged in an asylum. Rodrigo, on the other hand, took the opportunity to stop his studies and run in circles around them.

"This. What future have we if we're all dead?"

"Adi," Mélina admonished.

It didn't matter. Gabriel was too young to understand, and Rodrigo laughed as loud as the birds sang. She glanced at the kitchens and nodded at one of the soldiers who was watching them. Suspicion darkened his face, but Adi merely smiled.

"We'll need to tread more carefully," she said, setting Gabriel on the ground. He couldn't quite keep up with his older cousin, but he tried. "As British help gets closer, the French get more dangerous.."

Which said a lot, considering the brutality with which they treated the populace. Amelia wasn't the only woman Adi had hidden since Lambert and his ilk marched into Carvalho. A quarter of the village had disappeared from prying French eyes and grasping, greedy hands. A fact that no doubt angered Lambert even more.

His men couldn't find a brothel, and the village had no willing women. Not that the French cared about willing. The soldiers hadn't forced themselves on anyone that she knew of, but it was only a matter of time, she feared.

"We're leaving Portugal before the quarter moon."

Two weeks, roughly. Grayson probably wanted more time, and the quarter moon might hinder them, but they couldn't wait any longer. Adi grasped onto hope so strongly, she thought she might burst. It filled her until she wanted to scream into the ocean once more.

"What changed?" Mélina whispered. She grabbed Rodrigo by the collar and turned him back for the bench.

"Mama," he whined but reluctantly obeyed. Adi let Gabriel plop onto the ground, one hand tight in her skirts, the other drawing shapes in the dirt.

"I took a moment to enjoy the morning." She very much had. She'd enjoy all her mornings like that. Waking with Grayson's lips on hers. In fact, Adi couldn't think of a better way to start every day. "I decided if we didn't move now, then when? How much longer can we stay? Until the French slaughter us, too? Until our new government decides we are nothing more than Napoleon's slaves?" She shook her head. "If not now, Mélina, then when?"

Adi couldn't help it; her gaze slipped to the gardener's

cottage. Grayson slept now, but the fact that he remained, even after confessing his true purpose in Portugal, told Adi he'd keep his promise. He could've left any time. He'd healed enough; he had no ties to the land, the people.

Except maybe her. And his promise that he'd take them far from French hands.

"Tell no one." She caught Mélina's gaze. "No one, Mélina. I'll arrange everything."

"You're mad, Adi." Despite her words, Mélina nodded.

"You've been talking with Mama." Adi tried for a smile, but her lips smirked instead. Now that she'd decided, confidence made her arrogant. She'd have to moderate that—they didn't need her negligent.

"We're worried about you. You and your gardener." Mélina's eyes narrowed. "Does this have aught to do with him?"

"Do you trust me, Mélina?"

"That's not the answer I'd hoped for."

"Do you?"

"Yes," Mélina sighed. "I trust you."

"Then believe me." Adi leaned down and kissed Gabriel's cheek as she lifted him again. "And he's not my gardener."

***

Grayson slipped from the cottage in midafternoon. The soldiers didn't much enjoy the heat, which made them inattentive, careless, during the day.

It also made it easy for him to sneak past them and into the village.

Given the French couriers that continued, uninterrupted, , Grayson knew Lambert had heard of the British invasion and what happened in Évora. He hadn't mobilized yet, which concerned Grayson. Only a small garrison had been stationed here, along the southern tip of the country. Closer to Spain, however.

He had no idea if that meant anything, and he cursed himself for not seeing the connection—if there was one—sooner.

Perhaps Sebastião hadn't meant French troop movements in Portugal, but between Portugal and Spain. A stretch? Possibly. But, as Grayson kept beneath the olive and oak trees, ensuring the shade hid him from some eagle-eyed soldier, he wondered. The company wasn't inexperienced. The entirety of the French army had fought, and won, multiple battles.

Still, if Lambert wasn't mobilizing now that even Grayson had heard of the British landing hours to the north, why not?

Junot, and by extension Lambert, had made damn sure the countryside knew who was in charge. Shame they didn't look too deep. Even Grayson felt the angry waiting of the populace. But the French seemed content to believe what the pro-French government, a hundred miles north of here, told them.

Portugal was Napoleon's. Napoleon, Junot, and Lambert didn't care about much else. They believed they'd defeat the British without much trouble, boast of their superiority, and continue to conquer the continent.

Above him, birds fluttered from tree to tree, and he wondered if Philip the bird was among them. He couldn't tell. But he promised himself that when he returned home, he'd ask Philip—his brother, not the bird—about the different species and actually listen to his explanation.

He made good time from the villa, not that the road boasted much traffic. Or any, as far as he could tell. Skirting the outside of Carvalho, he looked for Maya again. He hadn't been able to spot her in the villa despite the multiple rooms he'd entered. Wherever she hid, she did as good a job of it as Inês.

No one walked the square or hawked their goods in the market. A quick peek around the buildings showed the guards at their stations, but nothing else. Not even Padre Lucio stood outside the church. In fact, no noise came from inside, either.

Grayson searched every alleyway and street, each balcony of each building, but nothing. No one suspicious stood out, and he couldn't see Maya or anyone who looked like her.

Frustrated, hot, and thirsty, he returned the way he came. Once back at the villa, he let himself into the cottage, cooler though he hadn't left the windows open. Apparently, the outside tile had something to do with keeping the temperature down inside.

He carefully lifted himself onto the table, then sat and finished the small bit of orange Adelaida had brought that morning.

The door swung open, startling him so badly he dropped the last bite of orange slice, grabbed his khanjar, and crouched, ready, in one breath.

"Oh." Adelaida looked stunned in the afternoon light. She had one hand on her chest, and the other clutched the door handle so tightly, Grayson wondered it didn't snap off.

"Ah." He straightened, ignoring the twinge in his left side. "You startled me."

"I startled you?" She shook her head, but her lips twitched. "I came by earlier, but you weren't here."

It almost sounded like an accusation, but it held more curiosity than anything. Grayson sheathed his dagger and eyed the orange, now crushed beneath his boot. Damn.

"I walked the village," he admitted.

Adelaida stepped into the room and quietly closed the door. "You found Maya? Or whoever looked like her?"

"No, no one." He shrugged, offering her the chair. From what he saw each day, she didn't rest except in the few moments she visited him. Even then, their time was hindered by the knowledge someone might've followed her, a soldier, or some enterprising servant out for a reward.

"Everyone's heard of Évora," she whispered, sinking into the chair with a weary sigh. "It's terrified us. It's also strengthened our resolve."

"What are they planning?"

She looked up at him, eyes dark and serious in the shadowy interior of the gardener's cottage. "They plan nothing, Grayson Conrad." She didn't sound haughty or arrogant. She sounded confident. "*I* plan."

His lips twitched, more with respect than humor. "I know. I've seen it. The people respect you."

They worshipped her, from what he saw, which made his heart swell with pride. To command such respect and adoration, especially given the circumstances, spoke of a trust that went deeper than a name. Her family might've been here for hundreds of years, and they might refer to her as *dama*, but that meant little compared to the unwavering respect the villagers had for her.

"More people arrived, several from Lisbon with news. We're housing them in the village until we figure out what they want."

"How do you know that?" Grayson stilled, connecting his earlier thought to what Adelaida had just told him.

"Padre Lucio brought the news just before Lambert's luncheon. That's what I came to tell you." She glared up at him, looking every bit the *dama* she was. "Padre Lucio doesn't trust them, given the timing. Carvalho is small compared to other villages, and not exactly on a main road from Lisbon."

"You don't trust them either," he said, settling against the table.

"My trust is hard-earned these days." She waved that off, holding his gaze. "It's hard to know what to believe."

Rather than asking if she believed in him, he asked, "Why are they here? Did they say?"

"Escaping the French, which is easy enough to believe." She stood, still a good head shorter than he, and watched him, head tilted just the slightest. "We used to have visitors, people in search of chocolates or wine. The rich who could afford to travel, who wanted to eat and drink the very best while overlooking the cliffs."

"Considering you were the chocolatiers to the Crown, I believe that." He traced a finger along her cheek.

Despite the heaviness of their conversation, Grayson needed to feel her skin beneath his fingertips. He tried to limit his touch; he didn't want to make her uncomfortable. But from the first, she drew him in like no other.

Her wit, her strength, her passion.

"It helped sustain the village." Her breath hitched as he ran his thumb along her jaw. "There's an inn just north of the villa; you can't see it from here, it's on the opposite road. We used to have guests year-round."

"I'm sure these visitors aren't here for the chocolate and wine. Safety?" He shrugged, voice still low. He pushed out the words despite wanting only to kiss her. "Food? Both are scarce."

"Information," she breathed. "Are you going to kiss me?"

He didn't need to be asked twice. Leaning down, he pressed his lips against hers, let her soft breath fan over him. Yes. This. Her arms wrapped around his back, and she stood on tiptoe. Her passion exploded over his senses as he deepened the kiss. Her fingers dug into his back, her mouth hard against his.

He drowned in her taste, in wanting her.

"I trust you, Grayson." She kissed the corner of his mouth. "I believe in you." She kissed the other side. "I—" She broke off, hands on his chest, eyes unreadable. "Why is that?"

"I won't betray that trust, Adelaida." He wanted to utter a joke about having a trustworthy face, but nothing came out. So he pressed his lips to her forehead and held her for a long, long moment.

"I don't know why Lambert hasn't joined Junot north of here, nor why he's stationed so far south of Lisbon." He sighed and admitted, "On my walk around the village, I'd wondered if it had something to do with your proximity to the Spanish border."

"Spain, rather, the citizens of Spain, have been battling the French for a year. We've heard many stories, but they're nearly two hundred miles away." She shook her head, then rested it on his chest. "However, with the arrival of these strangers, it makes more sense."

Very little made sense anymore, but he agreed.

"What made you think of our proximity to Spain?" He heard the frown in her voice. "Even before you knew of their arrival?"

"I couldn't figure out why Lambert wasn't mobilizing. If the village has heard of the British landing, then he would have as well. He would've known first, given the frequency of dispatches."

"He's waiting," Adelaida agreed. "Supplies? Reinforcements?" She jerked back. "Information."

Information? He hadn't thought of that. "I'm guessing supplies and reinforcements." Oh. A chill snaked down his spine despite the heat of the day. "Unless you're right, and he's waiting for his own spy. These people from Spain? From north of here?"

"I don't know." She shook her head, but that resolve returned, hardening her voice. "I promised Gabriel we'd leave." She laughed a little and relaxed, but that fire within her burned bright.

"And I promise you we will." He grinned and twirled her suddenly, lifting her onto the table. "How many *barca de pesca* has the village?"

"You think to use them?" She rested her head back on his chest, tightening her arms around him. "Why did I believe you and not those who've newly arrived?"

He had no idea. Especially after he'd lied about his name and origins. "I'm grateful you did," he whispered. "I was in no shape to fight an entire garrison."

"You believe you could've taken them all?" She sounded derisive but quiet still.

"Probably not, but, given my life would've hung in the balance, I'd have tried." Kissing the top of her head, Grayson tried to answer her, but he had nothing more. "I wouldn't blame you if you hadn't," he finally admitted. "Trusted me, that is. You had no reason to. Especially after you learned the truth."

"Hmm," she hummed, as she often did when she didn't want to answer. "The *barca de pesca*?"

He accepted the change in subject and stepped back, bending only slightly to meet her gaze. He wondered how sturdy the table truly was—could it hold the both of them? Clearing his throat, Grayson wrestled his mind back to the subject at hand. What had she asked?

"The *barca de pesca*," he repeated. Right. "Are there enough for everyone? I'm afraid we'll need to travel light, but I promise, whatever we need, my family will provide."

"Just like that?" She eyed him, head tilted. "You'll take us away from here, feed us, shelter us, clothe us, provide for us?"

"Yes." He had a long explanation about the importance of helping and giving back, but he just kissed her instead, a quick, light peck. "Just like that." He grinned.

"All right." She grabbed his shirt. "Now kiss me like you mean it."

Fourteen

Alone in the sweltering confectioner kitchens, a half mile from the villa, Adi methodically rolled the dough for Colonel Lambert's *pastelarias*. It was quiet work, redundant, and she didn't usually mind.

Except these were for the colonel, and she minded everything that man asked for. She'd agreed, of course. She hadn't any choice. He'd asked for pastries and chocolates, but even kindness was an order. With new people in the village now, strangers Adi wasn't yet sure about, she needed Lambert content. The self-righteous bastard.

Wiping her wrist along her cheek, where sweat beaded from the late-morning heat, she slowly tried to breathe out her constant anger at the man. She lost that battle every single day.

Looking over at the fires burning low and constant in the small arches beneath the long clay counter, she debated adding another log. Not yet. They needed the pots of cream and chocolate simmering, not boiling. Her family's ancient recipes, their legacy.

Yet she'd burn it all down in a heartbeat if it meant defeating the French.

The sun glinted off the richly tiled walls, the grand archways that worked well in keeping the interior cool. A breeze reached the room from the beach, moving through in a gentle caress. She'd already sent everyone home for luncheon and rest. Not many bakers remained. It made creating their chocolates harder, but Lambert didn't care about that.

Quiet settled over the kitchens, an empty echo that reminded her of those no longer with them.

"There you are."

Startled, she jerked from her work. Grayson stood across from her, his ubiquitous gardener's hat gone, his beard trimmed neatly. Adi couldn't read the look in his gaze, but it made her heart skip a beat.

"You move like the darkness." But she grinned, relieved someone kept her company, interrupted the sounds of the ghosts.

"When I couldn't find you at the villa, I worried." He stalked around the wide marble worktable, all grace and ease. Her hands tightened on the rolling pin, only to abandon it. "I eavesdropped on the kitchens—Karlotta sent Élea to keep you company, and I followed her here."

She tried to convince herself anyone would've done for company. Even Inês—well, maybe not Inês. But anyone else. Well, not the French, either.

The simple truth was, she craved Grayson's presence.

Adi licked her lips, hot and dry in the August heat. That's what it had to be. The heat of early August, of the kitchens, of her work. Not Grayson's presence. Not the fire in his beautiful eyes. Not the way his mere presence made her acutely aware of her body's every reaction to him.

His kisses from yesterday still burned through her.

"She came to keep me company," Adi admitted, breathless. She ignored the scalloped and tulip-shaped tins that were waiting for her pastry dough, the pots in need of tending. "But I sent her home." Grayson rounded the table, each move smooth and graceful like a dancer. Or a fighter. Her mouth went dry. "It's not every day I can give her time away from her duties."

He reached out and brushed his fingertips over her cheek. "Do you want to be alone?"

The words, as sinful as her chocolate confections, slid over her arms, raising goosebumps in their wake. Her heart raced, and Adi swallowed hard. Around the question that no one else had ever asked. Around the touch that sent wildfire through her veins. The promise in his every move.

No, she didn't want to be alone. Adi shook her head, ignoring her dough, her work, the workers who'd return far too soon.

"No," she breathed, caution well and truly tossed into the wind. "No, I do not."

"Good."

She half expected him to say he'd brought Lua for company. A teasing joke that always made her smile. But he merely moved closer. One step, a single step, and the sun shone off his dark hair, the ends curling along his collar. Another, and he moved back into the shadows, a hairsbreadth away from her.

Adi met his eyes, her skin tingling for his touch. Heat pooled between her legs, and she fully turned to face him. Grayson made no further move. In a rush of realization, Adi knew what he waited for, what he wanted. Her. He waited for her. Her choice.

"No one's ever offered me a choice." She hadn't meant to say that realization aloud. Now that it lay between them, all her breath rushed from her. Her heart beat loudly in her ears, like a procession making its way down the streets. Adi was thankful she was already flushed from the kitchens' heat.

"We're dealt one hand," he whispered, taking hers and brushing his thumb over her knuckles. "It's up to us what we do with that."

"Until you washed up on shore, I didn't—" She shook her head. Adi had no idea what she was trying to say, but the words crowded her lips, waiting to burst free. For the first time in her life, she spoke from her heart, not her head. "I lived my life in every dutiful way that was required."

Swallowing, she squeezed his hand and made her decision. It wasn't hard. In fact, Adi realized she'd made it the moment she helped a waterlogged pirate from the beach into the caves.

"I cursed the French for invading and taking everything from me. My husband, my livelihood, the comfort of my own home." She stepped forward, bold and wild and confident. Oh, it terrified her, but it exhilarated her at the same time. "I had no idea it'd bring me you."

She saw his grin, there and gone in a heartbeat. Predatory. Then he kissed her.

It burst through her. That same tempestuous storm that brought them together now swept them closer. Adi didn't know what she wanted, how much *more*, but she knew she wanted Grayson. The passion he offered but never demanded. The trust and confidence he reminded her that she possessed. She wanted his mouth on hers. Wanted to taste the lips that pulled wide in a daft grin or pressed thin in a scowl. Feel his warm breath against her cheeks, his skin beneath her fingers.

His hands cupped her cheeks, his tongue sweeping along her lips. Adi opened for him, meeting his kiss and letting go. She whimpered against his lips, stepped closer, and pressed her body to his.

"Grayson," she moaned as his hands combed through her hair, tangling in her braids.

Suddenly, she found herself in his arms as he carried her to the very end of the table. In another dazed breath, she realized she sat on it, his mouth on hers, hungry, demanding. Yes. Oh, yes. It burst through her, devastating and needy and so very wanted. Adi didn't think she could describe it, not with words in any language.

"Adelaida, are you sure?"

Sure? She nearly laughed. Breathing hard, Adi pulled back, even as she wondered how he managed to say her name with such passion it made everything in her melt.

"I'm not sure of much anymore. But right now? Yes. So don't you stop, Grayson Conrad."

He grinned, that darkly charming smile that sent shivers down her spine. "Yes, ma'am. Your wish is my command."

That sparked something in her Adi didn't understand but craved. She had no idea what to do with that feeling, so she held it in reserve. For next time. Next time?

Adi pressed her lips to his, just a touch, the simplest of kisses. Then she pulled back and looked at him. His gaze had darkened, and it pulled her in. The intensity, the watchful stillness tingled over her skin. His hands settled on her hips, burning through her clothing. He tugged her closer, or maybe pushed her back. Back against the table, his solid presence trapping her. Adi shivered, wound her arms around his neck, and pulled him closer.

His lips moved hungrily over hers—or maybe hers did. She couldn't tell and didn't care. She wanted him. Wanted the feel of his skin sliding against hers, wanted to taste him. Explore all he was and all he offered.

But then his hands were on her legs, warm and calloused as he rolled up her skirts, only to drop gracefully between her legs.

"Oh." Had she managed to say that aloud? Adi had no idea, because Grayson's mouth was on her inner thigh, and his fingers were caressing her and—good lord in heaven. She braced her arms on the worktable and opened her legs.

His fingers slipped into her wet heat, and Adi shuddered. He pressed against her nub, slow, even circles that made her weak, even as pleasure shot through her. Before she realized it, her orgasm washed over her, leaving her gasping for breath.

"Grayson," she moaned, arching against him. She wanted more, wanted that pleasure to rush through her until she couldn't think.

Grayson didn't sweep her off her feet. Thank goodness, because Adi didn't know how she'd react to that. She'd never been swept off her feet. Not something she thought she'd like, frankly. He tugged her to the edge of the table and urged her legs around his hips. His mouth was hard on hers, bruising in the most delicious, provocative way.

Adi shuddered. Pleasure burst through her veins, hot and grasping, and for the first time in her life, she felt throbbing need overwhelm her senses.

She clawed at his back, desperate to rid him of his clothes and feel his skin on hers. He danced his fingers up her bare arms, awakening her nerves. Grayson pressed his palms to her lower back, urging her closer. He nipped at the sensitive skin just behind her ear. She shivered, and his tongue darted out, caressing the light bite. He kissed her neck and across her shoulder until she pulled back, gasping, spinning out of control.

She loved it.

Adi gripped his shoulders, flushed with a dark, clawing want. She didn't need to ask; she simply knew. That same instinct shone darkly in his beautiful eyes. He wanted to slide into her as desperately as she needed him. That same throbbing need to taste and bite and devour pounded through him.

She kissed the side of his neck, tasted his arousal there. Breathed him in and hummed in appreciation and hunger. His eyes darkened, his fingers dug into her waist. She understood. Adi whimpered, a low sound in the back of her throat, and arched into him.

"Don't hold back. I want it all." She rocked against him, felt his delicious hardness against her, and hissed out a breath. She scraped her blunt nails through the hair on the back of his head, craving his touch.

He growled and thrust against her. *Yes.* He kissed her long and deep, and Adi drowned in it.

"Never," Grayson promised. "Not with you, not ever." He reluctantly pulled back and met her gaze. The blue-green flame burned her.

He cupped the back of her head, pressed his palm to the curve of her spine, and held her to him. Adi thought she could get lost in his kisses, as if the last year of invasion and exile and terror were worth it because of the way Grayson kissed her.

"Beautiful," he breathed against her mouth.

His fingers combed through her hair, dislodging pins and braids. Adi kissed him back, mouth hard against his, wanting more, taking all. Grayson deepened the kiss; the feel of his warm skin beneath her fingers was as arousing as the scent of him. As the feel and taste of him.

He easily lifted Adi and once more urged her legs around his waist. She had no experience undressing a man—Mateus's valet had always done so, and neither of them were fully naked when they made love. Adi desperately wanted every bare inch of Grayson's skin against hers for as long as she wished, and damn the consequences.

"I want to taste you," she breathed against his mouth. "I want to touch you." She shook her head, shocked at her bold words. But this wasn't going to be enough, and she knew it. From the fierceness with which he watched her, Grayson knew it, too.

"Not here." His breath came short, his eyes dark as they held hers. "But I will undress you and make you come with my mouth and hands."

"Oh." The word was barely a sound. "I want that. I want all of that."

Where this confidence came from, Adi didn't know. But then, what was it he'd said about playing the hand they were dealt? She was tired of playing it safe. That had brought her Gabriel, her greatest joy, but it'd also done nothing against the French invasion.

"I want more."

"I promise you, Adelaida, I'll give you everything." He said it so sincerely, a dark promise etched on her skin, she believed him.

"Yes," she breathed and ran her fingertips over the rough linen covering his broad shoulders, along his spine. Grayson cupped her face and softened his mouth against hers—softened, maybe, but no less possessive.

Her breath caught. "Grayson." Adi shivered, fingers tightening on the nape of his neck.

"Adelaida." He leaned his forehead against hers, his fingers trailing along her sides. She shuddered, hips jerking against his, whimpering at the brush of him against her wetness.

She kissed him again, harder, nipping his bottom lip, and tasted a hint of desperation. Her fingers brushed over his cock. She was more confident than her experience warranted, but she liked this new, emboldened Adi. He quickly opened his trousers, one hand catching hers against him. He jerked at her touch, as her nails grazed his skin and shoved the barrier out of the way. She stroked his cock, her fingertips caressing him.

She teased him, ran her fingers over the head of his cock, then scraped her nails down to his balls. They hadn't time for all she wished to explore, but this, oh, she wanted this. He shuddered against her, gasping out her name. Adi loved the sound of her name on his lips.

Cupping her bum, he lifted her hips. She breathed deeply of the heady scent of their arousal. Grayson slid his fingers into her, and Adi gasped, tilting her hips into his touch.

"Grayson," she moaned. "Grayson."

He entered her slowly, easing in as she adjusted to his size and length. She tightened around him, and he slid deeper into her heat. Her head fell back, and her breath caught. He ran his thumb over her, easily finding her pleasure, watching her with those fiery, intense eyes. Her lips parted, and she breathed his name, her hips meeting his with every thrust.

He drove into her welcoming body, and Adi tasted along his jaw, nipped his throat. He pinched her nub, and Adi dug her nails into his skin. He'd have welts there later. She didn't care; she wanted to mark him.

Grayson stroked harder, his thumb pressing down on her. Her orgasm exploded through her, a clash of light and pleasure and roaring blood drowning out her own cries. Adi ground her hips against his hand, nonsensical words falling from her lips. She tightened around him, drawing him even deeper, and she felt his control snap.

He kissed her, a sloppy, bruising kiss, and pounded into her. Adi welcomed him, held him close, and felt her own orgasm build once more. Just as she cried out, Grayson shattered in her arms, her name a cry on his lips as he pulled away.

Adi caught him. Or maybe he caught her. Either way, it was beautiful.

She gasped for breath and shook her head, as if that might shake some sense back into her. No use. The tingling pleasure of ultimate satisfaction settled over her. The warm, heavy presence of Grayson's embrace wound through her heart. She didn't think she ever wanted to leave.

Except—

"The table is digging into my legs," she whispered. Pushing his shoulder, she met his gaze.

He grinned, that quick smile that stole her heart. Oh. Oh, dear, she was in trouble. Sleeping with her pirate was one thing. And honestly, she truly needed to stop referring to him as hers.

But Adi knew it was far, far too late.

Straightening, Grayson fixed his clothing and combed his fingers through his hair. But it did nothing to tame his wild locks, and Adi quite liked that.

"I might never look at a kitchen table the same way." He lifted one leg and smoothed her stocking, tying the ribbon securely once more. Just above it, he pressed a kiss to her bare skin. His beard scraped along the inside of her thigh, and the contact made her entire body shiver.

Adi wondered if perhaps she wasn't as ready to resume her afternoon as she ought to be.

"At least we were far from the dough." She rolled her head to the side and looked down the marble table, where her abandoned dough and rolling pin sat, quite forgotten.

Grayson lifted her other leg and again tied her stocking and ribbon, kissing her skin before smoothing down her dress. Adi didn't even want to think about its wrinkles, but then decided she didn't care.

Not with the way Grayson's kiss burned through her, the

way his hands sat gently on her hips. Or the ease with which he helped her stand, holding her close against his body until she found her footing.

"I should finish the pastries," she whispered against his lips. "Before the dough spoils in this heat."

"Or your workers return." But he didn't release her, and Adi made no move to step back.

Not yet. One more minute. One more kiss.

Liar. Sex was one thing—she hadn't realized how she craved Grayson's touch on all her intimate places. How much she wanted him. His kiss, yes. She'd fantasized about that since meeting him. But this?

Madness, that's what it was. Pure madness. Yet her hands scraped through his hair, cupping the back of his neck, and Adi didn't want to let go. Ever. Which was ridiculous, of course.

Even when they escaped Lambert and settled elsewhere— England, probably—she still had her role as a *dama*. People needed her, depended on her.

Grayson kissed her slowly, as if eternity stretched before them. In no rush to stop or leave or abandon her. Tears pricked the corners of her eyes, but Adi ignored them. Breathing heavily, her blood racing from his touch, she finally forced herself to step around him.

What did he always say? One step at a time. They'd taken all their first steps, and she had no idea if there were any left for them. Nonetheless, she held out her hand. Tugging him along the length of the worktable, she resumed her position in front of her chocolate tins.

"I'll save a pastry for you," she promised, picking up her rolling pin. "We usually don't bake them this late, but the colonel..." She stopped and shook her head. "He requested them at breakfast for tonight's entertainment."

"Still not worried about the British?" he huffed behind her. "Every move that man makes gets stranger and stranger. He's waiting for something—or someone—else."

"Sebastião?" Adi worked the dough, coating it with olive oil as she rolled. "One of the new people supposedly from Spain?"

"Reinforcements from the sea?" Grayson stirred the cream, watching it intently. "I've no idea."

"We return to the village tomorrow." She eyed the fire but once more decided against adding another log. "I'm hoping Padre Lucio has more information."

Grayson stepped back and frowned. "How is this pot heated?"

"Clay," Adi laughed. She nodded to the arch beneath the tiled clay shelf. "Normally, all the fires are lit, keeping the surface warm longer. We don't need as much heat," she added sadly. "Clay conducts the fire and heats the pots."

"Huh." He nodded, clearly fascinated. "I've never seen anything like this."

"Kitchens are different in England?"

"Apparently." He turned back toward her and grinned. "How do you make them?" Grayson stood behind her, his hands on her hips. "Your chocolates and pastries?"

How was she supposed to think with him pressed so close? How was she supposed to do anything but melt against him? Adi leaned back in his embrace, unable to resist that momentary weakness.

Beneath her head, his shoulder supported her, strong and steady. He didn't move, save a quick kiss along the side of her neck. That simple kiss wound through her more tightly than anything.

Blinking her eyes open, Adi straightened, but Grayson didn't release her. He didn't stop her, either, but settled his chin on her shoulder.

"The pastries," he said, as if he hadn't crashed through every single wall she'd ever placed around her heart. As if he didn't make her body weak and her heart yearn. "You have a secret recipe?"

Adi laughed, a soft sound that made her lips curve in a slight smile. "Yes. Passed down from my father's great-great-grandmother. There are many pastry makers here; the convents are full of exceptionally talented women. But our chocolate recipes are second to none."

"I promise I won't steal the recipe." He kissed her neck again, lingering just below her ear. Again the brush of his beard over her skin sent shivers of need through her. "Or even ask about it."

"You're a strange man, Grayson," she whispered.

"Am I?" He sounded genuinely surprised. "I'm sure you have plenty of people wanting the recipe. Competition is no doubt fierce."

"Yes." She licked her lips, but what did it matter what she told him? Their time ticked down with every moment, every kiss, every intimate touch. Even when he kept his promise and ferried them all away, she had no guarantee of more. "Mateus, he wanted to know. Said it was my duty as his wife to share. And Inês, she was very adamant. But I'd made promises to my family, too."

"They didn't understand." She felt him nod, and his arms tightened around her waist. "They believe they were entitled to your secrets."

"You say that as if you carry some as well." Adi rolled the dough, still workable enough despite the heat and her neglect. She sprinkled more flour, a dwindling commodity as well, onto the cool marble table. "As if you have more than piracy and spying as your secrets."

She'd meant that in jest, but he stiffened behind her. The barest movement; his hands flexed against her waist, and his breath stopped for only a moment.

"You're wise beyond your years, Adelaida."

"Am I?" She pulled back and looked at him, though he kept his focus on her worktable. "I have a feeling that you aren't playing at not wanting to know. That you truly do not wish to. Why?"

"This is your livelihood. The French won't be here forever, and Dos Santos Chocolatiers, the chocolatiers to the Crown, will rise once again." He wrapped his arms around her more firmly and nodded at the table. "I won't spill your secrets."

"And I won't yours." She placed one hand over his, hoping he understood. "Whatever you tell me, I promise you it's safe."

Fifteen

Grayson stilled. He believed her. Her warm body pressed against his. Not in passion, though he still tasted her pleasure on his tongue, felt her body quiver beneath his hands. Wanted her again.

Her hand, covered in flour and calloused from work, conveyed a different warmth. Trust. Understanding. Hope.

"I don't want you in any more danger than you already are," he admitted. "You saved me on that beach, and I'll never be able to repay that. He pulled Adelaida closer against him, as if that might keep his own secret from bursting forth

"It seems, Grayson Conrad, that you forget I'm already in danger. As you say, Colonel Lambert already lives under my roof. His troops coerce my village. His arrogance knows no bounds. Despite the British arrival, he doesn't seem ready to move off anytime soon."

Adelaida didn't pull back. He half expected her to step away with a dismissive huff and finish her work. But her hand remained covering his. Her thumb brushed delicately over the back of his knuckles, as soft as her voice.

For the first time in his life, Grayson chose truth and trust.

"I made a promise to Esme, my oldest sister." He released Adelaida and turned to the fire, stirring the pot that sat atop the shelf that ran along the firepits. He wanted to ask what that shelf was called but somehow couldn't utter the question. Deflection, Esme would've said. Change the subject to one of frivolousness. "We promised each other, and then we made our younger siblings promise, too. The world is not as kind to outsiders as it likes to believe."

"I agree," Adelaida said softly, folding the dough and settling it into the metal cone cylinders. "People are not kind to each other, either."

Grayson watched the muscles of her back move, strong and sure, and wondered if this was a mistake. If the confession he was about to share would lose her entirely. But telling her felt right. Deep in his gut—his soul, his mother would say—it felt right.

"My parents met in Egypt." The scent of chocolate wafted up to him, rich and thick, a cloud of temptation. Grayson turned from it, turned from one temptation to another. He was drawn to her, and he didn't want to resist. "My father was contracted to marry my mother and take her from Cairo and the famine there to England."

She nodded. "This was before Napoleon?" Given the time frame and his age, Grayson knew she already understood. "I'm afraid I know little of Egyptian politics."

"Not many do. But this wasn't about politics, not entirely. Well..." He tilted his head and shrugged. All or nothing. He'd already decided to tell her. Had already leaped. "I guess you could say it was; my mother is the granddaughter of one of the Turkish sultans. Not the current one, a long-dead one."

Adelaida frowned and stopped her work. She tilted her head

and watched him. "I thought your parents met in Egypt. Was the Turkish sultan in Egypt?"

"They did. It's a long, complicated story, but her father was an Egyptian guard. He met the sultan's daughter in the palace, eloped, died protecting her, and sent her to Egypt."

"I see." Adelaida frowned. "I'd like to hear more of that story one day." She shook her head and gave a half smile. "But I see why you keep that secret. Though, for a pirate, I'd say that story is right up there with the best of them. Mysterious birth, secrets to keep." She nodded, that joyous smile playing around her lips. "Only trusting your siblings."

Grayson laughed. He wasn't certain what he'd expected when he shared the secret his family kept, but this simple acceptance wasn't it. He hadn't even told Landon, his only real friend. Though since Esme had married him, Grayson assumed she'd shared their secret. As Landon had never treated him, or any of them, any differently, it clearly hadn't mattered.

"You're the first person outside of my siblings to hear that story." He shook his head and walked back to the table, watching her hands coat the cones in olive oil. "Are you going to make your little chocolates, too?" He tilted his head toward the cauldron. "That's a lot of chocolate."

"It's almost our last," she admitted. "The French blockade blocked everything, even at the expense of the colonel's favorite sweet." Her lips pressed tight, but she merely shook her head. "We will, once the workers return from their rest."

"Do they always have a respite during the day?" Grayson pulled up a stool and sat beside her, content with this simple moment. "I've heard of that in Spain and Italy."

"In the summer, yes. Usually, we begin long before dawn and finish around luncheon. Cooler that way." She blew stray strands of hair from her face, and Grayson grinned. She hadn't fixed her hair after their passionate encounter. The strands clung to her neck and cheeks, looking wild and free. He liked that look on her. Wanted to see her like that always. "It was only at breakfast that Lambert spoke of the chocolates." She paused and met his gaze. "And today I wanted the quiet."

Did she always? He tried to halt his thoughts, but they raced forward like horses at the track. "Here," he said, changing the subject. It did nothing to dispel those foolish images of him and Adelaida in bed—on his lugger, may she rest at the bottom of the ocean, at his townhouse in London, anywhere. Everywhere. "Let me fix your hair before your staff returns."

"It's your fault." But she turned her head and over her shoulder gave him that smile, the one filled with laughter and happiness. "Is that why you don't drink wine?"

Grayson stilled his hands. "What do you mean?"

"On the beach, when I found you. I asked if you were drunk or something to that effect."

"You did?" He shook his head though she couldn't see him. "I don't remember." He snorted. "I don't remember much of that night, truth be told." His ribs throbbed at the memory of the pain. That, he most definitely remembered.

"No." She hummed. "I suppose not. But you said you don't drink. Is that because of your mother? I assume, given these secrets, she is not Christian?"

"No," Grayson admitted, the words slower now. "She's not. Then again, neither is my father. I assume he was raised as such; he never said. But he's not much of anything. There's a bit in there about the local vicar doing unmentionable things to a child, one of Esme's friends. And said vicar being summarily drummed out and turning up dead some months later."

"Unmentionable?" Adelaida repeated the word slowly, anger

clear in every syllable. Her hands clenched around the rolling pin so tightly, Grayson feared for the wooden cylinder. "Good," she hissed.

Yes, indeed. Neither he nor Esme knew what had happened to the vicar after he left the area. They didn't know how he'd died. Esme had threated to castrate him, then Mama had written the local bishop. Grayson didn't know any more of the story, other than the new vicar was not threatened, drummed out, or killed. As far as he knew, the new vicar and his wife still enjoyed weekly tea with Mama, though what they spoke of, Grayson couldn't imagine.

"Anyway, yes, that's part of it." He finished braiding her hair and began to pin the heavy strands around her head. It wasn't quite the way she'd worn it earlier, but he wasn't that talented.

"Where did you learn to braid a woman's hair?" He clearly heard the note of suspicion in her voice and swallowed a chuckle. At least she couldn't see his grin.

"My sisters. Esme, my older sister, she has my father's hair. Wild and curly and quite difficult to keep pinned. Since we're close in age, she enlisted my help in keeping it as presentable as it could be."

"You're so close with your family." She sighed, that wistful note back in her voice. "Go on, what is the other part?"

"My father, he has a problem with the drink."

"I see." She nodded but stilled when a pin slipped and stabbed her scalp.

"Sorry," Grayson muttered.

"I know many men like that," Adelaida continued, as if he hadn't wounded her. "Women, too. It consumes them." She paused, and he heard it then as well. The growing conversation of the returning staff.

Grayson rested his fingers at the nape of her neck, loath to release her. To disappear back into the villa and the gardener's cottage, away from this part of her life he couldn't share with her.

"Is that also why you refused *láudano*? Because you fear addiction?"

"You're more observant than you give yourself credit for, Adelaida." He pressed a kiss to her nape and stepped back. She watched him, her dark eyes serious but not judging. "Yes. Before meeting my mother, my father was a man of many vices—drink, opium, gambling, women." He shook his head as the voices grew louder. "Papa said it was hard to break the addiction, to stay away. A constant fight against the pull. So we thought it best not to try."

"You're a strong, brave man." She leaned over and kissed him, her fingers gentle on his bearded cheek. "I'm certain many don't understand that, either."

"No," he whispered, turning from her just as the first of the baking staff entered. He gripped the huge wooden spoon and slowly rotated it around the pot. "Not many except you."

Grayson doubted she heard him. He wasn't even certain why he'd added that. They lived in separate countries, with drastically separate lives. He was slowly taking over the family shipping business, with the odd foray into spying for the Crown. Adelaida lived under a French colonel's watchful gaze, barely keeping her family safe and fed.

It came over him again, that fierce need to protect her. Keep her safe, take her away from the brewing war. Once they left, then what? He'd settle her in London or near Nelda Hall. Then what? Leave her?

No. Never.

He wanted her with him. Wanted to be wherever she was. He loved—oh.

The breath rushed out of his lungs, and he stared into the pot of chocolate. Love? His mind warred with his heart, fighting over that word, but he knew the truth of it. Yes. He wanted her with him. Always. Because he loved her beyond breath, beyond reason, beyond sanity.

"Go home, *dama*," one of the women was saying. He turned his back more fully so no one could see his face. "Spend time with your son. We'll finish this for that colonel." She spat the last word. From the corner of his eye, Grayson caught the woman making a sign to keep evil away.

He suppressed a smile at the contrast of her very sincere worry for Adelaida and her visceral and very much sincere hatred of the French. Releasing the ladle, he caught Adelaida's gaze and tilted his head. He'd meet her outside. Slipping from the room before anyone could question who he was and what he was doing there, Grayson stepped into the shady back garden.

The air was cooler here, and the breeze so desperately needed inside the kitchens carried the scent of the ocean. He breathed deeply of the salt water. He'd spent so much time on the water after school. He and Landon had traveled for a year, but mostly over land, seeing northern England, Scotland, and Wales.

Afterward, he sailed with the company's captains. It was the best way he knew to learn the trade. And he'd loved it. Loved the rolling of the deck beneath his feet and the scent of the ocean breeze. It was his favorite scent.

Grayson's eyes shot open. No, no it wasn't.

He slowly turned toward the kitchens he'd just left. The scent of chocolate clinging to her hair—that was his favorite scent. The smell of passion on her skin as he kissed her throat.

Oh, but he'd fallen hard and fast and didn't know if he might recover.

"Did you walk?" Adelaida exited the kitchens, her headdress securely over her hair, her face still flushed.

He could see the marks from his beard against her skin, the faint redness cleverly disguised by the heat of the kitchens. Grayson swallowed and only then realized he'd extended his hand for hers. He'd fallen, all right. Right over the cliff.

"I did." He cleared his throat. The feel of her hand in his settled around him, as natural as breathing. As they fell into step along the winding path toward the road, he let that feeling wind through him. "Thought taking Rémy might attract too much attention, and I wasn't sure he'd let me twice in the same week."

She laughed and rested her head against his arm. Scandalous, he might've said if anyone were on the road with them. But he settled on intimate, tugging her closer. His hand wound around her waist, and she snuggled firmly against him.

Mine.

"Why did you come?"

The words were as soft as the breeze, and Grayson took a moment before answering. He pressed his lips to the top of her head and slowed their pace, though neither moved in a rush.

"I wanted to see you," he admitted. "With someone snooping about, I worried."

"Snooping?" she giggled. "I think you mean *espionando*, not *bisbilhotando*."

"Eh." He shook his head carefully so as not to dislodge her from his shoulder. "Both mean 'snooping'; *espionando* just means in espionage. Skulking," he added in English before reverting to Portuguese. "Also a good word, though I'm not sure of the translation."

They strolled in silence for a bit. He mentally rehearsed a dozen different openings but didn't wish to ruin the moment. This was the first and most likely last time they'd be alone together like this. Only the two of them walking along a tree-lined path with no one around, hidden by the olive and oak trees.

"I missed you, too." The words were nearly lost in the breeze, but Adelaida looked up and met his gaze. "I should get used to it; you'll be gone soon one way or another." She didn't smile as she had previously, and Grayson didn't either. "But I'm glad we have now."

Now. Yes, they had this moment. Perhaps even the next. After that? He had no idea, but he didn't want to lose her.

Grayson stopped beneath one of the large oak trees the region was named after. He cupped her cheek and pressed his lips against hers. She kissed him with the same desperation he felt but had no words to convey. The same hungry need that burned through him.

"Not here," she breathed. Gasping, Adelaida shook her head. "As much as I want you again, I want you naked and under me, where I can take my time tasting you."

"Yes," he growled. "Yes."

"I don't think once is enough, Grayson." Her eyes darkened, and she closed them. "I'm afraid it'll never be enough."

Take her away. Keep her with him. *Keep her safe.* Adelaida, Gabriel—all of them. Then what? He had no idea.

"I don't know how many will agree to leave," she said, resting her head on his chest, arms about his waist. "Mélina and Rodrigo. Mama. Most of the staff, I think. If they stay, Lambert will kill them for our desertion, and everyone is tired of being held hostage by the French. I haven't had the chance to speak with Padre Lucio since the Spanish arrived."

"Find out," he urged. "We're running out of time."

"Why?" she snapped. "You don't even have a way to keep that promise." She sighed. "I'm sorry. That wasn't—"

"You don't need to apologize for being right. Or even

wondering how." He offered a strained chuckle that told of his own concern over that one minor point. "When I made that promise, I had simply assumed we could leave. The logistics are harder than I first thought."

"You are arrogant," she said softly.

"Yes." He shook his head and brushed a hand over her cheek. "It's easy to be that way when things *come* easily to you. I never worried about popularity, merely did what I wished, forged my own path, so to speak. So long as I hurt no one, what did it matter?"

He hadn't fully realized just how arrogant he'd become until being stranded here. Unable to defend himself, to do more than suffer through his bruised ribs. Forced to rely on others, those not of his blood. His was a tight-knit family, keeping secrets out of necessity.

Relying on Adelaida, on the generosity of strangers, humbled him. Even as he fell deeper in love with her.

"I might not have always gotten my way, but I did often enough that when I didn't, it didn't matter." He blew out a breath and frowned. Adelaida had been right to call him arrogant.

"And now?" Again, a soft, quiet question.

"Now?" He tried to smile, a quick grin to hide his true thoughts. Instead, his lips lifted in a small upward tilt. "Now I promise I'll find a way. For you."

He felt that promise deep in his soul. Adelaida kissed him, her mouth warm and greedy on his. He could kiss her forever Pulling back, he pressed his lips to her forehead, holding her close.

"Besides, my sister and her husband are on that ship waiting for me. Oh." He laughed, annoyed by that realization. "I hadn't thought of it before now, that they might be among the strangers seeking refuge in the church." He paused, then shook his head. "No, I don't think they're in the village."

"You believe they wait for you though it's been three weeks?" Her voice held an incredulous tone that only made Grayson smile. He couldn't wait to introduce Adelaida and Esme. Esme was going to love her.

"Yes." That he knew. "The *barca de pesca* are our best bet. Small, easily maneuverable, well able to hide from French ships."

"They love you that much." She searched his gaze, and he wondered what she looked for. "I'm jealous of such devotion."

"I think you sell yourself short, Adelaida." He kissed her forehead again and stepped back. Taking her by the waist once more, he led her along the path. They hadn't many more steps before they needed to separate, and Grayson wanted to take each one with her. "The village listens to you. The servants worship you. Even Inês, though I admit I've yet to see her interact with anything other than her pianoforte."

Even that he only heard through the doors or windows. Her curtains remained drawn, and her doors locked. Strange, that, but even the French left her alone.

"Be glad," Adelaida said, offering a slight smile. "The French leave her be because she's a vicious harpy. I'm surprised they didn't kill her outright. I had to beg for her life, though now I'm not sure why I did."

The trees parted, and the villa came into view. Grayson stopped just inside the shadows, uncertain if they remained out of sight. He needed her safe; he needed her in his arms.

"Tomorrow we return to the village?" he asked though he knew the answer.

"Tomorrow," she whispered, her lips pressed hard to his. "Grayson—"

She stopped. Brushing his fingers down her cheek, he waited

for her to say more, but she merely kissed him again, quick, hard, a promise.

"*Boa tarde*, Adelaida."

Sixteen

A delaida lay awake most of the night, replaying her afternoon with Grayson. Her body still trembled with the memory of his touch, and she desperately wanted him inside her again. Heat pooled between her legs, but Adi resisted touching herself. Not only because Mélina, Rodrigo, Mama, and Gabriel slept beside her. And Lua, whose cold nose rested against her ankles.

She didn't think her own touch would be as satisfying as Grayson's. No, she knew it wouldn't, not when merely remembering his hands on her thighs sent thrills shooting through her. She spent half the night fantasizing about their illicit rendezvous in the kitchens. How much she'd wanted him against that oak tree, even though she'd have preferred him naked beneath her as she explored his body.

Definitely not the time or place for such thoughts, but they refused to let her sleep.

Adi tried to focus on his confession, the secrets he held so dearly, had shared so freely with her. But all that did was make the ache in her heart grow until her throat closed and tears pricked the corners of her eyes.

She tried to focus on anything else. The mysterious newcomers. Those claiming to have fled from Spain and further north near Évora. Could one be looking for Grayson? He'd dismissed that, and she believed him. Perhaps they truly searched for sanctuary, and she worried too much about their arrival.

The British being here, or several hundred miles north, at least, added to Adi's paranoia. Lambert's curious lack of urgency about their arrival worried her. He hadn't mobilized, and the frequency of his dispatches remained the same. Why? What did he wait for? What order did he anticipate that made him remain here, so far from the fighting?

It infuriated her that Lambert hadn't left. He'd already taken everything they owned—all they hadn't buried in the tunnels, at least. If he ordered his men to march north and reinforce Junot, no one would be surprised. The fact that he hadn't only solidified Adi's fear that he was waiting for something.

At least that fear fueled the angry fire already burning within her.

What was Grayson's English word? Skulking? How odd.

They'd skulk themselves, she decided. Untangling herself from the too-crowded bed, Adi slipped to the open window and looked over the grounds. The lanterns dotted the darkness, casting small pools of light on the marble terrace. She just made out the pair of overnight guards leaning against the pillars.

They watched the water, no doubt waiting for British ships. Carvalho sat beside a natural deep-water bay. It was why they could bring the cacao and wine directly onto the beach and through the tunnels. Forty miles north lay a series of fortresses built three hundred years ago.

Invasion after invasion. At least this invasion she could protect against.

Perhaps it was time to bring her remaining family in on Grayson's plan. She looked over her shoulder at them, sleeping peacefully on the mattress on the floor. Lambert had already shipped off the fine wooden bedframes.

They were leaving. All of them. No one would stay under French rule. She'd ensure that.

Chin tilted in determination, Adi let the ocean breeze wash over her, cool her from the sticky night. Returning her gaze to the grounds, she looked again for anything—or anyone—out of place. There, just off to the side, sat the gardener's cottage. It welled within her, that overwhelming need to sneak downstairs, slip outside, and find Grayson. Feel his arms around her and kiss him until she forgot everything else.

Adi hadn't realized she'd actually taken several steps for the door until she heard Lua softly woof at her.

Curling her hands into fists, she clenched her jaw and dug her bare toes into the floorboards. What was she thinking? Foolish. But, oh, did she want Grayson's arms around her. Adi looked out the window again but couldn't see anything more than trees from this distance. Foolish to want him, yes. More foolish still to fall in love with him.

"Oh, Adelaida," she muttered into the darkness. She rubbed her eyes, but the feeling remained, settling around her heart and squeezing. "You're a fool."

She returned to the window, and her head thunked against the windowpanes. Standing there, waiting for the sunrise, she planned their escape. She wouldn't sneak out early and deliver Grayson's food. No, she needed to speak with her family first.

She washed and dressed for the day, then returned to her

window. Just as the first rays of sunlight touched the sky with pink light, Gabriel stirred.

Within minutes, the rest of them were in various stages of wakefulness. Adi calmly kissed Gabriel and cuddled with him as the maids arrives. He clung to her this morning, fussy and sleepy. Adi kissed his cheek and whispered promises against his skin. He barely settled before Joana fetched him.

Kissing him once more, she realized he couldn't understand the dangerous step she took.

"I'll keep you safe," she promised her son. "No matter what I have to do."

Her remaining family watched her as they readied for the day, but they said nothing. Could they feel the change in the air? Or did that only settle around her?

Adi didn't know where or how to begin. She hadn't wanted the position of head of house, but Mélina mourned Théo, and her mother had been so angry with Papa's leaving—*desertion*—that someone had to step up and claim it. When she returned with Inês and the few staff that remained, the village was in an uproar over the French invasion, and half the staff wanted to join the Portuguese army.

But the memories of Mateus's joining, of the slaughter the army faced against the French, had been fresh, and Adi stepped into her new role. She hadn't thought about it, had merely done so. Now, as she waited until only the three of them remained, she took that next logical step.

Protect her family. Protect them all.

Karlotta and Mélina watched her warily but didn't say a word. They stood close together, in case of eavesdroppers. Maybe Adi wasn't the only one who felt that change. That...anticipation.

"We're leaving Portugal."

Well. Not quite where she'd planned to start, but these days Adi found herself jumping in headfirst more often than usual.

"So you said." Mélina waited. "How?"

Adi held up a hand. At least she had their attention. "What do you know of the Sebastião tale?"

Her mother waved an impatient hand. "What does that have to do with leaving?"

"What do you know?" Adi insisted. "It's important, Mama."

"He's to return in Portugal's greatest hour," Mélina huffed, no doubt in an effort to move Adi along to the important part. The leaving part.

"You don't believe that," Karlotta snapped. Adi wondered why she was so angry—angry now that was. Since Papa's leaving, Mama snapped and fumed often. Then again, none of them had dared hope. Carrying the shreds of crushed hope was a burden none of them wanted. "You never have; it's a fairy tale."

"I'm sure it is," Adi agreed calmly. "But someone claiming to be Sebastião has contacted the British."

"I think you better start from the beginning." Mélina's eyes narrowed. She took Adi's hand and squeezed. "And quickly, before the guards look for us."

Adi did. She told of the storm and finding Grayson—Paulo, she made sure she called him that. And of his eventual confession that he was here on assignment from the British Crown, sent to discover this Sebastião.

"He didn't know the legend, only the name."

"You trust him?" Her mother looked less angry and suspicious and more curious now. It was a change Adi liked. Her once happy, laughing mother might return. "Your gardener?"

"Yes." He wasn't hers. She bit that admission back. Because Adi desperately wanted him to be hers.

"Yes?" Mélina demanded, her arms crossed over her waist. "Only that? Simply yes?"

"Yes."

Oh, yes, she trusted Grayson. With her life, her son's life. Her heart. But Adi bit back that admission, too. No sense bringing any of that into this conversation.

"What else aren't you saying?" Karlotta asked.

"There's much," Adi admitted. "But right now, we need to keep an eye on Inês and Maya."

Her mother harrumphed in that same annoyed half snort she always used when dealing with Inês. Mélina, as observant as anyone Adi knew, slowly nodded.

"You think she's Sebastião?"

Adi jerked her head around and narrowed her eyes at Mélina. "I don't know. I hadn't before this conversation," she admitted, her mind racing. It made sense, she supposed, why Maya had been in the village. Maybe she was looking for a British contact with food and medicinal herbs. "I suggested keeping an eye on them because Paulo thought he saw Maya, or a woman who met her description, in the village when we went last week. He's since returned to the rendezvous place, but no one was waiting there."

"He's gone with you to the village?" Her mother's voice had risen, and Adi poked her in the arm.

"Lower your voice," she snapped.

"Adelaida."

"Mama, do not." The warning came sharp and deadly. Even the breeze stilled. "I am doing this to keep us safe. To keep Gabriel and Rodrigo safe. The British have already landed, if the rumors are true. No one yet knows how they'll fare against the French. Either way, we're caught between our French oppressors and new overlords. We might never have a say in our own lives again."

The words tumbled out, fears she hadn't dared put a name to and suspicions she hadn't fully fleshed out until now, this conversation.

"Papa fled with the monarchy and every rich landowner in this country. Even as we planned his funeral, the village questioned us. We're lucky Padre Lucio didn't ask any questions about the body. The only reason the village remains loyal to us, specifically, is because we stayed. We're under the same French rule as they are. We share with them what little food the gardens supply. We keep them employed as best we can."

"She's right, Karlotta," Mélina said into her mother's stunned silence. "It's why you didn't leave with Henrique. Théo heard you arguing—you were against leaving the land and our people to the French, but Henrique already had it in his head that he needed to see to the Brazilian lands."

All the breath rushed out of her mother in a single woosh. Her shoulders stooped, and her head bowed. "He's always been like that. Gets an idea in his head and won't see any other way. He thought he needed to protect our people there from the rich merchants who wanted to make money—*more* money." She grimaced and shook her head. "He refused to understand that we had obligations here, too."

"They've promised not to rise up because I've asked. I've shared stories of what the French did to the Portuguese army. Because we fled, and everyone knows there's no returning. Not now." Adi's voice caught, and her throat tightened. Friends and staff, neighbors, everyone. Killed. She shook her head. "They agreed we needed a better plan against so well-equipped and trained an army as the French. They did so because we stayed true to our promise of protecting them."

The sun brightened the room, and Adi knew that any minute the guards would pound on the solid oak door, demanding their presence. Breakfast needed serving; the colonel would be wanting his morning pot of chocolate. Bardot would want coffee and fresh bread and grape preserves.

"And right now, we can all escape." She paused and bit back a smile. "Not right now as in this minute," she amended. Grayson said his sister and her husband wouldn't abandon him, and she believed him. He also seemed confident in using the *barca de pesca* as their means of escape, and Adi desperately needed that confidence. "But we can. First, we need to discover this Sebastião and find out if they're working with us or the French."

"All right," her mother sighed. "Tell us why you think Inês— or Maya—is a part of this."

"And tonight, you can tell us more about this Paulo," Mélina added with a twinkle in her eye Adi hadn't seen in more than a year.

Denial sprung to her lips, a spluttering sort of refutation, but Adi couldn't utter a single word. Instead, she dug her fingers into the pockets of her gown and grasped for a plan.

"I don't know that they are," Adi admitted. "I'm basing this off what Paulo saw." And, oh, it was difficult to call him Paulo when she now thought of him solely as Grayson. When that was the name she'd gasped in pleasure. "His description, and the glance I caught of the woman, fit Maya. But then from a distance, half the village does as well."

"I'll do it." Karlotta sighed and looked heavenward. "Lord, give me strength."

"Do what?" Adi needed her mother to say the words. She wanted no mistakes or misunderstandings.

"I'll find Inês and speak with her. Though these last months have been nice, not having to do so."

They believed her. Adi breathed a sigh of relief and let all the hope she'd held tight in her heart break free. The worry that

Grayson wouldn't keep his word. That all this Sebastião nonsense was a ploy for food or shelter. Or even information, but for whom?

She believed him, deep in her heart, but nearly a year of living in constant terror had worn on her.

Her mother left the room with a quick admonishment that they both hurry. Mélina turned for Adi and watched her carefully.

"You trust this Paulo?" The words came sharp and fast. "Deeply, in your heart and soul?"

"Yes." Her heart skipped a beat at this question, but Adi swallowed the words that wanted to tumble from her mouth. Those weren't for Mélina. Only for Grayson.

"Why?"

"You think I'm being foolish. Rash." She gave a tart laugh. "Yes, I know. I've told myself the same things. That he could lie about any of this, and I'd never know. That for his own sake he might promise me things I want so desperately."

"You still trust him. Why?"

He made her feel alive. For the first time in her life, Adi felt her choices were hers. To love Grayson or not. Enjoy his body against hers and explore the passion between them. That was her choice.

Well, maybe not the loving him part—that happened quite against her will. And was very much a surprise. Apparently, her heart had different ideas than her head.

"I'm not so foolish that I believe the storm brought him to me." A small part of her did, of course, because that's what happened. However, saying it aloud would make her sound as mad as Rainha Maria.

"Adelaida Karlotta, do not lie to me."

Adi's lips twitched. "Mélina, I'm not. I believe him because he asks for nothing but offers everything. I can't explain it all; not now, we haven't the time. Trust me."

Mélina eyed her but nodded. "Let's get to the kitchens before they notice we're missing." She spun sharply for the door. "And tonight, you can tell me what else there is between you and Paulo."

Adi flushed, but luckily Mélina had already exited the room, breezing past the annoyed guards.

She was absolutely not going to confess anything about her relationship with Paulo. Or Grayson.

<hr>

She couldn't slip away until midmorning.

Karlotta and Mélina watched her with apprehension, though Adi gave nothing away. She moved around the kitchen and their remaining staff with her usual ease as she gathered Lambert's breakfast.

She'd become somewhat of an expert at setting aside food without looking suspicious. Not that the guards ever noticed. Manuéla might've, but she never uttered a word, nor even looked at Adi askance.

With a quick kiss to her mother's cheek, Adi slung her basket over her arm, slipped out the side door, and hurried around to the cottage. The birds sang freely, as if they hadn't a care in the world. Adi envied them that as they followed her down the shaded path, chirping along.

The door eased open the moment Adi arrived. Her heart jumped, but she slipped inside.

"You're late." Grayson's hands cupped her face, and he kissed her hard. "Are you all right? The guards didn't detain you? Gabriel is well?"

Her heart skipped for a different reason: his kindness and worry. "I'm fine. We had a delayed start to the morning."

He kissed her, that hard, fast, hungry promise of more. The basket bumped against his side—his right side, thankfully. Adi could only wrap one arm around his back and pull him closer.

"I missed you," she admitted, the confession a breath in the dim interior.

"I almost left the cottage a dozen times last night." Grayson's slight laugh warmed her. "It's not hard to slip past the overnight guards. And there are fewer of them than there are entrances."

Why didn't you? The question wanted to break free, but she held it back. Instead, she let the longing settle around her heart, and she found the humor in the situation. It'd been a long time since she'd been able to do that.

"Were you going to climb up my trellis and tap on my window?"

"You don't have a trellis." His grin widened, that beautiful, daft smile that melted her heart. "But I did think about it."

Adi laughed, feeling so carefree she might've forgotten the world contained anyone but the two of them. "And you'd have surprised Mama, Mélina, Rodrigo, and Gabriel." She tilted her head, her fingers brushing along his beard. "Though not Lua, who seems to like you."

Grayson took her hand and kissed her fingertips. "Is she the only one?"

"The birds seem to as well." Adi tipped her head toward the door, where they continued to sing in the rapidly warming morning.

He laughed and tugged her against him. "All well and good, but not who I was thinking of."

"You don't even know my mother."

That earned her another laugh, short and surprised. He

walked her back to the table with a low growl that ignited the fire in her veins.

"I'd toss you onto that bed, but even the mice leave it alone." He pressed her against the table, trapping her hips between his hardness. His hands settled on her waist, his teeth nipping along her jaw.

"How much time do you have?" he whispered along her skin, his breath a warm tease.

"Not long." Adi combed her fingers through his hair, holding him to her. She kissed him hard, though she felt their lack of time as keenly as ever. "I need you."

That was all it took. His mouth on hers, demanding, possessing, his hands bunching up her skirts. She was already slick with need, and he groaned against her throat.

"I'm going to have whisker marks on my skin again." But then he slipped a finger into her, two, pressing hard to her nub.

"Is that a complaint?" He rubbed her nub in fast, hard circles.

"Definitely not."

"Adelaida."

One-handed, he fumbled with his trousers, and in the next breath he entered her. Their coupling was fast against the table. Adi held on to his shoulders, her legs wrapped tight about his waist as she met his every thrust.

Pleasure burst over her, and she sank her teeth into his shoulder, muffling her cry of release from alerting the household or even the birds outside. He moved faster, and Adi slipped a hand between them, rubbing her nub until pleasure burst through her again. Grayson pulled out, gasping her name as he came over her thighs.

She kissed him as he regained his breath, letting her own pleasure seep into her bones. "I don't think there's a better way to begin the day," she whispered against his jaw.

"Perhaps in a bed, where I can watch you come again and again."

"Yes," she hissed, thighs clenching at the image, the raw need burning through her. "I want that very much."

He straightened and grabbed a handkerchief, then cleaned them both up. He kissed the inside of her thighs before helping her stand and kissing her lips. "As do I."

"I need to return to the village," she admitted, lingering over his kisses, once more uncaring about his whiskers against her skin. "You'll drive me?"

"Of course," he said, as if it were as natural as breathing.

"We should have more information about Sebastião. Or at least who might be interested in the old myth."

"What?" He grabbed for her hand, but Adi stepped out of reach. "Adelaida, no."

"We don't have all the time in the world." She stopped at the door. "We all have our parts to play."

Before he could utter another protest, Adi slipped outside into a deceptively glorious morning.

Seventeen

H e hitched a skeptical Rémy to the cart as the kitchen staff loaded what they could into crates and baskets. The French soldiers watched them as if they loaded gunpowder instead of olives and oranges.

In the hour since Adelaida's leaving the cottage, Grayson had cursed himself, her, Lambert, Junot, Napoleon, and everyone in between. Mostly himself for placing her in such danger.

Arrogance, that's what it was. He'd believed in his abilities to the exclusion of all else and hadn't thought a storm could stop him. He also hadn't thought much beyond finding out Sebastião's information and returning home.

Now he found himself square in the center of a convoluted French operation that made little sense. He cared more for Adelaida than he thought possible. And while Grayson wanted to take down the entirety of Lambert's garrison, he wanted her safety more.

It wound through him, how much he needed her safe. Tangled up in his heart, ignored his head. He wanted nothing more than to leave Portugal with her in his arms.

She didn't look at him as she supervised the loading, but then he'd expected that. What worried him were the curious looks her mother and sister-in-law cast his way when they thought no one was watching. Certainty settled in his gut.

She'd told them about him.

At least that he wasn't a gardener from the north, looking for work and food. Grayson doubted very much she'd breathed a word about the passion they shared.

Careful not to touch her in any untoward way, he helped her into the cart. Eyes on the ground, though he kept the guards in sight, he moved slowly, for show. The French expected a hunched man with a limp who had trouble lifting himself into the cart. No more, no less.

Most people expected one thing and saw only that. Grayson was an expert in offering them what they wished. He'd enjoy their stunned reaction when they realized the truth. But Adelaida had snuck through his barriers with her smile and laughter, and he'd never looked back.

Rounding Rémy, he scratched the suspicious donkey's nose and promised him all the carrots he could eat once they left Portugal.

Grayson settled into the seat, made a show of his pain, and picked up the reins. "What are you scheming, Adelaida?"

"Scheme?" She offered a laugh. With her back straight and her gaze on the road ahead, her lips nonetheless curled upward. "What you said yesterday, it made me think."

What had he said yesterday? He remembered quite a few confessions on his part, sharing secrets he'd never told another soul. He remembered tasting her passion, hearing her cries, feeling her clench around him. The way she'd pressed against his side as they strolled back from the kitchens, the intimate togetherness that had kept him sane throughout the long night.

"About leaving," she clarified. "The sooner the better. I agree with you—Lambert is waiting, and whatever he waits for will not bode well for us."

"Good." The constant band around his heart loosened just the smallest bit, and he breathed a little easier. "I meant it; I'll take you and anyone who wishes to join you to safety."

As safe as England could be, with the constant threat of French invasion. The Conrad name went far; they had contacts in parliament and the monarchy. Bringing the village—what, a few hundred people?—wouldn't be any trouble. He'd ensure that.

"Before that, we need to discover Sebastião." She made a small movement with her hand, and he clenched his jaw to keep silent. Her protest battered his control, but he held his tongue. "Either someone in the village contacted the British with a promise of information, or someone is using the village for protection."

"All right." He breathed out his anger. Well, he tried to. Mostly he huffed out a breath that did nothing at all.

He forced himself to acknowledge that anger for what it really was. Fear. Fear for Adelaida's safety, fear for her involvement. In his mind, he knew that—his heart didn't want her in danger at all. Wanted her safe and happy and laughing.

He'd needed help, washed up on that beach with battered ribs, and she'd appeared. His Angelic Adelaida. She'd become so much more than that since.

"You still suspect Maya?" His tone was as even as he could manage.

"I hope to see her," she admitted. "It'll be best that I do. I can listen to your description all day long, but the simple fact is that many women dress like her. Without confirming her identity, we have nothing."

There was more, he felt it, but he let Rémy plod along at his usual, labored pace.

"Mama has agreed to find Inês and speak with her."

What a terrible idea. "And you think that's a good idea?"

"No, but we have no others. Lambert received more dispatches today. At least one overnight and two curiors this morning. They're preparing for the British."

"Yes, I've seen them coming and going, never staying for more than a drink. Strange that." He ran a hand down his face and rested his elbows on his knees. He was far from comfortable, but at least it gave the impression of weakness. Or perhaps merely poor posture. "Has he said anything?"

"Lambert?" She gave a sour laugh. "No. Nothing we've heard, though Mélina swears he and Bardot are more interested in wine than in battles."

Surprised, he snorted. But then, Adelaida often showed a cutting wit. He liked it. "We're a hundred miles from Lisbon. Other than terrifying the countryside, I still don't understand why he's stationed himself here."

"Food and drink." She made a disgruntled sound. "He is a man of routine, however. I think his dispatches are upsetting what he considers a very plush position." She shook her head, then waved her hand about her face as if swatting a fly. She knew her role here all too well. That realization cut through him, fueling the anger that boiled within. He hated her in such danger.

"Mélina, she sings for them each night, but they never speak of anything important."

"I've not heard anything from the soldiers. A bit of gossip about that lack of women in the village. They're mostly asleep at night."

"I don't understand how they've managed to conquer the

entire continent." She huffed again, and her lips pulled down in a scowl. "Lambert and Bardot, they talk while I serve breakfast."

His hands clenched the reins, and it took everything in him to keep his eyes on Rémy. He hated that she served them. Hated that she stood anywhere near them.

"What do they say?" he asked, his jaw clenched. It wasn't an even and reasonable tone. Damn the French.

"Grayson." She breathed his name so softly, he thought he misheard.

His head whipped around, and only at the last minute did he remember his position. Swatting at imaginary flies, he looked straight ahead. She never called him Grayson in public. Always Paulo.

"I hate that you have to be here," he growled, forcing his gaze back on a plodding Rémy. "I hate that you aren't safe in your own house. That they took so much from you."

"When you washed up on shore, I didn't think twice about helping you." Her words came so quietly, he strained to hear them. "You could've been anyone, but I helped you anyway, and I don't regret that. The French were here long before you, but perhaps there was a reason I found you on the beach that night."

"Fate?" He tilted his head. The anger remained, simmering beneath his skin, a constant reminder he was helpless to cool. It didn't help that he was paralyzed here, unable to fight. One man against a garrison? Even he wasn't that foolish. "Serendipity? Providence? Luck?"

"If you like." Her lips curled upward now, easing the lines around her mouth. "At first, I thought you were as much trouble as the French. You lied to me, and your very presence caused more harm than good. If anyone discovered you, we were all doomed."

"Adelaida—"

"I could've done without you both—you and the French," she added, not letting him speak. "Perhaps this is how it's supposed to be. Fate or luck or destiny, whatever you choose to call it. There's a reason you washed up on my beach as I walked in the storm."

"What were you doing in that storm?" He'd never asked, though she'd asked him. "It was vicious, certainly not beach weather."

"I wanted a moment." She chuckled, a soft, light sound. "I like thunderstorms. And I like the beach." Another soft breath, not quite a sigh. "I screamed into the ocean that night. Screamed and screamed until my lungs ached. And it felt marvelous."

"Screaming into the storm?" The village came into view, deserted and eerie in a way it hadn't been last time. It settled in Grayson's bones like an omen.

"It was either walk in the storm or scream at Lambert." She glanced at him sideways. "The storm seemed the better option."

"Indeed." He smiled, a short-lived grin. "Where is everyone?"

"I don't know." Her voice chilled, and she shivered. "This can't be good."

Adi watched the French cart continue toward the garrison. The moment the small crowd of children congregated at the road between them and the market square, she turned for Padre Lucio.

"What's happened?" She tilted her head toward the deserted market. "Where is everyone?"

He shook his head, pale and wan, looking as if the strain of the last months had finally caught up with him. "The soldiers come here more frequently. They take everything and don't pay. The fishermen's daily catch. The vegetables you bring."

He hesitated, but she knew what would come next.

"The women." Her words were flat, angry. It'd long been her fear, the fear of every woman in Carvalho, of everyone here.

"*Sim, dama*. They don't care about the sanctity of the church, the sanctuary we offer." He looked ready to fight the French single-handedly, and she nearly grinned.

Except fury blinded her. It rose from deep within, that cauldron of hatred she'd tried to suppress for months. For the good of her people, her family, her son. Her nails dug into her palms. Her jaw clenched so hard, something popped.

"*Dama!*" Padre Lucio looked alarmed as he took her by the arm. "Where's your driver, shall I have him take you home?"

"This ends, Padre." She waved him off, ignoring her slight dizziness from the heat of the day, her burning anger, and the nauseous knowledge she could stop this.

Grayson had wandered off in search of anyone in the village. He'd been reluctant, but she'd insisted. Padre Lucio wouldn't speak with Grayson lurking about, and they needed far more information than they had.

"Lambert stays here, a hundred miles south of Lisbon. Why? No one knows, but he hasn't joined Junot's forces." She looked at the children playing and laughing, though no one had yet ventured down the street for their food. That in itself sent shivers down her spine. "He waits for something else."

"You think the British will retreat here?"

"No." She hadn't thought about the British marching this far south. "I think he has other plans. Junot sent him here for a reason." She uncurled her fists and tried to work through his reasons.

"We're close to Spain," Lucio whispered, though no one save

Rémy stood nearby. "The new arrivals speak of such brutalities by the French." He scowled. "Spanish troops, too. You think he wishes to launch a second invasion from there?"

With her eyes on his, Adi slowly shook her head. "It's always a possibility, but everyone's heard of the British naval victory. News of that spread fast."

"What more does Junot need? He's slaughtered us, stolen our people and our food. They've taken everything."

"Food," she realized slowly. "Supplies. Having a natural deep-water port away from the British is ideal."

She could've smacked herself it was so obvious. Here she and Grayson had discussed a dozen reasons for Lambert being here, but this made the most sense. Though, of course, smuggling also sounded plausible.

"We're far enough from Lisbon. It'll take the British time and manpower to get here." She nearly laughed, but the first of the villagers had appeared at the mouth of the road. She'd need Grayson's input on military tactics; she had no idea if that was even plausible. However, as she spoke the words, they sounded right.

"You see the people every day," Adi said as casually as possible. "If they had the means to leave Carvalho, would they?"

"*Dama*, truly?" He watched her shrewdly, but the spark of hope in his tired eyes told Adi all she needed to know.

"Discretion, padre," she warned. "I promised the village we'd be safe and would survive this invasion." She smiled at the woman in front of her. "And I mean to keep that promise."

"*Dama*." The woman offered a quick curtsy as Adi handed her a basket of vegetables and herbs.

Grayson's gardening had helped immensely. They severely lacked the staff to keep the villa running at the most basic level. Gardening, though important for their survival, hadn't been a priority. Fishing, yes. Rationing their stores, definitely. They had a variety of trees—oranges, apples, pears, cherries, olives, and figs. That had sustained them these long months.

The vegetables from the small patch of garden the kitchen managed had expanded greatly with the help of a single extra person.

She didn't dally listening as those few who had information shared it as quickly as the words allowed. Adi smiled and nodded, offering what encouragement she could. This visit, unlike last week's, energized her. She could see the end of this ordeal, and she grasped it with both hands.

Grayson wandered back into the street. She couldn't hear him, of course, not over the noise of the children. She looked up just as he rounded the corner. He nodded, his gait easy and smooth, and stood with Rémy while Adi finished with the villagers.

"*Dama*," Padre Lucio said as the last of them hurried off, disappearing before the soldiers returned from their own deliveries. "Are you certain?"

"About leaving?" The only other thing she'd ever been more certain of was Grayson. "Padre, I don't speak in jest. Nor would I ever offer false hope. We aren't deserting Carvalho. We're protecting our people."

He nodded, and though his questions were obvious, he said nothing except, "When?"

"I'll send my gardener with word." She nodded at Grayson, who watched her from the side of the cart. "If you trust me, trust him."

"As you wish, *dama*." Padre Lucio nodded and took his own crate of fruits before disappearing into the church.

"The French are at the next street." Grayson helped her into the cart and hurried around Rémy. "What did you and the good father speak of?"

"The French are taking everything," Adi whispered as the pair of horses came into view. She wanted to take them, too. Would horses fit on a *saveiro*? She had no idea, but she'd be damned if she'd leave her precious horses for the French.

"I noticed the lack of anyone in the market." His voice sounded grim, hard.

"They steal everything." Anger, fear, unadulterated *rage* blinded her. Padre Lucio hadn't said it outright, but Adi knew the soldiers were kidnapping women. There were stories of French soldiers roaming the countryside, raping the women and pillaging everything they could carry. "I'm afraid those we've tried to protect have also been discovered."

Grayson stilled. When she chanced a glance at him, his face was dark with rage, and she thought he might leap from their cart onto the French's. Attack them with his bare hands.

"For months, I've catered to Lambert and Bardot. I've given them everything they asked for and more. Mélina didn't have to sing and play for them; she did so in order to keep them entertained."

Bitterness choked her. Fury blurred her vision. No more.

"I'm sorry, Adelaida."

Something in his voice broke through her rage, and she narrowed her eyes at him. He didn't look at her but ahead at the road. Though he sat hunched over, every muscle remained taut. "I refuse to lose another person. We aren't deserting our heritage. If we die, no one will be here to rebuild."

She swallowed and tried to open her fists, but they seemed permanently clenched around her skirts.

"Did Padre Lucio say anything more? Did anyone offer information?"

"You didn't find Maya?"

He gave a brief shake of his head. "I didn't expect to. Not her specifically. Figured if she, or whoever purported to be Sebastião, hadn't met me at the rendezvous point by now, they'd given up. Maybe now that word spread about the British it doesn't matter?" Another shake of his head. "I don't know. But if the information was that important, then I agree. Why give up?"

"Hmm. But why go to all the trouble of smuggling out a letter that promises information only to give up?" So many things she didn't understand about this. "And how? How did your people find it?"

"I've no idea," he admitted. "Hilton never told me. But then, he has a vast network."

"His focus, you said, is in the Americas? I don't understand how this letter came into his possession."

"He said he intercepted it, I don't know," Grayson admitted. "He's excellent at his job, from what I've heard. If he says it's important, it is. Important enough for me to agree to run the French blockade and find Sebastião."

"The padre said something that made me think Lambert is here to protect Junot's supply line."

"This far south?" He blinked in surprise, those beautiful blue-green eyes wide on hers. In another blink, he returned his gaze ahead. "How so?"

"We're a deep-water bay, easy to land a ship, or ships, and unload onto the beach."

"That means Lambert expects fighting this far south." Grayson urged Rémy faster, though the donkey did as he pleased. "Even farther than Lisbon, but...ah. Yes. Into Spain. Whatever happens with the British forces, Lambert is expected here—to protect the secondary supply route. Use their Spanish allies if need be."

A chill worked its way down her spine despite the already sweltering morning. "I told Padre Lucio we're leaving. He'll spread the word."

"Good. We'll need the *barca de pesca* in position before anything. But first, I'll need a couple nights for planning. It's been a while since I navigated by the stars alone."

He paused, and while Adi wanted to ask about the stars, she held her tongue. Sitting atop a cart with the French behind them was not the time for an intimate discussion.

"Will you teach me?" The question escaped before she knew it.

"Yes. I'll teach you to sail by the stars, navigation, anything you want." He grinned but didn't look at her. "Whatever you wish."

His promise, as the villa came slowly into view, took hold of her heart and squeezed. Oh, she was in trouble.

Eighteen

I t swept through her. Adi didn't know what that something was—fear or anticipation or exhilaration. A combination of all that and more. The ride back from the village went faster than she thought Rémy could walk. Yet there they were, suddenly arriving at the stables.

Grayson unhitched Rémy while the French watched with flushed faces and overconfident scowls.

"Where's Pierre?" she whispered so as not to be overheard. "He's usually so protective about the horses in this heat."

"He was here earlier," Grayson said as he rounded the horses.

Adi helped, though she had little idea what went where. The stable hands had always taken care of this before, and when Lambert marched in, Pierre had taken over without so much as a blink.

"Strange he isn't here." He always was. Always.

"Maybe Rémy really did bite him in the balls." Grayson snorted.

Covering her mouth so as not to laugh aloud, Adi cleared her throat and tried not to show any emotion. Instead, she petted the horses and silently promised them safety from the French. Wrestling her laughter, and that strange agitation, beneath her normal cool exterior, she turned to her guards.

"Where's Pierre?" she demanded in her best lady-of-the-villa voice.

"Not your concern," one snapped.

The other, however, looked concerned. When his friend caught sight of him, he turned for the barn door and stood guard there.

Interesting.

Adjusting her headdress, she swept from the stables without a backward glance. Pierre wasn't here, and at least one man knew it was unusual. Reassignment? No. Drunkenness? Possibly, but he'd been here earlier.

Special assignment? That made more sense. But where and why? *Porra*, she should've looked at the rest of the stables. Had one of the French horses gone missing?

"*Dama*." Grayson walked slightly behind her, but she resisted looking over her shoulder. "Walk slower, Adelaida, I can't walk that fast, or they'll know I've been faking."

She instantly slowed her step. "Was one of the horses missing?"

"Yes. The one farthest from where we stood," he muttered. "Pierre must've taken that one."

"Why?" She gave an aborted shake of her head. "One mystery after another."

"Maybe he left in search of the mattresses." Grayson's humor often made her smile, but today she feared she might erupt into uncontrollable laughter.

That was the problem, her lack of control. For nearly a year, she'd controlled everything. Her words, her tone, her facial expression. The household, the village, the people. Herself.

She'd only broken once, screaming into the storm with all she had.

It brought her Grayson.

It brought her hope.

"I'll meet you in the cottage." She said the words before she fully knew what they meant. Rash. Reckless. Everything.

He looked shocked but bowed respectfully and walked in that direction. Adi didn't watch him. Rather, she turned sharply for the kitchens. She'd almost forgotten what it was like walking in her front door.

Karlotta and Manuéla conversed by the fire, where the omnipresent pots of soup just now began to simmer. Adi swept her gaze over the room but couldn't see Mélina, Rodrigo, or Gabriel. Joana was missing as well.

Her stomach dropped.

"They're in the nursery," her mother called with a significant glance at the guards.

Adi nodded, smiled at the room, and hurried up the back stairs. Until Lambert's arrival, she hadn't even known these steps were here. Funny how a French invasion showed her more about her house than she'd known her entire life.

Not only the servants' stairs. The secret passages, too. She'd always known of the tunnels between the wine cellar and the beach; they never kept those a secret. Except from Lambert. The passages between rooms, however, she doubted even her father knew of.

"Mama!" Gabriel rocked on unsteady legs before he launched himself into her arms.

"Ah, my precious *anjinho*." She scooped him up, kissed his cheek. "What have you been doing up here?"

She caught Mélina's gaze. "Joana overheard one of the French soldiers." She nodded to the girl. "They're looking for a spy."

Cold, Adi hugged Gabriel tighter. She smoothed a hand over his head, more to soothe herself than him, she suspected. "Did they say who, Joana?"

"*Não, dama.* Only that they suspect everyone now that the British have arrived."

Nodding, Adi kissed Gabriel again, held him close a moment longer, then set him back down. Once more, she needed to leave her precious boy. She hated that. No matter how necessary it might have been, leaving her son so often broke her heart.

"Stay with Tia Mélina, Gabriel. And listen to Joana." She pressed a kiss to the top of Joana's head in thanks. "I'll need an alibi for the rest of the day. No one can find me."

"*Sim, dama.*" Joana looked fierce and certain. Her thin shoulders straightened, and her jaw rose. "Those bastards will never find you."

Mélina looked shocked by the coarse words, but she echoed Joana's sentiment. "Not even Karlotta?"

"No one but you two." She eyed Rodrigo. "And you, Rodrigo. You promise?"

"*Sim, tia.*" He looked surprised, confused. Adi hated to include him, but there was no help for it. "I promise."

Kissing Gabriel once more, she whispered, "I love you, *anjinho.*"

Her strange unease had only increased. She raced down the back stairs, turned into one of the hidden doorways to the pantries, and then into another that led outside, where she paused to listen for anyone lurking.

She pushed the door open a fraction, looked around as much as that allowed, and disappeared into the trees. Slipping between oak and fig trees, she rounded the back of the cottage, checked the area, then opened the door.

"What's wrong?" Grayson swept her into his arms, closing

the door with a decisive thud. "You're out of breath; did anyone see you?"

Gasping, she shook her head. "No."

"Adelaida," he began in a warning tone that held more than a bit of concern. "What's happened?"

"Did you learn more about Pierre?" Adi tried to control her breathing, but her heartbeat refused to steady. She wanted to blame it on the closed-in air of the cottage, but she knew it was more than that.

"Yes, our friends from this morning had a lot to say on the matter. Apparently, he's gone south, to Cape St. Vincent." Grayson slowly walked her to the table, and Adi let him, trying to understand her wild emotions. "I think he's scouting the terrain for Lambert. No mention of bringing supplies back."

"I don't understand any of this," she admitted. "It's so far south from the British landing, assuming the rumors we've heard are true."

"Even if they landed closer, it wouldn't matter. Lambert is here for another reason." He urged her to sit in the cottage's single chair. "A supply line is difficult enough to maintain, let alone one spread out over hostile territory. And no one knows where additional troops might be stationed."

He crouched before her, rubbing the wrist of her one hand then the other, as if he feared she'd faint. Adi nearly laughed; she'd never fainted in her life. But she wasn't about to stop him from touching her.

"You think he's here to supply Junot from the south?" Her breath had mostly calmed, but her heart continued to race.

"I don't know, but from what the soldiers are whispering about, it's the only option." He kissed the inside of her wrists, and Adi's heart nearly stopped. "At least, the only one I can think of with what little information I have."

"What are you going to do with that information?" The question barely made it past her lips before she regretted the words.

How selfish was she? She'd known Grayson less than a month, and she didn't want him to leave. She wanted to escape Carvalho with her family and her people and keep them safe. Wasn't that what everyone wanted? Safety?

Adi knew Grayson's reasons for being in the country, and they weren't to fall in love with her. Oh, that hurt. But in the months since Lambert's arrival, she'd become an expert at hiding everything about herself behind a very strong, very thick wall.

"I'm going to let Hilton know." His hands tightened around hers. "And I'm going to get you out of here."

"And then?" Why, oh, why had she opened her mouth again? She longed for the answer, but she feared it wouldn't be what she wanted to hear.

"What do you want, Adelaida?"

She nearly laughed. "Safety. I want my son to grow up in freedom. I want my family safe. I want my people fed and happy." Shaking her head, she tried to dam up the words, but they burst forth. "I don't want it to be like it was before. I want more. I want you."

Oh, God, why had she said that?

Before she could backpedal or take the words back or even figure out what came next, Grayson kissed her. His mouth was on hers, his hands cupping her face, and her entire world righted.

I want this, she thought, kissing him back. Her hands tangled in his hair, and she held him close.

"You have me." Grayson trailed his fingertips over her neck, helped her from the chair, and walked her backward to the table. "One day, I'll make love to you in a bed. On a real mattress." He brushed his lips along her jaw, a featherlight touch that made her tremble with clawing, possessive need.

"We won't leave for the entire day." The words gasped out as he easily lifted her onto the table. "I want you beneath me, Grayson." She hiked up her dress, yearning for his touch. "Mine for the taking."

He growled, a wordless sound of need and possession and want—and, oh, Adi wanted. He danced his fingers up her bare thighs, leaving goosebumps in their wake. Pressed his palms beneath her arse, urging her closer. He nipped at the sensitive skin just behind her ear.

"Grayson." She shivered, and his tongue darted out, caressing the light bite. He lightly kissed her neck, a tease that wound her need for him tighter and tighter within her. "Don't hold back."

***

He didn't. Couldn't.

She gripped his shoulders and pulled back, glaring at him in the afternoon light. He hated the uncertain light of the cottage. The grime that covered the windows and obscured her from his greedy gaze. Her cheeks flushed, and her fingers dug into his arms with that same dark need that pounded through him.

Her eyes darkened, her fingers gripping him even harder. She understood the fire that burned within him because it burned in her, too. She whimpered, a low sound in the back of her throat, and arched into him.

Grayson had no words. So he kissed her, hoping she understood all he wished he had poetry to convey. Cupping the back of her head with one palm, he pressed the other to the beautiful curve of her arse. Her fingers combed through his hair, her mouth hard and taking against his. He deepened their kiss, and the feel of her warm satin skin beneath his fingertips was as arousing as her scent. As the feel of her mouth on his.

"I hate sneaking around. Hiding in shadows." His finger slid into her wet heat, and she hissed, arching her hips so he could slide deeper.

"We'd truly scandalize the household if they knew we conducted ourselves like this." She nipped his throat, pushing his coat off and tugging at his shirt, exposing his own skin for her to touch, to taste. "I don't care."

His cock twitched, and he forced himself to take a moment. "You're mine, Adelaida." He cupped her face and kissed her softly but no less possessively. She was his as surely as he was hers, and he promised her then and there that nothing would tear them apart.

"Yours," she agreed. "As you are mine."

He deepened the kiss again, felt her legs widen to accommodate his stance and her heat, her glorious heat, through his trousers. He pulled back just enough to whisper against her lips, "Yes."

Arousal caught him, hard and relentless. It pulled him inexorably toward the goddess in his arms. *His.*

Beneath his touch, Adelaida shivered, her breath catching, her fingers tightening on the nape of his neck. He leaned his forehead against hers and trailed his fingers along her spine, grasping for the control he'd never before doubted in himself. She shuddered, her hips jerking against his, that low whimper shooting straight to his cock.

"All I want is you."

She kissed him again, harder, nipping his bottom lip, a hint of desperation in the kiss. Her hands jerked at his trousers and quickly pushed them down, her nails grazing against his skin. Her fingers stroked his cock, caressing him.

She teased him, ran her fingers over the head of his cock, then scraped her nails down to his balls. He shuddered against her. Cupping her arse, he pushed her dress out of the way. He breathed deeply of the heady scent of her arousal and slid his fingers into her heat. Adelaida gasped his name, tilting her hips into his touch.

"Grayson," she moaned, "Grayson."

He pulled her to the edge of the table. She raked her nails across the small of his back, and he hiked her legs higher on his waist. Words crowded his throat, promises of love and worship and adoration. Of protection and hope and a future. How he needed her more than anything in this life or the next. How he couldn't lose her.

Grayson swallowed them all. Not now. Those words weren't for now. He didn't know when, but not now. He entered her slowly, savoring the feel of her slickness. She tightened around him, and he slid deeper into her heat.

Her head fell back, her breath caught. He ran his thumb over her nub, watching her. Her lips parted, and a look of pure ecstasy crossed her face. She breathed his name, her hips meeting his with every thrust. In awe of her beauty, of her passion, of her driving need, he moved faster. Thrust harder into her welcoming body, tasted along her throat, nipped her lips.

Her nails dug into his skin, and he knew he'd have welts there later. "Yes," he hissed.

He thrust harder, his thumb pressing down on her nub. Her orgasm crashed through her, and she ground her hips against his hand, nonsensical words falling from her lips. Her teeth sank into his shoulder, and he shuddered. Then she tightened around him, drawing him even deeper, and his control snapped.

He kissed her, a sloppy, bruising kiss. He was pounding into her now. It wasn't long, already on the edge as he was, before he fell. Shattered in her arms, her name a cry on his lips.

Adelaida held him, gasping, her body still wrapped tight around his. He blinked, breathing in the arousal-tinted scent of her neck, her pulse still pounding by his lips. He kissed the spot and tried to find the shreds of his control, the mantle he covered himself with to fool the rest of the world.

The happy, light man with the lightning-quick wit and an answer for everything. Apparently not the man Adelaida knew.

"Grayson." His name on her lips sounded as soft as a prayer, as tempting as a promise. She cleared her throat and shook her head, and he wondered if she was scrambling for control as well. If she grasped it as tenuously as he, her own hold slippery, too.

He smiled ruefully and slipped out of her. He fumbled for his coat, found his handkerchief, and cleaned them up. Kissing her softly, letting that touch tell her what he had no words to express, Grayson lifted her off the table. Her knees buckled, but he easily caught her, holding her close as she smoothed down her dress.

"Don't leave." He wanted to swallow those words back, but no. "Stay."

Her eyes found his in the dim cottage, and she nodded. He debated letting her have the chair again, their typical stance—her sitting in the single chair, he leaning against the table. Not today.

"Come on."

She laughed when he pulled her under the table and urged her onto her side. "You're mad."

"You only now realize that?" He kissed the nape of her neck as she settled against him. "I've slept here for weeks; it's rather cozy."

Her giggle wound through him as inexorably as the passion in her kiss. "Yes, I see that. Lovely pillow."

"Alas, we must share. How unfortunate." He puffed up the pillow she'd smuggled from the villa, put one arm beneath it for added comfort. "And a blanket, don't forget." Grayson normally used it to mitigate the rough wooden floor, but now he settled it atop them.

"Hmm." She rolled over and faced him, her fingertips soft against his beard. "No mattress, however."

"Well, technically there is one." Grayson caught her fingers and kissed them one by one. "However, as I value my life, I wouldn't recommend it."

"Are you always so confident?" She frowned, clear even with the shadow of the table over them.

"No." The admission surprised him. But then, she'd broken through every barrier he possessed. "I should say yes, I was. Arrogant, perhaps. Your choice. Confident I could slip past the French and land here without any trouble. Confident I could sneak into the village and out again, exchange food and herbs for information. Confident I'd find my contact here, on Portuguese land I was definitely unfamiliar with."

"And now?" Her voice held a note of coolness, but he knew her better than he had even a week ago.

Whereas he kept the outside world at bay with a quick grin and a witty quip, she did so with that cool lady-of-the-villa voice. No one looked past it because they expected to hear it. No more, no less.

"Now I see how that arrogance nearly got me killed." He exhaled, urging her head onto his chest. Her fingers rested over his side, where his ribs had finally, mostly, healed. "I never fully appreciated the dangers of the sea before that night."

"And your mission?"

Grayson wished he could see into her eyes, not merely hear the evenness of her voice. But then, he didn't want her looking at him, prying beneath the surface. Though he had a feeling it was far, far too late.

"It took weeks for me to heal enough to even leave the cottage. I had a lot of time to think," he admitted. "Perhaps that was part of it—believing I could come here for a single night. Two, maybe, even a week at best."

She remained silent, and he knew she waited for more. The lightness of her fingertips over his ribs reminded him of her strength. Her belief in him even after she learned he'd lied about his name and his reasons for being here.

"It's humbling," he admitted, "realizing I couldn't take care of myself. Of you. I've been injured before, but I always had other ways to protect those closest to me."

Grayson caught her hand and held it against his lips. Deeper confessions lay between them, but he didn't know how she felt. If admitting his love for her would keep her in his arms or chase her away.

Arrogant he might be, but coward he was not. Grayson leaped.

"I love you."

Nineteen

Adi stilled. His words vibrated through her like ocean waves. Constant and steady and welcoming. He continued to hold her hands, his heartbeat steady beneath her touch.

That restlessness returned. She didn't know whether to leave the cottage and race along the beach or kiss him or—or she didn't know.

"Oh." The word whooshed out of her in a single breath.

Once again, she was not impressed with her own reaction to something monumental Grayson said or did. Pulling back, she studied him in the hot afternoon. The sun didn't reach beneath the table; no air moved in the closed-in cottage.

She tried to blame her reaction on that, but she knew better.

"I was hoping for a bit more of a response." His lips curled up in a small, self-deprecating grin, evident even in the shadows.

"You're not saying that out of a misguided sense of duty or honor or—I don't know. Englishness?"

He snorted. "Englishness? No." His lips brushed her palm, her wrist. "I'm saying it because I want to marry you."

Her mouth snapped closed. Eyes wide, she stared at him. "What?"

"I'm not saying it because of whatever you're thinking."

Adi had no idea what she was thinking. Her mind had blanked for one painfully long moment. In the next, visions tempted her. Of her and Grayson far from Carvalho, safe and happy and laughing on whatever an English beach looked like. Of Gabriel racing beside them, laughing and happy. Longing welled within her and closed her throat.

"I'm saying it because I love you." He kissed her gently and rolled her atop him. "I'm saying it because I want a future with you."

"A future?" Adi shook her head though she wanted to reach for his promised future with both hands. "I didn't think we'd survive this occupation," she admitted. That declaration was as terrifying to say aloud as it was held deep in her heart. "I promised my people, my family, we would." She'd made them promise in return, forcing them to conform so the French didn't shoot them all. "I asked so much of them with no idea how I'd keep my promises."

"You kept them alive, Adelaida." His fingers settled on her back, keeping her grounded. "No one could ask for more."

Oh. Oh, that's what this feeling was. Not the on-edge fear of plummeting over a cliff. The fear she already had fallen and no one stood below, waiting to catch her. Rather, that every single one of the walls she'd spent a lifetime building up now scattered beneath her feet. Grayson had done that.

"I lied." She rested her head back on his chest, listening as the steady thump of his heart beat against her. "Until you washed ashore, I didn't know how I was going to save anyone."

"That isn't an admission of love," he pointed out. "Or a denial."

Beneath her lips, his skin was warm and tempting. "A lifetime of this?"

"You're very suspicious." His lips pressed to her forehead, and his hands held hers, steady and confident. Her choice.

"A pirate washed onto my beach." She grinned down at him. "It's hard not to be suspicious."

One kiss to each hand. One to her nose. One against her lips. "A lifetime," he promised. "I swear it."

"Good." She kissed him, letting the love and passion she hadn't fully acknowledged pour into that kiss. "Because I love you, too."

The relief that filled her made her laugh aloud. Smiling around their kiss, she giggled.

"I love your laugh."

"I haven't laughed in a year." She pressed her lips back against his. "It's strange. I didn't think I'd remembered how. You make me laugh."

"I promise I'll make you laugh every day." Grayson rolled them again, kissing along her jaw. "Smile every day." He pulled back and cupped her face. "Make love to you every day."

"Don't make promises you can't keep," she warned.

"You're used to that, aren't you?" He nodded, serious where she tried for humor. "People not keeping their promises."

"Yes." The admission stabbed through her remaining walls with eerie precision. "Promises are easily made. Easier broken. Simple words of agreement that mean nothing after they're spoken." She swallowed hard, then admitted what she'd never told anyone. "Mateus promised many things. Little promises, nothing big. He never kept any of them."

"I'm sorry, Adelaida." Grayson's lips were warm on her now-cold fingers. "It's easier to keep those big promises—harder, I think, for the smaller, everyday ones that you can pretend you didn't make."

"Are you certain." She didn't ask it as a question. She asked it with everything in her, body and soul.

"That I love you? It terrifies me." He huffed a breath that passed for a laugh. Adi was grateful he didn't joke about this. Not this. "Like I could drown in you."

"I know." She rested her head on his chest again and closed her eyes.

"I can see a future with you, and I want that." His arms tightened around her, secure and confident. "I want it so badly I can taste it."

The temptation kept her up at night as well, dreaming of a better future. Of any future. One with Grayson. One that included laughter. Oh, she wanted that. Wanted this feeling, the comfort of his arms, the joy that burst through her heart. It wrapped around her, and Adi embraced it.

"I want that, too."

"I don't want you in danger," he said slowly.

Eyes still closed, she remained still. Soaking in this one more moment. "If Maya, or Inês, is Sebastião, I want to know what sort of information they have. I want to know why they contacted the British."

"Instead of the Portuguese forces?" He sighed but didn't release her. She liked that. "Or anyone else? Or even how she—or whoever—managed to send a communique from Carvalho to London?"

"I have a lot of questions," she agreed. "I'm still uncertain Inês is Sebastião. Of all the people in the village, in the entire parish, she's quite literally the last person I'd expect."

"Does she speak French?"

Adi eyed him in the light but merely shrugged. "Yes. What does that have to do with anything?"

"I've no idea. I'm trying to slot all the pieces together but not having much luck." He frowned, eyes unfocused as he stared at the underside of the table. "Does Lambert know that?"

"I doubt it." She rolled beside him, trying for a comfortable position on the floor. No such luck. "How do you sleep here?" She folded an arm under the pillow, but it did little for her hip on the hard floor. "This is incredibly uncomfortable."

"It is that," he agreed far too cheerfully. "But sleep is sleep."

Lips quirked upward, she giggled. "If Lambert knows Inês speaks French, I doubt he cares. He knows we do, so I'd assume he'd think she does as well. If he bothers to think of her at all."

Her time in the cottage ticked down, and Adi hated that. She didn't want to leave Grayson's embrace. However, if they didn't solve all these little mysteries—Pierre, the new arrivals supposedly from Spain, Sebastião—they'd have no more time at all.

"When they first came, Inês made a huge fuss. I begged for her life. Pleaded with Lambert and even Bardot not to shoot her outright." She sighed and looked over her shoulder. She couldn't see the sun from here, but she knew it was well past luncheon. "She stays in the conservatory now. Out of our way, away from the French. We leave food at the door twice a day, bowls of water for washing. No one, not even the staff, has seen her."

"For the sake of argument, let's say Sebastião is Inês." Grayson looked behind her as well, frowning. He sighed and rolled from beneath the table.

She took his proffered hand and stood, shaking dust and dirt from her skirts. Her braids had fallen loose, and Adi grimaced. "Go on." She dropped her hairpins onto the table and began the arduous task of braiding her hair. "Let's say Inês is Sebastião."

"You took everyone who wanted to leave with you when? December?"

"Just after Christmas, yes." There had been no celebrations that year. Only fear and misery as they'd trekked over two hundred miles in bitterly cold wind. "We thought it'd be safer farther south, so we took what we could. Food, gold, clothing. It took us—" She shook her head. "I'm not sure how long, honestly."

"And Lambert arrived in February? Let me." He brushed her hands aside and finished braiding her hair. "If Inês, or Sebastião, I suppose, found a way to secret a letter in February, even March, that's five or so months for it to find its way from here to Hilton's hands in London."

"I want a word with your Hilton." She glared ahead as Grayson pinned her braids. "I want to know many things about this letter that's brought you here."

"I'll arrange an introduction," he promised. Adi very clearly heard the smile in his voice. "You need more rest, Adelaida." His lips brushed the nape of her neck, and she shivered.

"That wasn't one of your promises." She frowned, exhaustion warring with that fiery need for survival.

Chuckling, Grayson kissed the side of her throat and wrapped his arms about her waist. She loved that feeling. The shivers of anticipation that danced up her spine, that made her nipples harden.

"Anything you want," he whispered against her skin. "I promise it's yours."

"A bold declaration, Grayson Conrad."

"A promise I intend to keep, my love."

"It's odd," she whispered.

"Keeping my promise?" She heard the frown in his voice. "Or loving you?"

"Both," she admitted, frowning now herself. His arms tightened around her, and she knew he didn't like that answer. "But what I meant was how odd it feels to be both terrified and content at the same time."

"I can't imagine what it's like living beneath the same roof as the invading army." Grayson leaned back and smoothed wisps of hair from her cheeks. "The strength it's taken to survive this long."

"When Lambert and Bardot first arrived, we worried they'd simply kill us all. They had their own cooks to make any food they wished." Adi closed her eyes and all too easily remembered those early days. "We barely settled in here before they marched into the village."

"They specifically chose Carvalho?" Grayson hummed. "They must've known about the natural bay."

"Possibly," she agreed, her bones cold with the memory of those first months. "Obviously, he never said why he chose here. But he held his men under control well enough that they didn't take our women. So we didn't put up too much fight when they stole from us."

"You kept the village from revolting, and that saved lives."

"Yes." A well of pride straightened her spine. "Even when we starved, we waited, listened. I was afraid they'd kill Padre Lucio outright; the French Empire isn't known for its love of the clergy. But Lambert didn't bother."

"I wonder if that's because he had other plans." Grayson hummed again. "Have you noticed Pierre leave any other day?"

"I only interact with him on village market days." She shook her head and stepped from his embrace. As much as she wanted his arms around her, Adi needed to think. Plan out their next steps.

Their. Oh, that was a nice thought. "It's nice to have

someone else to think these things through with," she added, smiling over her shoulder.

He returned her grin. "I find it best, yes. How about any other soldier?"

"None of the kitchen guards," she said slowly, trying to remember. "The days run together; however, I'm sure we would've noticed a change in routine."

"Even if they claimed one was sick, it wouldn't have raised any alarms," he agreed.

"No, they're very unhealthy." Adi tapped her fingers against her waist and stared out the window. She missed Gabriel. "When they arrived, they were half-starved, cold, sickly. I thought it was part of the reason Lambert let us be. For the most part."

"Because he was sick?"

"Because we had food and medicine, a warm, dry climate in which his men could recover." Her lips twisted into a bitter grimace. "One more advantage for him."

"If you'd rebelled when they first arrived, Junot would've only sent more troops, Adelaida. He'd have wiped out Carvalho in retaliation."

"I know," she snapped. Sighing, she rubbed her forehead. "I know," she said, softer now. "It was one of my arguments to quell the village."

"Tell me about Gabriel?"

His question surprised her. "What about him?"

"He's one of the reasons you fight so hard. He's your son. I want to know him." Grayson sighed and pushed off the table, prowling around the empty room until he stopped before her. "I don't want to cut him out of your life, Adelaida."

She hadn't thought that. But she hadn't known what to think. "I've protected him for so long," she whispered. "Kept him safe, away from the suspicious eyes of the soldiers. I feared he'd be the first target if they wanted to teach us a lesson."

That fear choked her every morning, setting ice in her blood that not even the fire of survival could warm. "Joana, one of the scullery maids, took over his care when Lambert arrived. She keeps him safe, plays with him. I owe her my son's safety."

"I promise." He took her hands and held tight, warming her with his pledge. "I'll keep them all safe."

"I know." She licked her lips, swallowed around the over-whelming love and affection she felt for this man. "I know you will."

"Tell me about him?"

"Gabriel loves to laugh." Her lips curled upward, and the simple joy she felt whenever he did so eased her fear. "He loves the birds, tries to chase them with his little legs."

"We'll have to learn all the names of them." He made it sound so simple. Leave Portugal, return to England, learn the names of birds. As a family. Oh, but her heart yearned for such a thing.

He glanced out the window and frowned. "Do you have to return?"

"Not yet. Not until I have to serve Lambert his dinner. I needed this afternoon with you so we can figure out how we're all leaving. You'll speak with Padre Lucio tonight?" Adi frowned, working through all the ways this could go wrong. But if she kept on that path, she'd accomplish nothing. Had months of spying on the French, of promising her people, taught her nothing?

"I'll have to, yes." Grayson leaned against the table and gath-ered her into his arms once more. She might never grow tired of that, of the comfort his arms provided. "The guards don't patrol the road between villa and village."

"That doesn't surprise me. They've no reason to do so." She

waved a hand in dismissal. "Why expend unnecessary manpower on useless patrolling of trees and wind?"

He looked surprised but slowly grinned. "You really have led them into complacency." He chuckled. "I am more impressed with you as each day goes by."

She offered a slight curtsy. "Thank you. It's why I was able to run into that storm," she added, serious now. "They didn't follow. Where was I going to run to? Without my family? Without my son? They knew I'd return." Adi shrugged. "Besides, that storm was wicked. Only a fool would've been out in it."

Grayson bowed low. "Look at us, a pair of fools."

Laughing, she shook her head. "You always make me laugh. Despite everything, even on that beach when I half dragged you into the cave, you made me smile more than I have all year."

"I'm glad." He kissed the back of her fingers, then pressed a kiss against her lips. "Now then. I'll speak with Padre Lucio tonight; we'll start moving the villagers."

"Yes, the caves would be best. He'll know who to move first. Those the French might not immediately realize are gone." She tapped her fingers against her lips, still tingling from his touch. "How long will you need?"

"Before we leave?" He glanced out the window again, but of course the dirty panes revealed nothing but smudged sunlight. "If you have any sailors who are used to navigating by starlight, send them first."

"That confident in yourself?" She eyed him curiously.

"It's been a while," he admitted. "And with so much at stake, and how quickly we need to move, it's best we rely on more than my calculations."

"Ask Padre Lucio," she urged. "He'll know who you need."

"Will they all leave? I don't want to leave anyone here for

French retaliation." He shook his head. "Or leave anyone starving and alone."

"I'm confident the majority will. I'll speak with those who won't." She'd anticipated that, having to cajole several of the fierier villagers into leaving, those she'd originally spent more time convincing not to rise up. "I'll need an excuse to return to the village, but we'll see who agrees first."

"I'll speak with the good father tonight," Grayson promised, kissing her softly. "And we'll begin moving everyone into the caves. They know the way?"

"Yes. We've used those caves for generations." Adi framed Grayson's face with her hands and kissed him hard and fast. "Be careful. I just found you; I don't want to lose you."

"I promise."

Twenty

As the sun sank deeper into the west, Grayson watched Adelaida hurry along the path and out of sight. His hands gripped the door in an effort not to follow her. But he'd promised. He might've ignored that promise and done so anyway had she not admitted she was used to people breaking their word.

How anyone could not give her everything was beyond him. The sun, the moon, the world? She only had to ask, and he'd find a way. But he knew she never would. She'd never ask for anything, and that angered him all the more.

She wouldn't because she believed in only herself. Oh, she hadn't said. She didn't need to.

Grayson closed the door and slipped his khanjar from his boot. He'd prefer it strapped around his waist, but he didn't want to alert the French to its presence.

Balancing the dagger, he worked through his exercises and let their conversation replay in his head. She'd promised the village their safety, and they believed her. From what he'd seen when he walked the village, no one would've betrayed her. He'd stake his life on that.

Inês, he wasn't so certain of, but he doubted she'd purposely place her daughter-in-law in danger. Through neglect, perhaps, but his view of the woman was heavily colored by Adelaida's dislike.

Apparently, everyone disliked her.

"Gah." He sucked in a breath at the sudden pain in his side.

Still not as healed as he'd like. It didn't matter; they had no more time. The moment the sun set, he'd sneak onto the beach and figure out his position in relation to where he believed Esme and Landon waited for him. Assuming they hadn't left.

Grayson almost laughed. Abandon him? Not likely.

Then he'd pay a very late-night visit to the village and speak with Padre Lucio about the fishermen and the *barca de pesca*.

He still needed to figure out how to group the ships together so no one drifted off, so the French couldn't spot their escape and stop them. And how the villagers might even make it down the path to the beach. Easier than the household, which was constantly under scrutiny. He could probably manage a few villagers at a time, but they'd need to leave en masse if they wanted to find his ship, evade the French, and make it out without casualties.

And then there was Rémy.

Grayson stopped again, teeth clenched around the now-constant throbbing in his side.

Even if his lugger wasn't at the bottom of the ocean, it wouldn't have been enough. The *barca de pesca* could hold... fourteen, fifteen people? And there were a dozen boats, which meant they were still woefully short.

Even adding more weight per boat, and praying to every available god and saint that none of them capsized, they still needed at least six more. At the very least. He hadn't asked about their numbers, only assumed that a couple hundred villagers remained.

Abandoning his exercise, Grayson returned to the table and the remnants of his supper. He finished his orange and figs and mentally mapped out where Adelaida might be at this moment. It was nearing Lambert's dinnertime—

The scrape on the door handle froze him in place. In the next instant, he grabbed his khanjar, melted into the shadows beside the door, and waited.

Adelaida wouldn't return, not when she needed to keep up pretenses.

Also, that wasn't her touch. He knew that as intimately as he knew the way she sighed his name. Grayson waited, flat against the wall as a hundred scenarios played out in his mind. Lambert had discovered Adelaida's sneaking out, or one of his soldiers had. She was already being interrogated, and Lambert had sent a soldier to discover what was so important in the cottage.

"*Olá*?" a voice called, soft and hesitant. "Paulo?"

Mélina.

His heart dropped. "You're lucky I didn't gut you." He didn't sheath his dagger but did step into what little light remained. "What's wrong?" His stomach knotted, and he spoke quickly, his voice harsh with demand. "Where's Adelaida?"

"Adi is fine." Even in the evening light, he saw her frown, her curious scrutiny. "She's serving the colonel." She spat that last word.

He pulled her into the room and closed the door. "Did anyone follow you?"

"No."

Grayson waited a moment, listening hard. Of course, hearing anyone who might be sneaking about behind that thick oak door was impossible, but he listened anyway. His heart pounded in his ears, and nothing he did calmed it. Fear for Adelaida closed his throat. While he knew Mélina wouldn't do anything to place her sister-in-law in danger, her presence didn't calm his fears.

He opened the door and looked out. It wasn't ideal, but then, nothing about this situation was ideal. No one loitered on the path, and no telltale flash of a bluecoat gave anyone away.

"Why are you here?" He eased the door closed and turned toward Mélina.

She watched him, calm but nervous. No matter how still she held herself, she couldn't hide that. But her chin tilted in defiance, and that same fire he saw in Adelaida burned in Mélina. Survival.

"Adi has made a lot of promises over the last days." Her voice cooled, and he sheathed his dagger. "She claims you'll help evacuate us from under the French thumb."

"Yes."

"You're very confident." She paused. "Arrogant."

That stabbed through him, but he merely crossed his arms over his chest. He'd rather not think on his arrogance and the trouble it heaped down on him. More importantly, down on Adelaida. "I promised Adelaida I'd find a way to have you all leave. Those who wish to."

"And have you?" she challenged.

"I have." Mostly. Sort of. "I have a ship waiting for us beyond the French blockade."

"Oh." She snorted. "A ship. All we have to do is run the blockade. How easy."

"You don't believe me." He nodded, wondering if Adelaida had shared misgivings with Mélina that she hadn't shared with him, or if Mélina was naturally suspicious. "I don't blame you. But talk quickly; we haven't much time."

"Who are you really?" she demanded. "Why are you here? How do you plan to sail eight hundred and fifty souls from here to your ship? Your ship," she added, "that's beyond the French blockade."

"And Rémy," he added. "I promised him he'd leave with us."

"Arrogant," she muttered again.

"Be that as it may, I'm confident in my plan." He paused, but Adelaida trusted Mélina, and he could as well. "What has she told you about this plan?"

"Only that you have one," Mélina admitted. She sounded quite put out, but Grayson couldn't tell if it was because of a lack of information or a lack of trust. "How does a gardener know so much about running French blockades?"

"How do any of us know how to survive the French?" he shot back. Then he paused and reminded himself she'd lived under the fear of French reprisals for months. He had not.

Arrogant. Adelaida had called him that, too. Conceited. She was right. Eight hundred and fifty people? Plus Rémy and any possessions they took? He definitely didn't have enough boats.

Instead of continuing their argument, he gestured for the chair. "It's not much, but it is a chair. Please, sit. I'm sure you're exhausted."

Mélina huffed, and even in the dark cottage she eyed him suspiciously. A joke about the chair not being a trap of some sort lay on the tip of his tongue, but he swallowed it. Now certainly wasn't the time for jokes.

Clearing her throat, she shook out her skirts and settled onto the chair. Clearly, this interrogation wasn't over.

"All right." She nodded. "Explain. How is it you have a ship waiting beyond the blockade?"

The less she knew the better, Grayson decided. "I'm here gathering information on French troop movement."

"Here. In Carvalho." Her words were flat, unimpressed. "Not in Lisbon with Junot."

"We were alerted to activity here," he confirmed. "It was important enough to take the chance."

"*We*? The government?" She snorted. "Bah, those fools." He didn't need to see her to know she narrowed her eyes. "Or the rebels, the *guerrillas*?"

He didn't know the term *guerrillas*, but it sounded like the word for war, *guerra*. "What has Adelaida told you?"

He couldn't imagine her telling Mélina and Karlotta much—not specifics, at least. Not about his true identity or his mission. She wouldn't put anyone else in danger. Still, she'd admitted she'd told them something to ease their suspicions.

"About Sebastião?" Mélina huffed again. "That's a silly legend no one truly believes."

"Someone believed it enough to use that name." He didn't believe in the myth himself, but then, he hadn't known of it before Adelaida told him. "It doesn't matter whether the myth is real or not; all that matters is the information."

"How long have you been here? What information have you discovered? If you didn't know the legend of Sebastião before Adi told you, where are you from?"

"I've been here long enough to know we're leaving before the quarter moon." Which was mere days away—five, six at most. "We can't wait any longer." He paused, debating. He needed Mélina on his side, not so much because he needed her support, but because Adelaida needed it. "It'll be more dangerous, but given the arrival of the British and the likelihood that more troops —French and British—are on their way, it's time."

He didn't say, nor had he shared with Adelaida, his fear that Lambert would slaughter them all to protect his supply lines. Grayson didn't want an Évora here, an entire town slaughtered.

He didn't want this town to suffer the same fate if what he and Adelaida suspected was true. That Lambert used Carvalho as a means to protect French supplies, an alternate route from the one coming in from the north.

"Are we to swim to this ship of yours?"

Grayson tried not to laugh, truly he did. Shaking his head as a chuckle escaped, he met Mélina's gaze in the now-dark cottage. "You have no trust, have you." It wasn't a question, and they both knew it. "I don't blame you. But I promised Adelaida I'd help everyone here escape, and I mean to keep that promise. The *barca de pesca* aren't ideal, but they're our only means."

"You're mad." The incredulousness in her voice did not help the situation.

"Oh, undoubtably." He rubbed a hand down his face but refused to admit how truly awful this plan of his was. It didn't help that it was his only plan. "However, I promised, and I never go back on my promises."

"And Adelaida?" Her voice hardened; a note of protectiveness stilled him.

"What of her?"

"Are you leaving her on this ship of yours? Dropping her off —where? You haven't said where you're taking us." She stood, poked him in the chest with her finger. "I have a lot of unanswered questions, Paulo."

"I'm sure you do," he agreed, stepping back from her fury. "But I won't hurt Adelaida. Ever. And I'm not leaving her on my ship. On any ship," he promised. "We'll be safe, I promise you."

She huffed again, clearly disbelieving, but said no more. The moment stretched before she huffed once more. "All right."

"I don't know what that means," he admitted. "All right what?"

"All right, I believe you." She hummed and walked for the door. "At least, I believe you won't do anything to harm Adi."

"I'd protect her with my life."

The door opened slightly, and Mélina waited. "I believe you."

Grayson doubted she'd believed anyone in nearly a year, so he took that to heart. "Thank you," he said sincerely as she slipped out the door.

He waited only a moment before following her out of the cottage. He watched her disappear into the shadows toward the rear of the villa. No matter how he wanted to follow Mélina, watch Adelaida, ensure her safety while she served Lambert his dinner, Grayson held himself back.

He promised her he'd see to his own role in this escape. Blowing out a frustrated breath, he turned in the opposite direction.

The sky wasn't as dark as he'd like to navigate by starlight, not so soon after sunset, so he headed for the village first. Once again, he saw no one on the road between the villa and the village. He hadn't expected anyone, but the lack of people slithered down his spine.

Keeping beneath the trees, Grayson hiked down the hill toward the village. He and Landon once hiked Scafell Pike, the highest peak in all of England, with plans to visit Snowdon in Wales. They never made it. Given Portugal's elevation, something he hadn't thought on before climbing the cliff from beach to villa, the entire country eclipsed any British mountain.

Breathing hard by the time he reached the village, Grayson headed directly for the church.

Padre Lucio awaited him by the side door. Though Grayson had never entered a Catholic Church before, he hadn't time to look around.

"You are the *dama*'s gardener?" In the candlelight, the padre eyed him suspiciously. "You don't look like a gardener."

"I—all right." How did one respond to that? Grayson wanted to know what the padre thought he did look like, but there wasn't time. "We leave by the quarter moon," he said.

"I've spoken with the villagers," Lucio said quietly. They stood in a small alcove with individual tiled seating against the wall. It was cooler here than outside, and the high arches of the room made everything echo. "They believe in the *dama*, trust her." Grayson heard the reverence in his voice. The villagers worshipped her. They'd follow her anywhere for keeping her promises, for keeping them alive during this occupation. "Everyone is agreeable."

"All of them?" Surprised, Grayson looked around, as if he expected someone to jump out and contradict Lucio's words. "A —*Dama* was afraid some might hesitate."

"*Sim, sim.*" Lucio nodded, pausing as they both listened at the door. No sound emerged, but with the garrison close by, it seemed neither wanted to chance a soldier patrolling the church. "She is a good leader. The people, they listen." Lucio waited again, as if Grayson might object.

"She keeps her promises," he said as Lucio's head tilted in the slightest bit of curiosity.

"*Sim,*" he said again. "And she's promised us safety. We'll leave now to ensure our legacy."

Grayson had not expected this conversation to flow so easily. He couldn't say why he thought there'd be more arguing, villagers waiting in the church for a chance to protest this exodus.

This ease of agreement was a testament to Adelaida's powers of persuasion. Of the village's trust and faith. In her.

"I'll need any fishermen who can pilot a ship by starlight," he told the padre. "We'll leave together, but first we need to chart our course. Send them tomorrow night; I'll meet them by the caves."

"As you wish."

"Everyone can take only what they can carry." He stopped and thought of Rémy and the horses. "Have any of them animals? Dogs, cats, pets?"

"A few, I believe."

Pressing his lips together, he nodded. "Bring them, too. We leave nothing for the French."

"And the church?" Lucio gestured into the church proper, with its arching vault ceilings and intricately carved columns. Even from here, Grayson could see the carved wooden pews and the marble statues. "The French have already stolen much from the villa, the people."

Would the French steal the pews? He had no idea. Another quick glance showed empty areas along the walls. He had a feeling they already buried things, hid them from the French. "Bury whatever you can between now and Saturday," he insisted. "We don't have any more time, Padre."

"Better to bury them for our return than leave them for the French to loot." His voice rose in anger. "They've taken so much already. Chalices and rosaries, gold from the poor box."

Grayson rested his hand on the padre's shoulder and squeezed. "We'll return, Padre."

"I see why the *dama* trusts you." Lucio eyed him with a glint in his dark gaze Grayson couldn't decipher. "I'll send the men at dusk tomorrow. They'll meet you at the caves."

With a final nod, Grayson slipped out the door. He wouldn't let Adelaida down.

Twenty-One

"Bury?" Adi watched him in the predawn light. Shaking her head, she stretched her wrists and nodded. "We buried much when we heard they headed this way. Gold and jewels, statues, linens, our best cutlery and china."

"I'm sorry." Grayson crouched before her, holding her hands.

"Those days were hard," she whispered, as if the days before and after hadn't been equally so. "We rushed through the tunnels, and it'd been cold, too—far colder than usual." Though Adi still wasn't certain if that had been her fear of French occupation or the actual weather. Or maybe it was the bone-chilling fear of being discovered.

She rubbed her forehead, letting the memories rush out now. "And that door between the wine cellar and the tunnels." She shook her head and met his gaze, dark and worried in the dimness. "You know, it was once an ornate, beautiful thing." A lavish construct that spoke of their place in society. "It'd taken us days to remove the thing piece by piece." Even now, her arms ached with the memory. "We replaced it with a door that matched the cellar's interior."

Now, only a small latch, cleverly hidden by a stack of empty wine barrels, showed where the door sat. Adi hadn't cared much. It was a door, no more no less. And removing the ornately carved beauty meant the French wouldn't steal it.

"How deep did you bury things?"

"In the caves? Not very—too sandy and wet. Though the tide doesn't come up that high, there are people who remember the earthquake and tidal wave. We only buried small bags of gold and jewels, heirlooms. Easy items to find and carry if we needed to." She curled her hands around his. With the hope of leaving looming over them, Adi hadn't slept well last night. Even now, nerves jumped in her stomach.

She half expected Lambert to burst through the door—their bedroom, the kitchens, this cottage door, it didn't matter—with his pistol at the ready. A recurring nightmare she could never dispel no matter how she tried. Sitting with Grayson, his hands warm and sure around hers, Adi tasted freedom.

"In the tree line, we buried the statues, cutlery, china, even our best linens. Not deep; it's difficult to dig too deeply in the soil." She frowned. "I thought Padre Lucio had done the same. The church is bare compared to what it once was."

"I didn't look," he said, then he paused. "But I don't spend much time in Catholic churches."

"It's no matter." Trinkets, compared to the lives of her family and the villagers. When they all disappeared, Lambert would order his troops to sack the villa, the village, the church and steal what they hadn't already. "You're meeting the sailors tonight?" She nodded as she calculated her own plans. "I'm uncomfortable keeping the villagers in the caves, even for a single day."

Uncomfortable? Scared. Terrified.

"I've seen soldiers patrol the beach. Have they searched the caves?"

"They know of the caves." Adi ran her fingers through his hair, letting the soft strands curl about her fingertips. Every day like this? Freely touching him? Kissing him whenever she wished? It tasted as delicious on her tongue as the promise of freedom.

"But they don't know of the tunnels."

"Tunnels?" His head jerked up. "What tunnels?"

"The tunnels connecting the cave and the villa?" She frowned. "I just spoke of them."

"I didn't make the connection," he admitted. "I thought you meant tunnels and caves interchangeably."

"Oh." She allowed him to pull her up. "It's how I met you in the caves that first day. The tunnels connect the villa and the beach, we use them to bring our casks—wine, cacao, peppers—into the villa. Easier than hauling them up the cliffside."

Grayson lifted her onto the table and kissed her jaw. "And the French, they know nothing of this?" His lips trailed along her throat. Her eyes fluttered closed, and she tilted her head.

More. She wanted so much more of this. This intimacy between them. It settled around her, deeper and more profound than sex. A quietness that warmed her from the inside out and made her smile.

"We are very good at hiding things from them." Her fingers tangled in his hair, and she held him close. "It's easy when they believe us already conquered. I'll leave the wine cellar unlocked. The door is hidden in the wall; the latch is behind a small stack of empty barrels. The key is atop them."

His laugh brushed against her skin, warm and gentle. "My clever Adelaida." His lips pressed against hers. "My Angelic Adelaida."

"Angelic?" She laughed and pulled back. "I'm not sure about that."

"You rescued me from that storm. I've no idea how you even knew I was there, but you did." Another kiss, deeper now. "For weeks, the only time I saw you was at dawn or dusk, and the sunlight was just enough to make you look like an angel."

"Not angelic enough." She held him close, kissing him one more time. "Not with this need I have for you. It claws in me, hungry for more."

"I know," he growled, pulling her close. "I might never get enough of you."

She knew that feeling all too well. How did one survive drowning in passion when they were desperate for more? "I need to return. We're gathering as much food as possible for our escape, but we need distractions for the guards."

"Be careful." He held her close and tight. "Please, Adelaida. I know, I know—you've survived this long. But with only a handful of days left before we leave, I'm afraid Lambert might grow suspicious."

"I won't make a false step now," she promised. "Mama is speaking with Inês today, and I must clean Lambert's rooms. It's safer for me to do it than one of the maids."

"I like that man less and less the more I know of him," Grayson growled.

"I don't want him to accuse a maid of sneaking into his dispatches and kill her as a lesson." The thought chilled her, as it had since the beginning. "He keeps them locked tight; we can't look at them, but it's a fear."

So many things were. Fear that Bardot would grow tired of Mélina's disinterest and simply take her. Or that Lambert would order a selection of the staff executed. Or even one of them. For months, Adi had done every single thing Lambert ordered—or *requested*. She wouldn't stop now, not with so much hinging on keeping things as they were.

His hands tightened on her waist, and Adi didn't need to see him to know the anger on his face. When he spoke, the words were low and even, but that couldn't disguise his fury. "I'm going to kill him."

"I've thought that myself," she confessed, the words low between them. She'd never dared say it aloud. "But it'll change nothing. I want all of us gone, Grayson." She forced him to meet her gaze. "All of us."

His kiss was hard, greedy. She drowned in it, craved more. When he pulled back, Adi gasped for breath and held on to him until she regained her balance. "I'll see you at dinner." He kissed her again, swift and confident. "I love you."

"I love you," she whispered and slipped out the door.

Back in the kitchens, she moved for her mother and the small tray of plates she carried. The soldiers continued their disinterested watch, talking amongst themselves. She wondered what they spoke of, always quietly chatting, as if they stood at a market and watched people walk past. What could possibly be of interest in the same kitchens, with the same people, guarded by the same soldiers, day in and day out for months?

"Mama." She eyed the guards, who gave her only a cursory glance. "Did you speak with Inês?"

"No. The tray was already outside the door. Again." She scowled, her back to the soldiers as she fussed with the tray. "I was waiting for you or Mélina. Create a distraction, please." Karlotta's dark eyes gleamed with determination. "And make sure they can't hear anything."

"Distraction?" Adi's eyebrows shot upward. "All right. On your way, unlock the wine cellar."

Her mother's lips pressed together, but she nodded. "We'll meet you in the nursery just after luncheon."

"Meet us?" Adi's lips twitched. "Are you going to drag Inês upstairs?"

"Yes." With that, her mother turned and slipped the large key ring from the wall as she went. Adi watched until she disappeared around a corner.

Oh. Her lips pressed hard so as not to laugh. What she wouldn't give to see her mother drag her mother-in-law from the conservatory, up several flights of steps, and into the nursery. They all had their part in this.

She turned toward the staff and caught Manuéla's eye. Jerking her head toward the soldiers, she whispered, "See they're distracted. I don't care how—food, a rat, anything. Just make sure they don't realize Mama took the keys."

"*Sim, dama.*" Manuéla wheeled Lambert's breakfast tray toward her, then casually resumed the day's meal preparation.

Adi didn't wait around. She hurried up the stairs and waited for the cart to arrive. Taking it from the panel hidden in the wall, she wheeled it along the hall, past a pair of guards whose sole job, it seemed, was to ensure none of them trespassed into the colonel's wing.

Nerves danced along her skin, but neither the soldiers in the kitchens nor those at the end of this hall seemed bothered.

Five days. Five more days, and she'd be gone from here.

She knocked on the door, waited for the bellow, and plastered a smile onto her face.

Feed Lambert and Bardot. Dust their rooms and take their clothing downstairs for laundering. Smile, keep quiet. Offer a pot of chocolate, though they had precious little left. Five days' worth?

Adi entered the room. She'd make it last until they left. Shame she couldn't toss it in his face as a last measure of defiance.

"*Bonjour, lumineux!*" she called and began one of her final performances.

Grayson slipped into the villa, carefully avoiding the guards in the kitchens. Another set stood at three of the five doors, which continually surprised him. Given the number of soldiers in the village, four more—even two more—wouldn't have been amiss here. Unless Lambert didn't care about those entrances, which made little sense.

Whatever the reason—complacency or stupidity—Grayson used them. By now, Lambert had finished his breakfast. In an hour, after Adelaida finished cleaning his rooms, he'd walk around the villa and sit smoking under the olive trees. Sometimes he read outside, other times he looked over the cliffs at the ocean.

Grayson didn't necessarily want to go through Lambert's papers. As informative as they might be, it was also a great risk. But Grayson promised both himself and Lambert he'd steal them. Give Hilton something more on Lambert's very unusual location so far south.

Waiting around a corner, he watched Karlotta putter around the conservatory. As much as he wanted to see what Inês would say or do, they all had their roles in this escape. Down the hall, around corners, it took him longer than he'd have liked, but every footstep he heard made him pause.

He'd never bring French fury down on Adelaida, but neither did he want any member of the household to see him here. No sense starting rumors when they needed discretion.

He quietly opened the wine cellar door, then slipped down the stairs and into the cool room. The stack of empty barrels was easy enough to spot, and Grayson climbed up and grabbed the key from atop the last one.

He could see why the French ignored the door; it blended into the wall almost seamlessly. Adelaida and her household had done an amazing job. Padre Lucio's words came back to him—Adelaida was the strongest leader he knew. Grayson hated that she'd been forced to take it all on herself, but he stood in awe of her.

It didn't take long to slip through the well-oiled door and into the tunnels. Even without a lantern, he followed the path easily enough. The sunlit beach beckoned just beyond the staggered rocks that guarded the cave's entrance.

Easy enough he could slip through them tonight. Even better—the household could quietly disappear into them without any of the soldiers realizing.

Grayson turned and retraced his steps, pushing the partially closed door open and stepping into the cellar. He half expected a soldier there waiting for him, musket pointed at his heart. Thankfully, he was alone.

It was only when he eased open the cellar door that he heard it. The shouting and riotous din as if the entire British army now stood face-to-face with Lambert's men. Grayson couldn't make out any individual words, only the commotion that echoed throughout the entire lower floor.

He slipped his khanjar from its sheath and crouched low, peering out the crack between door and doorjamb. The hallway remained deserted. Still, the noise was enough to send a signal to his ship, far beyond the French blockade.

Heart pounding in fear for Adelaida, he squeezed between the open door and closed it behind him. Grayson didn't care about keeping silent, not now. Had Lambert somehow learned of their plan? Had the French received word about troop movements and decided now was the time to mobilize?

The closer he moved toward the kitchens, the louder the ruckus grew. Straining to hear any coherent word over the din, he searched for Adelaida. His stomach dropped when he didn't see her. Nor Karlotta. Mélina stood just off to the side, calm as ever, even as the kitchen staff, a pair of guards, and Lua raced around the room as if something had been set on fire.

Hand tight around the bone hilt of his khanjar, Grayson finally caught Mélina's gaze. She offered the slightest of smiles and mouthed, "*Berçário.*"

He did not know that word. "*O que?*"

She frowned and rolled her eyes. A quick glance over her shoulder showed no one paid any attention to her. Squatting slightly, she held her hand at her knee and repeated, "*Berçário. Crèche.*"

Grayson nodded and retreated from what was now very clearly controlled chaos. "The nursery?" he muttered and turned for the servants' stairs.

Between Adelaida's description of them and his own nighttime surveillance, it didn't take him long to race upstairs. Despite Mélina's calmness, fear pounded through Grayson's veins. They were so close to leaving, escaping the French and the famine the army had brought with them. Of keeping Adelaida and her family safe.

No noise emerged from the nursery. Had Mélina led him into a trap? He eased open the door, dagger at the ready...and stopped.

"Is Mélina supervising the kitchens?" Adelaida asked calmly.

"Aye." His lips twitched, and he sheathed the khanjar. His heart still raced, and the fear that Lambert had somehow discovered their plan had yet to dissipate. Swallowing, Grayson nodded to Karlotta, Rodrigo, and Gabriel, who sat wide-eyed on a trundle bed with Joana and a very irate Inês.

Inês, who was tied to a chair and gagged.

Ignoring them all, Grayson closed the door and crossed the room to Adelaida. Cupping her cheeks, he kissed her. He didn't care who watched or what they thought. He was going to marry this woman.

"You are brilliant," he whispered against her lips. "And beautiful." He kissed her again. "I love you."

Cheeks pink, a smile lighting her face, Adelaida giggled softly. "You're embarrassing Inês."

"Lucky for both of us, she's in no position to protest."

"If you don't mind," Karlotta interrupted in clear exasperation, "*I* am in a position to protest."

Grayson eyed the woman. She was as formidable as Adelaida, and he instantly recognized where Adelaida got her fire. Bowing, though his lips twitched in an uncontrollable and most definitely arrogant grin, Grayson didn't step from Adelaida's side.

"A pleasure to meet you."

Karlotta rolled her eyes, but her lips did move ever so slightly upward. "Arrogant."

He couldn't disagree there. "Where's Maya?"

"In the village." Adelaida met his gaze and nodded. "Waiting for Inês's British contact."

"How did she send the letter?" He turned to Inês. "How did you send the letter from here to England and know it'd land in the proper hands?"

"We were discussing that," Adelaida said amenably enough. "Then Inês...forgot her decorum."

Covering his smile with a hand, Grayson tried to look stern. Then he quickly gave up. "This is not at all what I expected."

"You're the British contact?" Karlotta whirled on him and stalked forward, her brown eyes blazing with fury. And fear.

"Mama." Adelaida stepped between them. Grayson rested his hand on her shoulder; he had no need for her protection. She merely lifted her chin. "Stop. We will discuss Grayson's reasons—"

"*Grayson?*" Karlotta spluttered.

"—for being here later. Right now, it's of no concern."

"Can she be trusted without the gag?" He most definitely did not want to step into the quagmire of Karlotta's anger. He also wasn't certain he trusted Inês not to scream bloody murder. The fury in her gaze landed squarely on him, and he seriously considered sleeping with one eye open from now on. Inês might not know how to wield a dagger, but he wouldn't put bodily harm past her.

"Probably not," Karlotta grumbled. She huffed a sharp, displeased breath but turned back to Inês. "We've run out of time, and I have many questions."

"Remove the gag," Adelaida agreed. "Inês, speak, and quickly." Her voice cooled, hardened. Grayson stepped back and watched. This was no longer his mission, but the safety of her entire village depended on its success. "If you raise your voice, I'll keep you gagged until we land in England. Maybe even after. I don't have the time or patience for your dramatics. I need answers."

"What do you want to know?" Inês asked in a cold, raspy voice. She looked down at them haughtily despite her tied-up position.

"I know *why* you contacted the British. How?" Adelaida stepped aside, and Grayson stood beside her. He took her hand and squeezed silently in support.

"Braga."

"Our butler from Douro?" Adelaida sounded surprised. "You said he died."

Inês sniffed. "When the French arrived, I saw no choice. If the British kept their word, I wanted passage away from here."

"For all of us?" Karlotta demanded. She stood straight and stiff, hands balled at her sides. "Or only you and Maya?"

"All of us," Inês insisted in that same cold, proud voice.

"Bah," Karlotta snorted, clearly not believing her.

"How did you send him to England? What ship?" Adelaida fired the questions at Inês who watched her with a deepening scowl. "How did you know who to contact? How did Braga speak with anyone, he doesn't speak English."

Inês's scowl didn't waver. "The letters were sufficient to open doors to the highest echelons of British government."

"Who did he seek out?" Grayson asked, though didn't expect an answer. Inês didn't even bother to scowl at him. Who did she know in the government that gave her such confidence in sending her butler there with only a handful of letters?

"All right." Adelaida shook her head and met his gaze. Grayson had nothing to offer save support. He could take over the conversation but would rather not. "We haven't the time for specifics. We'll discuss this later, once we're gone from Carvalho."

"I have many questions," he whispered, but he held them back for now. "You're right, though. We haven't the time."

"No," Adelaida agreed. She tilted her head, and Grayson untied the woman from the chair. "Inês, return to the conservatory. When Maya returns, don't send her back to the road. Keep her with you." She nodded to Karlotta. "Mama, get back to the kitchens. I'll be down shortly."

Grayson waited until the nursery was clear. Joana eyed him in wide-eyed wonder as she gathered Rodrigo and slipped down the servants' steps. Adelaida scooped up Gabriel and stood in front of him.

"Gabriel, *anjinho*, this is Grayson."

The boy watched him, head buried against his mother's neck, eyes wide. He didn't blink, just curled one hand into Adelaida's gown. Grayson bent slightly and met Gabriel's eyes, smiling. The boy's lips pursed together in confusion, but he otherwise didn't move.

"It's a pleasure to finally meet you, Gabriel," Grayson whispered. "I promise I'll keep you and your mother safe."

Twenty-Two

I t washed over her like a gentle wave. Holding Gabriel while Grayson introduced himself, only the three of them left in the nursery, Adi thought she might cry.

Oh, there was the French, the fear that one of the soldiers would search the house after the chaos in the kitchens. Lambert appearing for no reason except he had the run of the household and had decided to hunt her down. Grayson being in the house, the nursery, his secret—their secret—out in the open now.

In that moment, none of it mattered.

Gabriel snuggled against her, warm and trusting. Grayson spoke of the three of them sailing on the water.

"And the stars," Grayson was promising now. "I'll teach you the names of all of them."

"Bold promises," she whispered. "Do you mean it?"

He lifted his gaze from Gabriel to her, his beautiful blue-green eyes solemn. No arrogance shone through, no conceit. "Adelaida, I mean every word."

He took her hand, lifted it to his lips. Cool and reassuring, his lips pressed a promise against her fingers. His other hand rested tentatively against Gabriel's back. Her son didn't move, which she thought a very positive sign.

"Every word?" Her heart sped up, and her breath hitched, but she tried to infuse a note of calm into her voice. She wasn't certain how well she succeeded. "I—" The confession caught in her throat. She swallowed hard and tried again.

"I never expected, well, you. You sparked something in me I didn't know lived inside." Her fingers tightened around his, and she grasped for the words her heart wished so desperately to say.

"I want more." She shook her head and felt Gabriel's eyelashes flutter against her throat.

"I'll give you everything," Grayson promised, and she believed him. Her heart skipped and then thudded hard in her chest. "I mean it, Adelaida. You've only to ask, and it's yours. My heart? Done. My soul? Already yours."

"Grayson." The word barely made it past her suddenly dry lips. "Marriage?"

"If that's what you wish, I'll marry you right now."

All her breath left her in a rush, and she nodded. His hand tightened around hers. "I didn't dare think about the future. I didn't think I'd have a future beyond this. Trapped in my own home, terrified of every single day. Worse in the nights."

They'd locked their doors, but if Lambert or Bardot truly wanted entry, even the solid oak wouldn't have stopped them.

"And now?" he asked.

"Now I want everything I thought I'd never have."

"Marry me," he said, and his true feelings rang strong in those words. "Marry me, Adelaida. We'll have Padre Lucio perform the ceremony before we leave." He frowned. "I'm not Catholic; will that be a problem?"

A giggle escaped her. "I've no idea. Not many in Portugal aren't Catholic." Frowning, she admitted, "At least they can't admit they aren't, not with the Inquisition still hunting people down."

"The Inquisition?" he repeated, clearly stunned. "All right. We'll wait." He gathered her close, being mindful of Gabriel, and kissed her. His gentle touch held promises for their future. "But we will marry. I promise you that."

"Good. I'll hold you to that." Adi wrapped her hand around the back of his head and kissed him hard.

"I love you," he breathed against her skin. "And I'll tell you that every day for the rest of our lives."

Adi believed him. She had no idea when he'd earned more than her trust, when he captured her heart, but she knew he'd keep his promise. All of his promises.

Grayson held her another moment, and the reality of this new life settled over her. The promise of a future not mired in fear and terror. In starvation and hopelessness.

"You'll protect Gabriel?"

He pulled back and watched her. "I'll protect everyone you love. Adelaida, we're all leaving. I promised you that weeks ago. I'm promising you that again."

"All right." She swallowed and nodded. "I do believe you. Only now that it's time."

"I know." He kissed her again and took her hand, leading her to the door. "I know. It won't be easy, but it will work."

Something nagged at her, as if she'd forgotten a single point. That one point that would unravel this entire charade and bring Lambert's wrath down on all of them. Adi couldn't grasp it even though it beat through her.

"I feel we're forgetting something," she whispered as Grayson eased open the door and peeked down the hall.

"Such as?" He looked at her but didn't dismiss her fears.

"I don't know," she admitted.

"I'll speak with Padre Lucio this afternoon and see if he's heard anything. I'm meeting the fishermen tonight. We'll plan our escape then."

It almost sounded too good to be true, but Adi nodded anyway. "All right." They slipped into the servants' entrance and down the stairs. "The villagers, the fishermen, the boats. Have we enough boats?"

"No." The flat word echoed sharply in the dark quiet of the stairs, but Grayson didn't stop. His hand squeezed hers, and she felt the tension in his admission. "We haven't a choice. Esme and Landon can't sail any closer, not with the French patrolling the coast. And we can't send the *barca de pesca* back for a second wave."

"All or nothing." The fear lodged back in her throat as they stepped onto the landing. "We'll make it work."

They had to.

Grayson had no idea how they were going to make this work. No matter how he calculated the boats, the people, the weight, he ended up with the same conclusion.

They were woefully short on boats.

Fifteen people per boat—twenty to squeeze—on the twenty-one *barca de pesca* in the harbor. Eight hundred and fifty people, Mélina had said. Not including pets, the horses Adelaida refused to leave behind, and Rémy.

Watching the sun set along the beach, he frowned. Did that include the household? Yes. Mélina would've made sure of that. All right, so technically they needed fifty-six boats. He'd settle for forty.

"Double," he muttered to the birds enjoying the evening

breeze. "We need double the ships we have. Philip," he said to a random tern pecking at the sand, "I wish I wasn't so good at math."

Arrogant, Adelaida had called him. She wasn't wrong. He meant his promises about taking everyone from Carvalho back to England—he meant every word—but he still needed a miracle.

The breeze blew softly today, another concern he'd rather not bring up. Wind. The *barca de pesca* had sails, of course, and from what he knew of them, they also boasted oars. Rubbing his forehead, he hoped the local fishermen had answers.

"No use borrowing trouble," he muttered to Philip, who was clearly uninterested in his problems.

He'd spoken with Lucio about the villagers, and everyone was prepared.

Check.

They each packed a single, small bag of possessions and brought any pets they might have.

Check.

Even now, small groups of villagers helped Lucio bury whatever they could under the suspicious gaze of the small garrison in the village.

Check.

That left the boats. He hated to cram so many on board; he feared capsizing. However, Grayson saw no other choice.

"Grayson?" Adelaida's voice whispered from behind him in the caves.

He jerked toward the sound. The smile he initially greeted her with dropped as the fear in her tone had him hurrying toward her. Stepping around the outcroppings, he gathered her to him.

"What's wrong? You've run all the way here? What happened?"

"The men are on their way," she gasped and curled her hands into his shirt. "But so are the troops."

"What?" The warm breeze he'd so enjoyed a moment ago now chilled him right to his soul.

"One of the Spanish we gave sanctuary to was a traitor." She breathed hard, the words tumbling from her mouth. "Padre Lucio sent one of the women to tell us. The Spaniard, he saw the padre taking down the statues. Maria ran all the way here to warn us."

A flow of colorful curses wanted to burst free, but there wasn't any time. "What happened? Did he tell the garrison?"

"Yes. I don't know how Padre Lucio knew, only what Maria told us." She paused, clearly terrified though she spoke clearly. "She said the padre confronted the man. Maria doesn't know what happened next."

"Is Padre Lucio still alive?" Grayson didn't wonder what the garrison would do if they discovered their clandestine escape. He knew.

"I don't know," she gasped. "We have to leave tonight."

"Send everyone through the tunnels." His mind raced, and he revisited his earlier checklist. So much for having time enough to plan this out. "Have them gather here with the fishermen."

"They're already on their way. I think." She shook her head. "I don't know; Maria didn't say."

"Where is she now?"

"With Mama. I'll send Joana with Gabriel and Rodrigo first. You'll watch over them?"

"With my life," he promised. "Send everyone now. Don't wait, Adelaida. I'll take care of getting them onto the boats." The boats. Too late for anything else now. "You can handle Rémy and the horses?"

"I'm not leaving anyone behind," she swore in a vicious

growl. "We have no muskets or pistols; the French confiscated them that first day."

"It doesn't matter." He kissed her hard, his own heart pounding, his mind racing. "No longer than a half hour," he warned. "Just get everyone out of there."

"I love you." She kissed him hard, and he tasted her desperation in that kiss.

As she disappeared back into the tunnels, he swore to both of them that it wouldn't be their last kiss. Not by a long shot. Not a moment later, Joana appeared, carrying a fussy Gabriel and a clearly scared Rodrigo.

"Joana, I need you to watch over them until I can get the boats settled." He crouched before the small, thin girl. The fire in her eyes had not diminished from earlier, and she watched him with a grave fierceness he'd seen burn through Adelaida.

"Are we going to die?" she asked in an eerily calm voice.

"Not today," he promised and kissed the top of her head. "Not even tomorrow. I promise you the French will not win today."

"*Dama*, she said that. I believe her." Joana nodded again and rocked Gabriel. "I believe you, too. What do you need from me?"

He wanted to tell her nothing. She was far too young, and she had precious charges to tend to. Cold dread slithered down his spine as Grayson heard himself say, "I need you to ensure the fishermen work fast. We have little time, and there are far too many of us. I need you to make sure the household and the villagers don't wander from this cave."

Joana paused, then nodded, her chin tilted. "*Sim, don.*"

Grayson blinked down at her use of the title but didn't quibble. Tapping his fingers against his thigh, he paced in front of the cave, but only a few moments passed before the fishermen hurried into sight.

"We heard," one said. Older, weathered, his hands well used to working the lines, he was clearly the leader. "What's our course, *don*?"

Again he let the title go. "What's your name?"

"Benedito."

Grayson held out his hand and shook Benedito's, offering what respect he could in the few seconds they had. "Grayson." He used his real name now; there was no need to keep it hidden anymore. He said what they all no doubt already knew: "There aren't enough boats. If you can't find more in one hour, I need everyone into these."

Benedito didn't look happy with that prospect. He also didn't look surprised. "There are no more. The French sank everything but what you see here."

Grayson cursed but nodded. "I was afraid of that. All right."

He quickly explained where his ship waited beyond the blockade. Benedito nodded, silent as Grayson explained what he'd hoped to calmly discuss tonight. But the sun was setting rapidly, and Joana already had a small group of silent but scared villagers grouped around her.

Rodrigo clung to her skirts, and Gabriel was whimpering louder than Grayson thought was safe. He stepped back and took the child from Joana's arms as Benedito consulted with the others.

"Follow Benedito, Joana. Make sure everyone is safe." He debated for only a heartbeat. "Leave Rodrigo and Gabriel with me."

"No, *don*." Joana glared up at him. "*Dama* entrusted me with their lives."

"Then you stay with me." He tried to suppress his smile but knew something showed on his face. Joana's eyes narrowed. Turning, he looked up and down the beach, but so far it remained clear. "Benedito, are you ready?" He bounced Gabriel in what was no doubt a vain effort to soothe the poor child. "We're out of time."

Benedito repeated the course Grayson had given him. Though he was confident in his skills, with so much literally riding on those course coordinates, he had hoped for backup. Another skilled sailor to help work through the currents and the location of the French ships.

"We'll see you on your ship, Don Grayson." His lips might've tilted up in a smile beneath his gray beard, but Grayson couldn't tell for sure. "Or in Hell. Either way, we leave this beach together."

Grayson laughed. "Let's hope for the former. My sister and her husband wait for me on board. When you arrive, tell them Grayson is slightly delayed."

"Slightly delayed?" Benedito repeated the English words carefully, sounding out each syllable. If he was suspicious of the language, he said nothing.

"They'll understand, and they won't give you any trouble."

Benedito shrugged and turned for the ever-expanding group of people. Still silent. Still waiting. Still no Adelaida or anyone from the villa. Worry churned his stomach, and he jerked his head at Joana.

"Listen to the *don*," she told an older woman who eyed him suspiciously. "And Benedito. We all leave together."

"What'd she say?"

"That Padre Lucio died stopping the Spaniard spy from bringing more troops." Joana frowned. "She didn't see it herself, but he isn't here yet."

Grayson rested his hand on her shoulder. "If he's alive, he'll be here. He might be overseeing the rest of the village."

Grayson had no idea, and he didn't want to give the girl false hope. On the other hand, he had no idea what went on outside this relatively small cave. He kissed Gabriel on his cheek, then handed him back to Joana.

"I need you to keep them here," he whispered, nodding to Rodrigo, who clearly understood what was happening. "Rodrigo, I need you to keep Gabriel quiet; can you do that?" The boy nodded, straightening. Grayson hated to pile such responsibility onto his young shoulders, but he needed to find Adelaida. "Listen to Joana, and stay hidden."

Grayson pushed away the fear that Lambert had found Adelaida and was even now torturing her for information. That the Spanish spy had spread more dissent. That the garrison had slaughtered the remaining villagers.

He pulled his khanjar from his side and turned for the tunnels. He hesitated, debating between the tunnels or the steps, but he didn't know what he'd walk into either way.

"The stairs, *don*." Joana urged Rodrigo behind a protruding rock, and the three of them disappeared into the darkness. "You can see more from there. I don't know what's happening in the house, but the soldiers might be patrolling the hallways."

"Stay hidden," he ordered. He'd broken his promise to Adelaida. He kept her son and nephew safe, but he'd also left them.

"No one will find us," Joana swore.

"Don't come out unless it's for me or Dama Adelaida." They'd either come together with everyone else or it was already too late. Grayson pushed that thought to the recesses of his mind.

Joana didn't say a word; she'd already disappeared into the shadows.

Hesitating once more, Grayson spun for the opening and ran down the beach. It was still empty of soldiers, and he couldn't hear any sound from Benedito and his small group after a dozen or so paces. They were all terrified.

The sun had fully set by the time he reached the stairs leading up to the villa. No soldier waited for Grayson as he took the steps two at a time. He didn't worry about slipping; he didn't think about anything other than finding Adelaida.

Deserted. In the second it took his mind to register the emptiness of the villa, where before at least two guards had kept watch, he also smelled smoke.

"You're brilliant," he muttered and raced around the building for the kitchens.

Twenty-Three

Adi had waited until the majority of the staff stood at the far end of the kitchens. The guards, who didn't seem to know anything about what had happened in the village, continued their discussion on the merits of keeping chickens versus pigs.

She could barely hear their separate arguments over the roaring in her ears. So much for slowly funneling everyone into the tunnels one at a time so the French weren't any wiser.

Mama and Mélina had already sent Inês and Maya into the tunnels and to Grayson. Half the maids had followed right after they plated the foot soldier's meal. Lambert and Bardot's dinner warmed in the pots, waiting for later.

Slowly breathing out, she listened hard for any sound other than the arguments. Nothing from outside—as far as Adi knew, only Maria had managed to escape the village and spread the word about the traitor.

Adi hated not knowing what else was happening in the village, if any of them still lived. If the French slaughtered her people as they had in Évora. If Padre Lucio still lived.

Breathe in. Breathe out. She caught Mélina's eye, who nodded and ushered everyone else out of the room. It took no more than a moment before the guards recognized the silence of the normally bustling kitchens. As one, they stopped speaking and turned toward her.

Adi didn't wait. She tilted the large pot of boiling water onto the floor, separating her—and the exit—from the guards. Grabbing the poker, she scattered the logs, pushing them onto the woolen rags that had been strategically placed around the kitchens.

The pots of olive oil would explode when the room got too hot, burning her beloved home. With any luck, sparks would land on the soldiers, setting them aflame also.

She didn't look back.

"Take the tunnels," she ordered the group. "Grayson is waiting there."

"Adi." Her mother grabbed her arm, looking up the stairs. "What about Lambert's papers?"

She'd thought about them but had dismissed stealing them. "Even with the chaos, they'll be too well guarded." They had only moments before the rest of the house realized the kitchens were on fire. "And I need to take Rémy and the horses. I'm not leaving them."

"I'll get the papers." Mélina urged the group through the cellar door and grabbed Karlotta as well. "Go. Take care of Rodrigo and Gabriel."

"Mélina!" Adi grabbed for her arm, but she slipped by.

"I'm not going to let them win." She paused on the steps only for a moment. "They're here for a reason, and I refuse to let that reason burn."

"Hurry," Adi whispered and whirled for the stables.

The last rays of the sun didn't quite reach the stables, casting the wooden structure in shadows. Only a single lantern illuminated the stalls where Jacques, filling in for a still-missing Pierre, saw to the horses. As she raced into the stables, she didn't have to feign breathlessness.

"The kitchens are on fire!" she shouted, waving her hands in a fine imitation of frantic disorder. Then she grabbed Jacques by the coat and dragged him toward the villa.

Jacques, who now clearly saw the smoke, didn't hesitate. He ran for the back of the villa, not pausing to see if she followed. Adi didn't watch further. She opened the stall doors for her pair of horses and Rémy.

"I wish I knew how to bridle you," she muttered, grabbing the proper equipment for later.

"Adelaida!" Grayson's voice stilled her, but only for a moment.

"What are you doing here?" she demanded, fear choking her. "Where's Gabriel?"

"Hiding with Joana and Rodrigo. The three of them are waiting for us. They won't come out until we're back." He stilled her shaking hands and hugged her, hard and fast. "I swear to you, they're safe."

"All right." She looked out the stable doors at her home, smoking nicely now. Enough to have mobilized the rest of the troops. "Any more word from the village? Here." She shoved the bridles at him. "I don't know what I'm doing."

He took one look at the situation and hurriedly bridled both horses and Rémy. "People arrived. One woman told Joana that Padre Lucio was dead, but she hadn't seen it for herself. Joana didn't believe her."

"Oh." All her breath left her, and she had trouble drawing it back in. She crossed herself and said a quick prayer for his safety. For all their safety.

"Hurry up. We haven't any time to dally."

"I'm not dallying," she snapped, taking Rémy's reins and leading him down the rear path to the beach. "I'm also not leaving anything for the French."

Grayson joined her, and she handed him Rémy's reins. "Take them down there and make sure they're on a boat. And keep the children safe."

She turned for the house, where the fire at last smoked enough to cause chaos. When Grayson grabbed her arm, Adi wasn't surprised.

"I'm not leaving you."

"Mélina went upstairs to take Lambert's papers."

He growled beneath his breath and shoved all three sets of reins into her hand. "I'll meet you there." He kissed her, his fingers tangling in her hair, his mouth hard and brutal on hers. Adi scraped her nails along his scalp and kissed him back with equal desperation.

"Don't you leave me, Grayson Conrad. You promised."

"And I always keep my promises." He smiled and pressed his lips to hers once more. Not enough—never enough—but they were quite literally out of time. "Besides, you promised to marry me."

"And I intended to." She pushed him along just as her mother raced from the house toward her. "Find Mélina. Please."

"I love you."

Grayson disappeared into the house, his dagger drawn. Shivering in the warm night, Adi handed Rémy's reins to her mother and hurried toward the beach path that wound down the cliffs. It'd take longer to rendezvous with the rest of the village this way, but at least she saved her animals.

"Where's Lua?" she asked just as her dog ran up beside them. "Is everyone else gone?"

"Yes. There's only us and Mélina." Even in the dark, Adi saw Karlotta glare at Rémy. "You move now, or you stay for the French, who will probably eat you."

Rémy moved.

"Marriage?" her mother asked as they made their way down the cliffside.

"The choice is mine, Mama. And I'm very happy with it."

It didn't surprise Grayson that everyone left in the house was now battling the fire in the kitchens. His Adelaida, she was brilliant. A part of him mourned her actions. She'd done what she needed to, but it couldn't have been easy, burning down her home. Even a part of it.

As he raced through the villa, ignoring the open conservatory door and the very obviously open wine cellar door, he listened for Mélina. He bit back his shout of her name. No matter how he wanted to call out, if she hadn't been caught, he didn't want to endanger her.

At the top of the stairs, he braced for a fight, but the men Adelaida had said stood guard to Lambert and Bardot's wing were nowhere in sight. No doubt in the kitchens. Good. That meant Mélina had either sent them there so she could more easily access Lambert's rooms, or they had already rushed down.

He moved quickly, each step more hurried than he'd have liked. But he didn't know which rooms Lambert or Bardot occupied. No matter how much faith he had in his own skills, he hadn't managed to infiltrate this wing. He hadn't wanted his presence to be a sign that the household rebelled. Not when

Adelaida worked so hard to keep things calm and her people alive.

"Mélina?" he called into the first room.

Probably not Lambert's, but he took no chances. He'd promised Adelaida.

Room after room remained empty. Even though he knew in his gut Lambert's was on the end, Grayson checked each one anyway.

The door stood open, which he found unusual. No Lambert, however—Bardot cornered Mélina.

"I let you live," he growled, hand around her throat.

Blood cold, he straightened and caught Mélina's eye. Her own widened, and she looked terrified.

"Let her go."

Grayson spoke in French so there would be no misinterpretation. Candles lit the room, and he wondered where Lambert had run off to. The kitchens? Why him and not Bardot? Rather, why one and not both? If the house caught fire, they'd all need to evacuate.

He'd keep an eye on the door in case of any sneak attacks.

"Who are you?" Bardot growled, squeezing harder. "Her lover?"

"I don't need to be her anything to tell you to keep your hands off her." Grayson slowly advanced, anger burning his blood. "Let her go. Now."

Bardot moved quickly, Grayson gave him that. In one breath, he dropped Mélina, turned with a pistol in hand, and fired. Grayson dropped. The impact against the wooden floor jarred his ribs and knocked the breath from him.

"Damn it," he grunted, pushing himself up.

Ignoring the pain, a very clear statement he was still not as healed as he wished, Grayson braced for Bardot just as the man leaped at him.

"Run!" he shouted at Mélina, who was already moving for the door.

Bardot jabbed him in the ribs—his bad side, of course. Observant, Grayson had to admit as he sucked in air. He still gripped his dagger, and even though he now hunched over in pain, he sliced at Bardot's legs.

The other man didn't expect it and growled in pain.

Grayson still didn't know where Lambert had disappeared to, but as he struggled with Bardot, he hadn't the breath to worry. Bardot grabbed him about the waist and pushed him into the wall, using the momentum to once more jab at his side.

"The hero isn't as capable as he thinks," Bardot taunted.

"The hero?" Grayson laughed around a gasp. Bardot continued to hit him with short, quick jabs. "I'm not the hero. Mélina is, and you let her go."

He steadied himself against the wall, waiting...waiting.

Bardot paused, glancing behind him at the door, through which Mélina had long since disappeared.

"Shouldn't have looked." Grayson stabbed him in the stomach, pushing him back. "You have no idea what these people are capable of," he spat.

Bardot clutched his stomach as he crashed onto the floor. Grayson didn't pause but raced from the room. His left knee had twisted again, and his ribs throbbed like the devil. It didn't matter. He needed to ensure Mélina had escaped and find out where Lambert hid.

Even as he thought it, he doubted Lambert hid. Had he followed one of the staff? Adelaida and Karlotta? Mélina even? He hadn't seen her holding any papers. Had she returned to Lambert's rooms? There were only two doors left.

Breathing heavy, his back straight despite the pain, Grayson pushed open the next door. It no longer mattered if Lambert saw him. After that fight with Bardot, anyone on this floor would've heard him.

"What are you doing?" he demanded as Mélina riffled through what was obviously Lambert's desk. She'd jammed a small dagger into the locks and pried open a half dozen drawers already.

"He has more papers here than I thought. And journals. Diaries." She met Grayson's gaze for a moment, eyes fierce. "I'm taking everything."

"All right." He looked around, listening for any sound of Lambert's return. No footsteps sounded in the hallway. Spotting a courier bag on a chair, he grabbed it and handed it to Mélina. "Hurry. We haven't much time."

"Is Rodrigo safe?" she demanded, haphazardly stuffing papers into the satchel.

"Yes. He's with Gabriel and Joana," he reassured her. "I promise you, they're safe. They're hiding from everyone until Adelaida or I retrieve them."

He kept watch at the door and glanced at her. He didn't want to ask. Almost didn't. "Did Bardot violate you?"

"No." She spat the word but shuddered. Her hands never stilled as they opened the many drawers of the secretary. "I promised him that after my mourning period I'd go to him voluntarily."

"I should've killed him sooner." Grayson wanted to vomit, not only from the pain in his ribs, but from what she'd gone through. She searched the drawers once more, but several remained locked. "Leave them."

"As far as he knows, I'm still in mourning," she promised as he grabbed her elbow and hurried her out the door. She didn't look in Bardot's room but kept her gaze straight ahead.

The hall had sunk into darkness now; no candles had been lit. The entire villa smelled of smoke, and Grayson faintly heard a buzz of activity as the French put out the fire.

"Where's Adi?" Mélina asked as they turned from the steps for the cellar.

"Taking Rémy and the horses to the beach." Grayson merely shrugged at her incredulous look. "She didn't want to leave anyone behind." Still no Lambert, and worry gnawed at him. "Where is he?" Grayson muttered.

"I don't know," she admitted.

"Get to the beach. Benedito is with the boats. He has the course. Make sure everyone who's there gets on one of those boats; we don't have any more." He looked around the cellar, half expecting a soldier to leap out and tackle him.

"Where are you going?"

"I'm going to find Lambert," he snarled. "And make sure Adelaida is safe."

He didn't look back as he raced up the steps. That was only a partial truth—he'd leave Lambert here to rot if it meant everyone else made it onto a boat. Unfortunately, Grayson had a feeling that wouldn't be the case. While the soldiers battled the flames, or the smoke, at least, he couldn't shake the feeling that the soldiers from the village had managed to get word to the villa about the exodus.

The path from stables to beach was a steep, winding switchback, one he barely navigated in the dark. Huffing from pain and breathlessness by the time his boots hit sand, Grayson pressed his left arm against his ribs and promised himself a nice, long recovery. Preferably in bed with Adelaida.

If they all survived the next hour.

That thought spurred him on. They would. He'd make sure of it.

The waning moon cast shadows along the rocks, but as he turned for the boats lining the beach by the cave, he saw Lambert. Several boats had already set out to sea; he saw their sails unfurling in the wind. Much to Lambert's obvious fury.

Lambert stood several hundred paces from him. Adelaida and Rémy stood another several hundred in front of Lambert. Judging by the angle of his arm, Lambert had a pistol aimed at Adelaida's back.

Yelling, Grayson pushed himself forward. He didn't care about his knee or his ribs. All he cared about was keeping Lambert's pistol away from her.

Lambert turned and fired. The musket ball hit the rocks on Grayson's side, barely missing him. The shot didn't slow him down, and he pushed harder.

Adelaida stopped, pushed Rémy toward her mother. *No!*

He had no breath with which to scream at her, and he didn't want Lambert realizing she'd turned for them. Even in the moonlight, Grayson saw another pistol in Lambert's belt, one he'd already reached for.

Harder, faster, Grayson raced down the last incline and leaped at Lambert.

Cursing as he tackled him, Grayson didn't have time or breath for anything more. He plunged his khanjar into Lambert's stomach, then rolled off him.

"Grayson!" Adelaida's voice echoed over him as he lay on the ground gasping for breath.

"I'm fine." The words barely made it past his lips. He looked over at Lambert, who gurgled obscenities at him. He watched Adelaida's shadow pluck Lambert's pistol from his belt and tuck it into hers.

In the blink of an eye, she knelt before him. Her fingers brushed through his hair even as she helped him sit up. He yelped in pain at the movement. Even if she'd been gentle, it would've jarred him. This time he feared he'd broken his ribs, not merely bruised them.

"Where's Mélina?" Her voice brushed his cheek, and she grunted as she helped him stand.

"Tunnels," he gasped.

Her arm slipped around him, and she took most of his weight. Grayson didn't look back at Lambert, even as he heard the man scrape along the dirt path. His knee gave out, and he almost took the both of them down.

"*Desculpa*," he muttered.

"This feels like the first time we met," she said, breathless. "You weren't in the best of shape then, either."

"I'm continually in your debt."

Her soft laugh drifted between them. "I'd say helping us escape more than paid that debt."

"Any more soldiers?"

"Not yet, but we have only a single boat left. Everyone else has already sailed."

Something in her voice told him there weren't as many people here as she expected. "Padre Lucio?"

She didn't speak, just shook her head.

"I'm sorry, Adelaida."

"From what the villagers said, he gave his life so the rest of us could survive." Her voice hardened with resolve. "I won't let his death be in vain. I won't let any of their deaths be in vain."

"You're a brave, wonderful woman, Adelaida."

"Joana!" she called as they approached the caves. Before she could draw breath for another shout, Joana emerged with Rodrigo and Gabriel.

"Into the boats," Grayson ordered as Adelaida helped him limp toward the remaining *saveiro*. The horses and Rémy already stood in it unsteadily. Benedito himself and a pair of men Grayson didn't know waited to sail them for his ship.

"*Dama*." Benedito bowed deeply as he helped Adelaida in beside Karlotta, who took both Joana and Gabriel into her arms, and Mélina, who grabbed Rodrigo the moment he scrambled on board.

Benedito helped Grayson next, which was just as well since he couldn't feel anything but the throbbing pain in his side. "*Obrigado*, Benedito," he managed as he collapsed beside Adelaida, who now held a clingy Gabriel.

"I burned down my home," Adelaida whispered, holding Grayson as close as she held Gabriel.

"You survived." He glanced at Mélina and Rodrigo, Karlotta holding Joana close. "You all survived. They didn't win because of what you did here today."

"We can rebuild," Karlotta whispered. "One day."

"And I took all Lambert's papers." Mélina paused and met his gaze. He nodded.

Lambert and Bardot were both dead.

Her fingers brushed her throat, where angry bruises were already forming. Adelaida rested her cheek on Gabriel's head and met his gaze.

"I never want to come back here," she admitted. "Even if it's Gabriel's birthplace."

"Nothing is set in stone. We'll see what happens with the British forces first. Napoleon won't live forever." He lifted her hand. "Nothing is set in stone," he repeated. "Except your promise to marry me."

"A promise I don't intend to break." She kissed him, the

truth of her statement inherent in the passion that simmered beneath the surface.

"I love you, Adelaida." He brushed a hand over Gabriel's dark hair.

"And I love you, Grayson Conrad."

Epilogue

"How will you climb aboard?" Adi eyed the ship coming clearly into view.

They'd managed to evade the French easily enough. Either they didn't patrol this part of the ocean, or they'd left the area, more concerned with the British farther north. Either way, she thought it fortuitous. Honestly, she couldn't handle any more excitement.

Her heart hadn't stopped pounding during the voyage.

"I have no idea." Grayson sighed but didn't move. "Probably the same way we'll carry up the horses. By rope."

She smiled as a face popped over the side of the ship. "Grayson Conrad!" The woman said something in English Adi didn't understand. Then, in French, "Aren't you a sight for sore eyes."

"My sister," he whispered. "Esme, I missed you!"

They did, indeed, haul Grayson, who clenched his teeth around a continuous moan of pain, up the side of the ship like they did Rémy. Rémy bore it with a stoic glare. Adi thought

Grayson might scream into the night until every French ship along the Portuguese coast heard him.

Finally, they were all on board.

"Is there anyone else?" Esme said, still speaking French. Adi appreciated being part of the conversation.

"No," she said. She looked back to shore, though she couldn't see her home from this distance. Not even the light of a fire. Perhaps the soldiers managed to put it out. She'd never know. "Those who stayed ensured the rest of us escaped."

She had no idea how many had escaped the village. How many Padre Lucio's sacrifice had ensured. She jerked her gaze from the horizon to meet Esme's curious one. "Are there any Spanish on board? The man who betrayed us to the French, he was Spanish. Or claimed to be."

"I'll have Marsters check. Everyone else is as settled belowdecks as we could get them." Her lips quirked upward in an eerie imitation of Grayson's smile. "We weren't expecting company, you understand. I'm sorry to greet you so inhospitably."

"I'm grateful you took in my people," Adi assured her. "We're all grateful." She felt Grayson shift beside her, his breath still coming too quickly beneath her hands as she held him upright. Two men walked purposefully toward him. "Is one of them your Colonel Hilton?"

"No, that's Landon, Esme's husband, and Marsters, his valet." Grayson nodded at them. "I'll introduce you to Hilton when we get to London. Mélina!" he called. "Keep those documents safe."

The satchel hung across Mélina's body even as she held Rodrigo tight.

"Landon, Esme, Marsters. May I present Dama Adelaida Dos Santos y Machado and her son, Gabriel. She's agreed to marry me." Grayson lifted his arm and wrapped it around her waist, pulling her closer.

Adi ignored the congratulations and turned for him. "I can't believe we made it. Maybe not all of us, but so many."

She had her people to check on. Mélina, who clearly needed medical attention and was even now being fussed over by Esme. Her mother, who clung to Joana and looked dazed. Benedito and the other sailors had disappeared below with the others, but she needed to thank him, too. She supposed she ought to check on Inês as well.

"One day, we'll rebuild." He pressed his lips to hers. "I promise you, Adelaida. Carvalho will not be forgotten."

"I love you."

Thank you for reading!

If you enjoyed this book, I'd really appreciate it if you helped others enjoy it, too. Reviews are precious and help persuade other readers to give my romances a try.

Sign up to my VIP list for a short story, *One Day with You*. This story, along with more short stories about Louise and Malcolm, are only available to my list. https://bit.ly/3kSzMjI

I send weekly newsletters with things like new releases, special offers, pictures of my dog, recipes, and other exciting news about my stories, research, and travel that I hope you'll enjoy as much as I do.

Stay Connected

ckmackenzie.com

 twitter.com/ck_mackenzie
 instagram.com/ckmackenzieauthor
 tiktok.com/@ckmackenzieauthor

Also by C.K. Mackenzie:

<u>Kaya and Paul: The Conrad Chronicles</u>

Husband of Convenience

Sins of a Rogue

A Lover's Promise

***

<u>Nadia and James: Part of the Conrad Chronicles</u>:

Smuggler's Captain

Her Captain's Honor

***

Conrad Legacy Series:

The Lady's Marquess